COLIN BATEMAN

CROSSMAHEART

D0808264

WITHDRAWN FROM STOCK

HarperCollins*Publishers*

Leabharlann Choatae Laoba

Acc. No. 00/5620

Class No. F

No. 6100

HarperCollins*Publishers*
77–85 Fulham Palace Road,
Hammersmith, London W6 8JB

This film tie-in edition 1999
1 3 5 7 9 8 6 4 2

First published in Great Britain as *Cycle of Violence*
by HarperCollins*Publishers* 1995
Reprinted five times

Copyright © Colin Bateman 1995

The Author asserts the moral right to
be identified as the author of this work

A catalogue record for this book
is available from the British Library

ISBN 0 00 651064 7

This novel is entirely a work of fiction.
The names, characters and incidents portrayed in it are
the work of the author's imagination. Any resemblance to
actual persons, living or dead, events or localities is
entirely coincidental.

Set in Linotron Meridien by
Rowland Phototypesetting Ltd,
Bury St Edmunds, Suffolk

Printed and bound in Great Britain by
Caledonian International Book Manufacturing Ltd, Glasgow

All rights reserved. No part of this publication may be
reproduced, stored in a retrieval system, or transmitted,
in any form or by any means, electronic, mechanical,
photocopying, recording or otherwise, without the prior
permission of the publishers.

This book is sold subject to the condition that it shall not,
by way of trade or otherwise, be lent, re-sold, hired out or
otherwise circulated without the publisher's prior consent
in any form of binding or cover other than that in which it
is published and without a similar condition including this
condition being imposed on the subsequent purchaser.

For Andrea

1

Miller was twenty-eight when his father died, too old to be considered an orphan in anyone's eyes but his own.

It was a shock for young Miller, but not half as much for him as for his father who had been repeatedly assured by the doctors that he was suffering from a stomach bug, and not the cancer he feared. They had been lying, of course, a betrayal of trust masquerading as an act of kindness. They had meant to inform his son of the finality of the condition, but had somehow never quite gotten round to it.

It had been a bad couple of years for the Miller family. Young Miller's auntie had been the first to go, a crotchety early spinster his mother had reluctantly inherited after their mother died. It was an imposition on her own young marriage that was accepted with the sanguine mixture of duty and resignation for which the Belfast Irish are famous. It seemed a blessed relief to everyone concerned, bar his auntie, when, after twenty years of rarely interrupted invective, she was struck down by a stroke which silenced, or at least made unintelligible, the constant commentary on the state of mankind which made her fascinating company only for those with the capacity to remove themselves to a different, higher plane. Even when her wheelchair was inadvertently left outside in a snowstorm and she froze to death it was difficult to detect much genuine remorse in Miller's parents. His mother shed tears, of course, but they dried quickly and her things were out the door and down the road to Oxfam before the week was out.

His mother's demise was equally sudden. She was struck

by a number 67 bus while out shopping and died later in hospital. At parties after she was buried – not to celebrate her demise, you understand, for she was mourned widely – Mr Miller would occasionally describe the tragic but straightforward circumstances of her death and then add cryptically: 'The funny thing is, there is no number 67 bus,' before narrowing his eyes and wandering off. Later he would laugh about it, fancying that he had planted unlikely suspicions in people's minds, but in fact they merely thought him strange, and a little bit sick.

With the auntie gone and the mother too, Miller's brother Tommy soon followed, unable to cope with his father without the interventionist policies of his mother. He made tracks for England, leaving as his only legacy Miller's broken nose, which he had inflicted when they had both fought over who could stand closest to the gas heater on a freezing winter's morning before school fifteen years previously.

Father and son moved from their large, spacious bungalow to a small terraced house. It suited his father: he made a substantial profit on the sale of the bungalow and the house was much cheaper to run and would enable him to save even more for the retirement from the civil service he was never destined to enjoy. But Miller hated it. It was a shabby terrace in a run-down neighbourhood, it was damp and in urgent need of redecoration, but neither of them possessed the gumption to take it in hand the way Mrs Miller would have. There was always next year.

The decline in his father was both gradual and sudden. Miller spent so little time in his company, beyond breakfast, that he failed to notice the slow reduction in his father's stature, the droop in his face, the tightening of skin against bone. He wasn't aware of the long periods his father spent asleep in the chair in front of the box, or the groans when he shuffled up the stairs to bed. At least that was how he imagined it was. Later he would wonder what would have happened if he had taken more time to look after his father, had somehow managed to postpone his death for a matter of weeks. He might never have moved to Crossmaheart at all and thus avoided all the heartache.

Things only really clicked when his father asked him to take a few days off work to look after him, and then when the doctor called to inject him with morphine and commented incredulously, 'You mean they didn't tell you? Dear, dear, that's bad.'

The realization that the house was a mess only struck him when the minister visited. Tommy was back, of course, but wouldn't stay in the house of death, despite the fact that the body was at the undertaker's. He'd come for the hooley – there was something much too Catholic about 'wake' – but he wouldn't stay overnight. Miller hadn't been bothered by ghosts yet, although he had been rendered completely unconscious by a different kind of spirit.

The minister, a tall, emaciated figure in his fifties, tried to be philosophical about his father's sudden passing. Or perhaps theological. He quoted extensively from the Bible. Miller Senior, in his day, had wavered between the Church of Ireland and its near neighbour Catholicism – he thought the difference between them wasn't worth spit, though he never specified if this was the actual spit of Christ or some sort of symbolic saliva – before falling back on an intemperate Orangeman's interpretation of the straightlaced Presbyterianism of his youth. Boiled down, what the minister said was, 'It was for the best.'

The lounge, with curtains drawn as much for the piles of empty beer cans and chip papers lying about as out of respect for the dead, seemed an unlikely place to be getting theological, and the minister was soon unsettled by it. He was wary of Miller's sallowness, deeper and more distressing than his own, disturbed by the pale, staring eyes of the young man which he interpreted not as an awkwardness in the face of death, but an embarrassment in the presence of a man of God.

'He was a civil servant then?'

He had a cup of tea by then, which he sipped tentatively, aware even in the gloom of the spots of turned milk swirling before him.

'I don't know so much about the civil,' Miller replied. 'He had a bit of a temper on him. I mean, he wasn't a violent man. He never hit me. When I was a kid and I did something wrong he'd talk it through with me, explain how I'd transgressed and how my actions affected other people.'

'Commendable, I'm sure.'

'Then he'd take me outside and throw me in the nettles.'

'I . . .'

A playful smile slid onto Miller's lips, which only served to unnerve the minister more. He took another thin-lipped sip of his tea and regarded the room. There must have been thirty empty cans. Musty newspapers were piled in one corner. A film of dust above the TV. Spiders' webs in the four corners. Where he looked, Miller looked, and realization dawned on the orphan. Before, minutes before, he had not been aware of the dust, of the cobwebs, of the grit on the carpet, of the sunlight weakly piercing the age-thin curtains, of the smell of decaying food and stale air. It had been his father's job to clean the house, to cook, to provide. He was newly retired. He was a widower. He had the time. Miller had his job, friends to meet, drinks to drink. He could have done them all, he could have helped do them all, but it wasn't his job. His dad had had to do it in the same way that his mother had to do it before him. It's what parents were for.

'We had a bit of a hooley last night,' Miller said by way

4

of explanation, being careful not to let any hint of apology creep in.

The minister nodded, and began: 'The nettles?'

Miller shrugged. 'Were you ever stung by nettles? The only cure for them was docken leaves. Dock leaves. You'd rub the sting with them. Did you ever do that?'

The minister shook his head.

'One of the ancient remedies – dates back to the Romans, you know. Get stung back then, rub it with a docken leaf. It's where the word doctor comes from, dock, you know?'

The minister nodded slowly, the way the nervy doctor had nodded when he examined his dad at the hospital. Tommy had arrived that morning and they sat together by the bed as the doctor examined the yellowed flesh and bones of his father, asking questions he must surely have known the answers to already. Had he been sleeping, had he been eating, a history of cancer? His father nodding, answering each question for him, at his most lucid in three days. And then the bubbling in the lungs started and when the doctor heard that he hurried them outside and a nurse took them down to a waiting room while they got him stabilized again. There wasn't much in the waiting room, a few split plastic chairs, a selection of crumpled paperbacks, a young man in a wheelchair. The nurse nodded at the man. 'Never mind Norman, he was in an accident.'

After ten minutes the nurse came back, this time carrying a tray with tea and biscuits, and they knew, because it had been the same with their mother, as if a cup of hot tea would make things all right. They ignored the tray, the doctor arrived, nodding, perspiring, as if he was about to make a meal of it, but when he had to say it he was admirably abrupt. Miller had expected him to say his father had been promoted to glory, like it was a good thing. Or that he had lost him, as if his skeletal frame had bounded off and was hiding in the nether regions of the hospital. But as

5

it was it wasn't much beyond, 'I'm sorry, he's dead,' and it was a relief. The doctor left. Tommy put his arm round him and they cried together, their first physical contact since he had decamped to England.

Norman said: 'Why don't you give him a kiss, you bastard?'

They held onto each other.

'Look at yees, ye poofy fuckers.'

The nurse appeared again and wheeled him away quickly. 'I'm sorry,' she said without looking at them.

Later his brother said, 'It's for the best.'

It was a Friday afternoon. It was raining heavily outside and the wind rattled branches against the downstairs windows of the Fitzpatrick Funeral Home. A young girl, long blonde hair, tied back, white shirt, black skirt, showed them the coffins. She seemed ill at ease. She left them alone to make up their minds.

'What do you think?' Miller asked.

'I think she's on a Youth Training Scheme.'

'She must have been sent here. Nobody chooses to become an undertaker, do they? It's all families.'

Tommy rapped the side of a coffin. 'Five hundred. Six hundred. They all look the bloody same.'

'You're only paying for the brass. What do they do, burn the coffin as well? Or do they turf the body out and get the coffin back?'

'Like you get a return on the empties?'

Miller shrugged. 'God knows.' He tapped one himself, a hollow, lifeless sound. Apt. 'It should say somewhere, non-returnable.'

Tommy laughed. 'Silly this, isn't it?'

'Daft.'

'He's gone now.'

'Aye, I know.'

6

'Dead as a doornail. Doesn't much matter whether we buy a coffin or have him stuffed and mounted on casters, it's all the same.'

Miller nodded. 'So what do you think, go for the cheap?'

'There's none of them cheap. People will think we're cheap if we go for the cheapest.'

'What does it matter what people think?'

'It would have mattered to Dad.'

'You think?'

'Well, it would have mattered to Mum.'

'What did we do for her?'

'I don't know, Dad did all that.'

'So what do you think?'

'I don't know.'

Tommy started tapping again.

'When in doubt go down the middle of the road,' Miller suggested.

'Or go the whole hog and get a mahogany one, spend a fortune and destroy the rain forest at the same time. He couldn't stand all that shite about conservation, remember?'

'He couldn't stand a lot of things,' said Miller. 'He couldn't stand you a lot of the time.'

'We got on a lot better after I left home.'

'On the phone, yeah. Once in a while. I remember when Mum first brought you back from the hospital, Dad took one look at you in her arms and said, "Where'd you get the monkey, love?" She didn't speak to him for weeks.'

The girl came back and led them into a small office. A desk, three chairs, an austere oil painting on the wall facing them as the brothers sat down. They discussed the details. Miller reached for his cheque book but she waved it away sharply. He thought idly about asking for a cash discount. For hire purchase terms. He wondered if she accepted Green Shield Stamps, and then if they still existed.

'I'll just see if there's an opening,' she said quietly, picking

7

up the phone. She really was quite pretty, he thought, but there was something odd about her make-up, thick and pale, as if she had perfected its application on her quieter customers. He wondered if undertakers had office parties at Christmas.

'Hello,' she said into the heavy black mouthpiece, 'I'd like to book a cremation for 11 am on Monday, please.' She nodded her head, slowly. 'I'm sorry,' she said politely, 'I must have a wrong number.' She replaced the receiver, took a deep breath and dialled again.

The funeral came, the funeral went. He saw it all through a blur of alcohol. He shook hands. He ate smart triangular sandwiches and devoured iced pastries. He shook hands and tutted a lot. Nobody came back to the house. They all went to the pub and drank his father's health, which he found surreal. The few relatives there remarked upon how controlled the young Millers were. They're putting on a brave face, they said. Their own friends, their own age, rallied round, made sure they always had company, had enough to eat. But, the funeral over, there was little more they could do. They had their own jobs, their own families. Come the weekend they could be supportive again.

Tommy went home on the morning after the funeral. Miller gave him a lift to the airport and made a vague promise about calling him once he heard anything about the will, if there was one. They shook hands perfunctorily, another first. And then he went home to the quiet house.

Too quiet, too quiet to think. He argued with himself over how to cope with death, believing that it should come naturally, but equally aware that although he felt a sense of loss he was more acutely aware of how he should be seen to be behaving rather than how he genuinely felt. And he had felt nothing beyond that immediate, tearful sense of loss at the hospital. He felt a lack of depth. As a child he

8

had once voiced concern about drowning in the bath and his mother had reassured him with, 'Don't worry, love, you're much too shallow to drown in three inches of water.' It was a phrase that came back to haunt him, in much the same way as his father had thus far failed to. He resented the fact that bereavement leave from work was only one week, when paternity leave was a month and maternity six. He resented the fact that German biscuits had not increased in size in keeping with the enlargement of the Fatherland, but he could do nothing about that either. Then again he had no wish to wallow in self-pity and began to contemplate an early return to work, where he could wallow in group pity, but they wouldn't hear of it, and he was angry with himself because he imagined they'd think he was just being the martyr by coming back early.

Marooned at home – his home now surely, half a home at least, shared with his brother – he threw himself into sloth. He failed to clean the house from top to bottom with an intensity which left him breathless. He made a point of not dumping his father's clothes or selling his valueless mementoes. He failed triumphantly to excise the fifties decor and coped with the accumulated rubbish and accelerating decay by ignoring it. He sat for days watching the TV, listening to his records. He barely ate, drank a little, but only alcohol.

A week after his father's death he got up in the afternoon and looked at himself in the mirror. Dank hair. Red-rimmed, sleepless eyes. A half-beard. He used words for a living, but for the life of him, for the life of his father, he couldn't decide on the words to describe his complexion – was it pasty-faced or pastry-faced? He thought it was probably pasty, but he liked pastry better; there was an air of potential about it. Later he thought of that as a half-baked idea, and the thought pleased him because it made him realize his mind was working again and the old playfulness was coming back. That night, washed, shaved, dressed, if not ironed, he stood in the garden breathing deeply in the sharp winter air and thought about getting back to the land of the living.

Or, indeed, the land of the dead. It had been another rough week in the city. A bomb had exploded in a crowded department store in Royal Avenue, killing thirteen people. Six men had been shot dead in a bookmaker's office in revenge for the bomb. And in revenge for the killings in the bookmaker's office two off-duty policemen enjoying a quiet drink had been shot in a country pub. Everyone expected the next piece of action would involve a young IRA terrorist being shot dead on the way to a possible hit, but no gun to be found near his body. It worked in cycles like that.

Miller returned to work at the paper. The *Post* was an evening paper, but the first edition was on the streets not long after 11 am, which meant the staff were mostly in as early as 6 am, which made it a morning paper. Miller didn't object to this particularly because he never required much sleep and nobody ever answered their phones before nine o'clock anyway and it left him plenty of time to tinker with his own column – and that line would be edited for a start – before he had to do any proper work. His column was a weekly one, occasionally a weakly one, and it made a lot of people laugh and a lot of people cry and it made him quite well known, if not across the city at least across the newsroom. Apart from the column he was a senior reporter and he covered for the most part activities in the city centre, mostly courts and killings. Since the city had been pedestrianized to try and stop the car bombs Miller raced about town on a battered mountain bike, armed with a bike phone, a notebook, a tape recorder and a small camera loaded with black and white film. His bike was known in the newsroom as the Cycle of Violence. When, occasionally,

Miller fell into a drinking spree and failed to return to the office, the bike was known as the Endless Cycle of Violence. If he was respected for anything, it was because he always came back with his story, or at least phoned it in, even while in the depths of inebriation, and it was always accurate and always fair. His spelling was rarely accurate and his complexion was rarely fair, but in his own way he cut a dashing figure racing across the city and he was popular with the ladies and gents alike, sexually with the former and socially with the latter.

Miller was greeted with a mixture of sincere sympathy and hardly concealed embarrassment when he arrived in the newsroom. The duty editor, Frank Galvin, shook his hand and asked him if he wanted to skip his column for that week, but Miller shook his head, his own head, and his hand, Galvin's hand, and assured him that he was well on the road to recovery.

'Well, we'll ease you in anyway. Wasn't that long ago I lost my dad.'

Lost him, Miller thought. Misplaced. Forfeited. Mislaid. 'Thanks.'

'Do you want to stick around the office or are you up to going out? Things are pretty tight out there.'

'Yeah. So I hear. No, I'm okay. I'll go out. Fresh air'll do me good.'

'Not much fresh out there. It stinks. Stinks of death.' Galvin was one for the stirring phrase, always had been, but then he looked at Miller with suddenly sad eyes and said, 'I'm sorry. Nothing personal.'

Miller laughed. 'Never worry.'

And, as so often after a storm, there was another one, and, literally, in a teacup. The Teacup, to be precise, a small, untidy, traditional snack bar on the corner of Cornmarket. Miller had been there a hundred times as a youngster, eating a big fry while his dad picked out losers from the paper and his mum did the shopping. He still liked to pop in occasionally for a late breakfast if he could get away with it. It still served old-fashioned fatty food. There was always a spillage of salt or sugar on the table and a steady rattle of gossip from the old aggies behind the counter. On his third day back, he found himself outside the Teacup on the way back to work from the law courts. It wasn't strictly on the way back to work, unless you were nuts, but he'd filed his story, the deadline was past and he felt like a rest. Few of the shops in the city centre still adhered to the old half-day closing on Wednesdays, pressed to open by the encroaching national chains, but with the rain and a frosty wind the centre was as empty as he could recall it. He had pottered round a record shop and a book shop, buying nothing, carefully securing the Cycle of Violence outside before entering each shop, before making his way to the Teacup. He ensconced himself at a table by the window so that he could keep an eye on the bike and ordered a fry and a pot of tea. They arrived together within five minutes, and he was just about to tuck in when he noticed a man outside taking more than a passing interest in the bike. He was an old man, to be sure to be sure, with frizzled grey hair and a red face. He wore a mac and white-to-grey sneakers and he had the wild blue eyes of a man of the streets. As Miller watched, the old man reached out and ran his hand along the wet saddle, onto the plastic bar and up onto the handlebars. His fingers, thick and dirty, rested on the bell. He looked suddenly up from the bell into Miller's eyes. Miller shook his head, raised his thumb and signalled for him to move on. The old man smiled back – surprisingly good teeth – and raised his hand to the glass. He dried a little portion of it by swirling it with the end of his sleeve and then pressed his nose against it so that it bent upwards into a pig snout. As his breath massaged the glass into mist, the old man's face began to disappear. Miller looked away and tried to

12

concentrate on his food. When after a few moments his eyes involuntarily darted back to the window he was relieved to see that the man had gone, leaving only the impression of his nostrils at the centre of a slowly dissipating cloud, but his relief was short-lived. The door opened and the nightmare was doddering towards his table, the loose sole of one of his gutties slapping on the yellow linoleum floor.

Miller pulled his plate protectively towards him and cast a helpless glance across at the waitresses who stood chatting, aware but unmoved, by the till. The tramp stopped opposite him.

'Do ye mind if I sit down, sonny?'

'No,' Miller lied with the honesty of politeness.

'You're sure?'

'Of course.' The second question was redundant, as he was already sitting, eyeing the food. Miller bent his eyes to the plate. Bent eyes, he thought, a good phrase. He could no longer smell the unhealthy sweetness of the fry; he smelt sweat and stale alcohol and could almost feel the chill of winter exposure off his guest. He sliced off some sausage, dabbed it in the egg and, without looking up, put the fork in his mouth. As he did so the old man let out a sickening, throaty rattle, which seemed to roll across the table towards him like a breaker on a polluted beach. Miller clamped his mouth shut around the food and began to chew rapidly, gerbil-like, staring at his plate, willing himself to swallow without being sick. As he forced it down he glanced up at the waitresses again but they were still chatting and he knew that he had lost.

He put his knife and fork down and looked up at the old man. 'Do you want to finish this?' he asked. 'I have to go.'

It was just a few moments before he realized the man was dead.

*   *   *

13

They called the ambulance. A crowd formed around the Teacup, alerted by the odd spectre of the emergency vehicle in the pedestrian zone. Inside, the old man lay stretched out on one of the tables while the paramedics examined him. The waitresses, six or seven of them in all, were grouped around the table like anxious competitors at a catering competition. Miller leant against his bike. His legs felt shaky. He was cold.

'Do you know his name?' a policeman asked.

Miller shook his head. 'Is that what they call natural causes?' he asked.

'Is what?'

'Him in there. Natural causes.'

'You have to be dead to die of natural causes,' said the constable, wisely.

'No, you have to be alive to die of natural causes.'

'That doesn't make sense.'

'Yes, it does. You have to be alive, before you can die.'

'A subtle difference. You don't get extra points for being pedantic, you know.' The constable nodded, satisfied with the mild admonishment, his biro still poised to make his first note. 'So you don't know him?'

'Didn't.'

'Don't.'

'Didn't.'

'Don't.'

'What are you saying?'

'He's not dead. Therefore your natural causes are irrelevant. I'm not saying he's not going to die very soon, but as of this moment in time, or that moment of time when I was in there looking at him, the old man is still alive. He is very sick, possibly of natural causes. It could, of course, be self-inflicted. He smells like a brewery. Worse, turps.'

Miller nodded slowly. 'I thought he was dead.'

The constable shook his head. 'Not yet.'

And, unasked for, tears began to run down Miller's face. The constable looked at him for a second, then flipped his notebook closed. 'Are you okay, sir?'

Miller nodded. He tried to say something but nothing would come. He had a big lump in his throat and he was scared to open his mouth in case it burst out.

The constable put a hand on his shoulder and said: 'Is there anything I can do?'

Miller shook his head, mentally screaming because he could not control himself. A woman, big, old, gruesome, emerged from the crowd which had now switched its attention from the old man lying flat across the restaurant table to Miller. She put her hand on his other shoulder. 'Is it yer da, love?' she asked and he tried to scream back, no, of course it isn't my fuckin' da, you think I'd have a da like that mangy ol' bastard, but still nothing would come and all he could do was cry some more and shake his head some more. I'm mortified, I'm absolutely mortified, please, God, give me my body back, he pleaded, but all he could do was lean back against the Cycle of Violence and weep some more as the ambulancemen brought the old tramp out on a stretcher and placed him carefully in the back of the ambulance. The policeman left him and began ushering the crowd back, waving his machine gun left and right. The woman, kind heart, gave him a little squeeze and faded away. The ambulance gave a brief blast of its siren, then began to move silently between the shops. Within a few moments Miller was left mostly on his own. With the departure of the spectators and the return of the casual, blissfully unaware shoppers, his body at last responded to his commands and he quickly wheeled the Cycle of Violence away.

Drunk, very drunk, Miller arrived back at work. He slumped against the back of the lift, then stumbled out on the news floor. He weaved his way between the desks silently, but there was something about the hideousness of his deportment, all hunchbacked and left-footed, that drew stares as he passed and by the time he had located his desk and sat down all eyes were upon him.

He switched on his computer, shuffled some papers, tried to read a press release, but he couldn't focus. He looked up suddenly, caught Alec Webb watching him. Webb turned away quickly. He nervously ran a hand through his thinning hair.

'Hey.'

Webb pretended not to hear.

'Hey, Kojak.'

Webb looked up. 'What?'

Miller's voice was thick. 'You won't answer when I say, "hey", but you look up when I say, "hey, Kojak". Have you got a complex about your hair?'

'No, Miller, I haven't.'

Webb ran his other hand through his hair.

'That's all right then.'

Webb nodded and returned to his work. He told himself to relax.

'Hey.'

Webb flicked a page of the report he had been reading.

'Hey, baldy.'

Webb looked up. 'What?'

'See? You have got a complex.'

Miller started laughing. He thumped the desk with his hand. 'Sorry, like, no offence.'

'No offence taken.'

Miller was suddenly aware of a presence behind him and swivelled in his chair. Frank Galvin stood there, hands on hips, mouth open, brow furrowed.

'From the sublime to the ridiculous,' Miller said.

'Miller?'

'Yes, ginger-bap?'

16

'I'm sorry?'

'I said, it must be a real pain having to go through life with ginger hair. Not being liked by anyone.'

'I . . .'

'My dad had a theory that people with ginger hair were taken out of the womb too soon. That they weren't done properly. What do you think? Were you premature, Frank?'

'Miller, I . . .'

'I, I, I, I.'

Miller stood, pushing his seat backwards, and set off across the newsroom. Halfway across, a telephone line, snaking out from beneath a desk, caught his foot. He stumbled forward, clutched at a desk, then slowly righted himself. He glanced down at the offending flex, still coiled round his foot, and after a moment's hazy reflection yanked at it. The phone came shooting off the desk and hit him square in the groin. With a wail he collapsed to the ground.

He lay there for about a minute, foetally curled round the phone. Reporters all over the newsroom stood by their desks watching. Galvin crossed to where he was lying and stood above him, shaking his head.

Miller opened one eye and watched him; the eye swivelled round the room, taking in as many faces as it could from its lowly position. Miller's hand moved slowly to his crotch and gently traced its outline. 'God,' he whispered, 'take away the pain, but leave the swelling.'

2

The door was closed, but unlocked. Marie Young pushed it open, stepped into the gloom and then closed it softly behind her. She leant back against it. No exertion, but her heart was beating fast with memory. Three weeks he had been gone, but it was still his room. It still smelt of him — no, smell was the wrong word, aura perhaps; it gave off an impression of him. His stuff was still all there. The police had been through it, of course. They'd left it in such a mess that Mrs Hardy had had to come and tidy it up herself, something Marie thought she would never have done for any of her other guests. It would have been bundled up, and out the door.

Marie pushed herself off the door and crossed to the bed. She sat down on its edge and ran her hand over the quilt. Here they had lain together. Here they had argued playfully over who would sleep on which side. It was a single bed and he had found it difficult to sleep when she was there, but he never complained; in the nights he huffed and puffed and sighed, but he never said a word. She drifted in and out of sleep herself, but she'd always been like that. In fact she slept better with him than with anyone she could remember.

She wondered who it was that had told the police. She didn't think Mrs Hardy knew; certainly she had never mentioned it, not even hinted at it, and she was a big, honest woman. Perhaps it was Tom O'Hanlon, the insurance man, on the top floor, who had taken a shine to her himself, been rebuffed, and now only glared at her over his newspaper on the few occasions he made it down for breakfast. Or the McCauleys, the unemployed couple in the room next to hers. They were friendly enough, in a reserved way. They carried their resentment at being unemployed very publicly; they were both teachers at the local secondary school until they were made redundant because of falling numbers of pupils. Education was never a big priority for the denizens of Crossmaheart. Most likely, though, it was Mrs Brady, the retired headmistress. She held the McCauleys in contempt because they were unemployed, barely registered the existence of Tom O'Hanlon and regarded Marie as little more than a hussy because she worked in a pub. Mrs Brady had not exactly caught them on, but she had seen her outside his room early one morning. They had passed each other in the hall without speaking but Marie knew that her face had burnt red, there, and later at breakfast too. Nothing was said, of course.

When he failed to return, the police spent longer with her than with anyone else in the house. They made it clear they knew the nature of their relationship, made it clear with their suggestive eyes and barely masked innuendo. They certainly hadn't accused her of anything, of any involvement, nothing of the kind.

Patting the bed, Marie rose, blew a kiss to the room and left. She went down to the breakfast room and sat opposite Tom O'Hanlon. He pulled the corner of the *News Letter* back for a second, but didn't acknowledge her. In a moment Mrs Brady and the McCauleys arrived together and sat around the table. The Radio Ulster news drifted in from the kitchen. They had long since given up listening for any word of him. He was no longer news, even though it had only been a few weeks. The empty seat spoke up for him. Sometimes she felt it was screaming at her. Sometimes she would reach under the table and run her foot down one of its dark legs, as she had done when he had sat there. Sometimes she had gone further, running her foot up into his crotch, she carrying on a conversation with Mrs Hardy or the McCauleys the whole time and he bursting red.

Mrs Hardy emerged from the kitchen laden with a hefty wooden tray and wished them all a hearty good morning. She set it down on the table and puffed out a blow of air from her flushed cheeks. 'I hope you don't mind having porridge this morning,' she said.

'I don't mind so long as it wasn't done in the microwave,' said Mrs Brady. 'I always think it's never cooked all the way through.'

Mrs Hardy turned away, winking at Marie as she did. 'I don't think anyone's ever been killed by a raw oat, Mrs Brady,' she said as she disappeared into the kitchen, the door swinging to before Mrs Brady had a chance to respond.

'I'll be mother then,' said Mrs McCauley, lifting the first of the bowls and passing it to Mrs Brady who accepted it without comment. Everybody called her Mrs McCauley, but Marie found it difficult. She was only the same age as her and, she thought, less intelligent. She thought of Mrs as a term of respect for an elder and better, not just something you used freely on any married person.

'Did you get started then?' Mr McCauley asked Marie.

Marie shook her head quickly.

'Started what?' Mrs Brady asked.

'Didn't you know, our Marie is going to be a writer?'

Mrs Brady snorted into her porridge. 'Of course, she's a regular polymath. Waitress, writer, goes without saying. Whatever next?'

'I am too,' Marie said and immediately regretted it. It made her sound like a petulant twelve-year-old. I am a petulant twenty-five-year-old, she told herself.

'What went wrong? You'd big plans to get started last night.'

Marie shrugged. She hadn't actually sworn him to

20

secrecy, but there was no need to bring it up in public, embarrassing her like that. Still, he probably meant no harm. Poor unemployed sod, she thought maliciously, and smiled keenly at him. 'I went out to buy a word processor yesterday, but I got drunk at lunch time and bought a food processor by mistake. I lost three fingers trying to type in the first sentence.'

Mrs Brady spluttered into her porridge. Tom O'Hanlon put down his paper at last, smiling in spite of himself.

'There's absolutely no need for that,' Mrs Brady admonished. She reached over and began to shovel heaped spoonfuls of sugar onto her porridge. Then she repeated the exercise for her tea.

'I see you're still on your calorie-out-of-control diet, Mrs Brady,' said Tom O'Hanlon, glancing surreptitiously at Marie for approval.

The McCauleys grinned at each other. Marie wanted to laugh but bit her lip, not so much to avoid giving offence to Mrs Brady as to withdraw her approval from anything O'Hanlon might say or do. The stupid, sulky man.

'My dear young man, I'm sixty-nine years old and I haven't had a day's illness in my life. Sugar may rot the teeth, but I fail to see what other damage it could possibly do to your body.'

'Excuse my ignorance,' asked Mrs McCauley, who had been biting her own lip for some moments, 'but what is a polymath?'

Mrs Brady shook her head slightly. Tom O'Hanlon studiously examined the remains of his porridge. Mr McCauley looked to Mrs Brady.

'It's someone who's an expert in more than one field, dear,' said Mrs Brady.

'Like a farmer,' added Marie, helpfully.

'Don't listen to her, dear. I was using the term sarcastically. If that girl ever produces a novel I'll eat my hat.'

21

'Get some fibre in the diet,' murmured Tom O'Hanlon.

Mrs Brady was many things but she wasn't deaf and she gave O'Hanlon a look that could cook porridge. 'It's my son's the deaf one,' she snapped hotly, 'and I don't need you to remind me of it . . .'

'I never mentioned . . .' Tom began.

'And how is young Brendan?' interjected Mrs McCauley, attempting to defuse the situation.

Brendan was far from young, touching forty, and had built a promising career for himself in a prominent charity for the deaf. He didn't visit his mother very often. Rarely, in fact. He wrote her a lot of letters. Always neatly typed. Mrs Brady liked this. It showed how efficient and business-like his attitude to life was, qualities she had always admired and which she had attempted to instil in him as a boy. Normality was the key to dealing with a disadvantage, she believed. She didn't know that he dictated the letters to his partially deaf secretary which meant that what he planned to say rarely made its way into the finished product. For example, when he would dictate wearily of his latest brain-storming session over budgets, she would read of his barn-storming exploits with budgies and grow concerned over his extra-curricular activities. When he wrote angrily of show-downs with his boss, she would hear of hoe-downs and think what a wonderful, relaxed job he had. When they did meet, annually usually, they had some wonderfully bizarre conversations. Brendan didn't like to travel to Crossmaheart; most everyone he met made fun of him because he was deaf. Even perfectly respectable adults. It was a strange town. It was never personal, which he didn't appreciate. They didn't mean any harm by it. They called a spade a spade and sometimes a shovel. Crossmaheart people made fun of everyone. Normal or disabled. Crossmaheart still had a Cripples Institute. There were no special people in Crossmaheart. There were no intellectually or physically challenged people. There were mentals and cripples. There were no single-parent families, there were bastards and sluts. There were natural-born mentals and mental cases, nuts who had made themselves crazy through wielding a gun in the name of one military faction or another. There were natural-born cripples and those who had brought it on themselves, gunmen who had been shot, gunmen who had shot themselves, bombers who had blown their hands off, thieves who had been shot in the legs by terrorists because they (the thieves) were a menace to society, and you could see them hopping down the streets, wearing their disability with pride like it was some red badge of courage.

'Brendan's fine,' Mrs Brady beamed, 'he's hoping to hear about a promotion quite soon.'

'Hear about it?' Marie asked.

'What?' snapped Mrs Brady.

'What?' replied Marie.

'What?' demanded Mrs Brady.

'What?' asked Marie.

Mrs Brady slammed down her spoon. 'Are you making fun of me, young lady?'

'Me?'

'I've a good mind to . . .'

'What?'

'Tan your bloody . . .'

Marie slammed her own spoon down. 'Is that a deaf threat?' she asked.

Mrs Brady paled. The McCauleys shook their heads in unison. Tom returned to his paper.

The kitchen door swung open again. 'Hot enough for you Mrs Brady?' Mrs Hardy asked.

After she had taken her pills, Marie popped downstairs again for a cup of tea with Mrs Hardy. It had become a bit

23

of a habit over the months. She didn't start in the bar till
eleven. Tom O'Hanlon was gone to work, the McCauleys
always went out early and Mrs Brady was closeted in her
room with Gospel tapes and a Bible. 'You do give her a hard
time, don't you, Marie?' Mrs Hardy observed, slowly stirring
her tea.

Marie shrugged. 'It's difficult not to sometimes.'

'Ach, I know, she's a miserable old soul, but there's no
harm in her. It might ease things a little if you could bite
your tongue the odd time. Just to keep the peace.'

'I know I should. It's just difficult, y'know?'

Mrs Hardy nodded her head slowly, but it wasn't really
an agreeing nod. She'd made her point.

'You know the police were back last night?'

Marie shook her head. 'What do they want now?'

'Ach, just more of the same.'

'Still no word then?'

'Nah.'

She could see him. Plain as day. Could touch him. Could
feel the hair on his arms. His chest. The morning-after beer-
breath. She shivered. 'What are you going to do? About the
room, I mean. It's been weeks.'

'Oh, I'll give it a while yet. I'm in no rush. Sure he'll
probably turn up safe and sound and what would he be
thinking of me if I had all his stuff out of there? He'll come
wanderin' through that door one day with a paper under
his arm and wonder where his tea is. That's the like of him.'

She makes it sound so romantic, Marie thought, so lovely
and unbelievable and romantic. Marie knew he would
never walk through that door. He would never whistle,
badly, the tune from *The Good, the Bad and the Ugly*. It was
Crossmaheart. People didn't reappear in Crossmaheart.

She could still see him, that last night in Riley's. He knew
he shouldn't really have made a habit of going in there, it
wasn't the right pub for his sort, but she was there and he

24

liked to watch her work and enjoy a bit of crack with her. He believed he had a certain degree of immunity because he worked for the paper. Sometimes the men would have a go at him because of something the paper had said, something they perceived as against their sort, but it all seemed good-humoured enough and he got the same kind of hassle across the road in his own sort of pub anyway. That last night they had been particularly busy; she'd been confined behind the bar instead of her usual free-ranging round the tables and she'd only been able to catch glimpses of him as he sat at a table near the door reading a paper and sipping a pint. And then when she could finally take a breather and think about buying them both a drink she had gone across with them but he'd been gone. Just gone. She didn't like to ask then, didn't like to seem too interested. The customers knew there was something between them, but she didn't like to seem too . . . taken in front of them. Bad for tips. Flirty as ever. She'd hung about long after closing, for he liked to walk home with her along the pockmarked streets, put his arm round her and snuggle her as the helicopters hovered overhead. But he had not returned. Nor had he been at home. And then the police had come.

As usual Marie walked to work. The McCauleys had given her a lift a few times shortly after she'd arrived in their battered old Volvo, but they weren't impressed by her tardiness and soon stopped offering. She didn't see what difference it made to them that she was a few minutes late, they'd no jobs to go to, but then she supposed that they'd trained and worked according to a tight schedule and it might be difficult to shake it off. Mr McCauley had been – was – a history teacher and spent a lot of time in the library, although he always moaned about its poor selection of books in his particular field. His wife was a domestic science teacher and did a lot of voluntary work in the town, helping with the elderly and the infirm. 'Doing my bit for the cripples,' she'd begun to say when asked about it, falling easily into the local way of things.

There was no rush hour to avoid. Those who worked, worked outside the town, in the city. Although it was generally accepted in the wider world that work started around 9 am, the situation was such in Crossmaheart that if you intended getting to the city for that time you left pretty much whenever you felt like it, because the chances were that you wouldn't get there on time. Outside the town, in every direction, were the checkpoints. They weren't permanent, like a wife, but time-consuming and unpredictable like a steady girlfriend with a roving eye. You could leave at dawn and be passed through with a salutary wave and be in work two hours early. You could leave with just enough time to drive at sixty miles an hour the whole way to the city, and be pulled over and your car reduced to a pile of nuts and bolts. You never took anything for granted.

But work, as such, didn't greatly concern the people of Crossmaheart. Nothing very much concerned them, besides fighting and rowing and collecting their unemployment cheques. Once a quaint picture postcard village, it had been swamped in a couple of years by the dregs of the city, guinea pigs in a scheme to alleviate the urban decay and religious mayhem of Belfast by shifting it to an idyllic existence in the country, with its own industries, its modern leisure facilities and enlightened infrastructure. The planners had taken everything into account, except human nature. They transferred scum from slums into scum with immersion heaters. They had hoped Crossmaheart would reflect all of life's rich tapestry, and perhaps for one bright shining moment it had; but then someone had stolen it. The factories soon fell prey to the gangs and the symbols of war, and the onset of recession finally closed them down. The leisure centre was bombed. The shopping mall fell vacant. The Main Street was still there, with Riley's pub and the

Ulster Arms doing the best business of all. Westwood's Bookmakers was enjoying a boom. And the glaziers did best of all because there was never a night when there wasn't a window smashed somewhere.

It wasn't that much of a walk to work anyway. Mrs Hardy's guesthouse was on the outskirts of town – still on the Main Street but at the far end of its ribboned development. As she walked along the cracked pavement Marie kept her eyes down, was careful not to trip. She knew people who made a living out of tripping over cracked flagstones and claiming compensation off the government. It wasn't her style. She listened to her Walkman. At the moment her favourite music was the second side of *Stupidity* by Dr Feelgood. She had listened to it every morning for three months. She switched on as she left the house, and the album finished with 'Roxette' as she opened the door of the pub. If anyone asked her how far she lived away from her work, she would sometimes reply, 'Stupidity,' and leave it at that.

As had become her habit, Marie glanced at the corner seat as she entered the bar, the seat where she had last seen him. Of course there was no one there, the pub was still not open. She went behind the bar, hung up her coat. Johnny Riley, son of the owner, Pearse, said good morning as she passed. He was studying a newspaper and didn't see her nod, so he said it again and this time she replied with a grunt.

'Rough night?' Johnny asked.

'Ish,' said Marie, getting a Coke and hitching herself up on a stool in front of the bar.

'Sore head?'

'Ish.'

'I don't know how you stick it, girl, working in here all hours, then wanting to spend all your free time in the pub as well. You'd think all this shite would put you off the drink.'

27

Marie shrugged. 'Sure what else is there to do in this hole?' she asked.

Johnny shrugged himself and returned to the paper. Marie sipped at her drink, swivelling in her seat to look at the table in the corner. The winter sun angling through the window illuminated that corner of the pub. Almost like heaven shining on it, she thought, then quickly told herself to wise up.

It was still early in the week so the lunch-time crowd was pretty small. Towards two, when they stopped serving food, a small, neatly dressed but haggard-looking man came through the doors. He stood for a moment, until his eyes got used to the gloom, then crossed to Johnny at the bar and ordered a pint. Crossmaheart is big enough, but it's a two-pub town. It's not the sort of place strangers call into for a quiet drink. To say that all eyes in the pub followed him is, well, the truth. Lifting his pint, aware that he was the focus of attention, he gave Johnny a faintly nervous smile and carried it across to the table in the corner.

Marie slipped off her stool, lifted her notepad, and crossed to him. 'Eating?' she asked.

He set his pint down, leaving a white moustache above his bare lip. 'I hadn't thought about it,' he said.

'Well, you'd better, we stop serving in a minute.'

'Oh . . . I see. Do you have a menu?'

Marie shook her head. 'We're having new ones done.'

'Oh . . . well . . .'

'You just tell me what you fancy and I'll see what I can do.'

'Oh, I . . . don't know. What about, ahm, something, uh, light, uh – Prawn Marie Rose?'

Marie looked at him. She shook her head slightly. Folded her arms. 'You're from Belfast, right?'

The man nodded, embarrassed. She turned back to Johnny and shouted. 'Man wants Prawn Marie Rose.'

Johnny shook his head. 'All out of prawns, love. Have to be Prawn Marie Celeste.'

'Prawn Marie Celeste?' asked Marie.

The man shook his head. 'I . . .'

'How about Chicken Masala?' asked Marie.

'I . . .'

'Any Chicken Masala, Johnny?'

'All out of Masala, love, have to be Chicken Masada.'

'What's Chicken Masada?' Marie asked.

'Basically it's your normal chicken, but after we serve it we tape all the doors shut and commit suicide.'

'Chicken Masada then, is it?' Marie asked the man.

'I . . .'

Johnny burst into laughter from behind the bar. 'Marie, will you give the man peace? He's only in for a quiet pint and something to eat.'

'I never said a thing,' Marie protested and smiled down at her customer. He smiled back, but there was a nervous sheen of sweat on his brow. 'So what's it to be? Will I do you a Mexican burger?'

'Uh, yeah, sure. Uh, what is it exactly?'

'It's the same as an ordinary burger, but I wear a sombrero when I serve it.'

She kept her face straight, but this time he gave out a big laugh. 'Sure,' he said, 'bring me that.'

'Right you be.'

She was about to turn when he said, 'Do all your customers get treated to this floor show?'

'Nah,' she said, 'only the blow-ins.'

Later, after he had eaten and the pub was quiet, she went back over to his table and apologized for taking the piss. He laughed and told her not to worry. He offered to buy her a drink. She said why not and sat down. She bought the next one. As she was reaching into her bag he nodded at her hand and said: 'When did you break it?'

'What?'

'Your hand. You must have broken it recently.'

She examined it herself. 'How the fuck do you know that?' It came out sharper than she meant. She put her other hand on his arm apologetically. 'I mean . . . I'm sorry, but . . . ?'

He laughed again – a nice laugh, she liked it – and took another sip of his pint. 'It's the hair on your hand. I had the same. When you break your hand, because it's all plastered up for weeks away from the sunlight, the hairs grow back black and thick. See mine? One hand you wouldn't notice the hairs, the other, look at them, like a bear's.'

'It's a good job I didn't break my jaw then,' she said, 'or I'd have a beard by now.'

'How'd you break it?'

'Don't ask.'

'I'm asking.'

Marie shrugged. 'I punched a wall.'

The man nodded. 'I'll have to keep on the right side of you then.'

'Yeah, well.'

'What brought that on?'

Marie looked at him.

'I'm sorry,' he said quickly, 'I'm being nosy.'

She stood up. 'Customers,' she said, nodding back to the bar, 'I'll have to run.'

His mouth narrowed apologetically. 'Sure. Cheers. Thanks for the drink.'

'You're a journalist, aren't you?' she said.

He nodded.

'I thought so.'

'How on earth can you tell?'

She shrugged. 'I don't know. Something.'

She went to work. When she looked later he was gone.

30

Johnny noticed that she was disturbed. Noticed her snatching a couple of vodkas too many during the night. He asked her if she was okay, but as ever she said sure and went on about her work, her mouth working away the whole time. He didn't know where she found all the chat. He knew she had ambitions to be a writer. If she ever gets round to it, he thought, it'll be a bloody big book.

She didn't remember at first whose bed it was. The room was lit only by the light from the hall snaking under the bedroom door. He lay beside her, his bulk, his builder's bulk and sweat. He had sulked for a long time because she wouldn't let him touch her and now he was snoring, big boomers that drew sympathetic replies from tankers in Belfast Lough.

Her mouth was thick with drink. She scrambled in the dark for the bedside lamp, then stretched across for her handbag. She found her pills, sat for a moment trying to work out if she'd taken one already that night, then swallowed one. She lit a cigarette and lay back.

It was about three. She couldn't be entirely sure because her watch had been running slow of late. Like my life, she thought. Like my bloody life. He was fat, he was as ugly as sin, and she had needed the company. Nothing had happened between them, and she was relieved that he hadn't tried to force the issue, because then she would have had to stab him. She hadn't stabbed anyone yet. She didn't go about looking for someone to stab. She went about looking for love and companionship and sometimes good sex. But if they were looking for trouble, they'd come to the right bitch. That was how she'd thought of it when she armed her handbag with a fork and a pointed steel comb. She always kept the bag within easy reach of the sofa or the bed or the car, unzipped.

*   *   *

31

He didn't come in the next day, but the next one, a Friday, he was back at the same table, at just about the same time, just nicking in before they closed the kitchen.

'You journalists like living on the edge, don't you,' she said when she went to take his order, 'cutting it this fine?'

'Goes with the job.'

'I thought you'd have blown back to the smoke by now. There's not many stay this long.'

'I'm working here. With the *Chronicle*.'

'The *Chronicle*?'

'The *Crossmaheart Chronicle*, the local . . .'

She snapped: 'You don't have to explain. I do live here.'

He blanched.

'I'm sorry,' she said immediately.

'Uh . . .'

There was a tear in her eye now; she could feel it, he could see it. 'I'm sorry,' she repeated, and the tear fell onto her order pad, soaking in. Just one tear.

'Did I say . . . ?'

'No, no,' she said, shaking her head. She sat down opposite him and said quietly. 'I'm sorry . . . I was . . . I am a friend of Jamie Milburn.'

He nodded. He put a hand on her arm. It felt warm. His hand. And her arm. 'I'm here to cover for him until he . . . turns up.'

'We were good friends, you know?'

'I never met him. I'm told he was a good reporter.'

'I don't know — about reporting. I don't know anything about reporting. But he was a good writer. He was helping me to write. I was writing a book.'

She liked him: he had a warmth about his eyes which belied his dishevelled, slightly wasted appearance.

'What's your book about?'

'It's about that old Irish blues singer, Muddy Trousers.'

He looked at her.

'Or was it Broken Waters?' she added.

'You're taking the piss,' he said.

She smiled. 'Only a bit. I hate talking about things I haven't written yet.'

'I thought Jamie was helping you?'

'He was. But it was mostly just talking, talking it through, talking about a plot and characters and grammar and poetry and all that. I had a cunt of an English teacher right the way through school, if you'll excuse my French. I loved English, but I learnt nothing. Until I met Jamie I thought Iambic pentameter was an Olympic sport. For five years I tried to impress people that I was really into that beat writer, Jack Caramac.'

He had a big smile on now. She liked that too. 'I think you'd make a good writer.'

She smiled too. She put her hand out to him. 'I'm Marie Young. I'm sorry for getting upset. I liked Jamie a lot.'

'Perfectly understandable.'

'There's no word on him yet then?'

He shook his head. 'I don't know if they're even still looking for him. They've enough on their plates down here as it is.'

Marie bit at her lip. 'He'll turn up.'

'I hope so.'

'And till then you're filling his boots.'

'So to speak.'

'Good. You seem nice.'

'Thanks.'

'I didn't mean it to sound so patronizing.'

'It didn't.'

'Well?'

'Well what?'

'I'm Marie Young . . . and you're . . . ?'

'Sorry . . . Miller.'

'Miller what?'

'Miller nothing. Nothing Miller. Just Miller.'

She crinkled her brow. 'That's a bit dramatic, isn't it?'

He shook his head. 'It's got less to do with drama than silly Christian names.'

'Are you serious?'

He nodded. 'Serious.'

'Well, how silly are we talking here?'

'Extremely silly.'

'What, like Glenn Miller?'

'No.'

'Windy Miller?'

'Nope.'

'Miller Lite?'

'You could probably go on for quite a while. But there's not much point, I doubt you'll get it. Not many do.'

'It's not, like, a girl's name, is it?'

'I'm not telling.'

'That means it is.'

'No, that means I'm not telling.'

'Go on.'

'Nope.'

'You're no fun.'

'I'm no fun.'

She tutted. 'I'll get it eventually.'

'I doubt it.'

'Do you want to go out for a drink one night?' she asked.

It came out of the blue so fast he almost said no. And it came out of her blue so fast she nearly kicked herself because she didn't want, didn't need, to get involved with another bloody journalist. Something moved her to it.

'You're asking me out?'

'For a drink. I want to ask you about writing.'

'You want to ask me about my name.'

'That too.'

'A night out in Crossmaheart?'

34

'We could go further afield. Up to town if you want. Something different.'

'I'm very busy for the next wee while. At nights, I mean. Things to sort out in Belfast, a lot of work here in Crossmaheart.'

'You don't want to go out, do you?' Half a snap. Then calmer: 'I'm sorry, I've embarrassed you.'

'Not at all, not at all.' He touched her arm again. Warm. Her arm. His hand. 'It's just that I am really busy. But what about, say . . . what, today's Friday. What about next Monday? That okay? Next Monday? Sure we could go up to the smoke. Talk about writing. Christian names. Whatever.'

She smiled.

'Okay.'

'If I don't see you before then . . . where'll I pick you up?'

She gave him her address and they settled on a time. They both smiled.

'Okay, now we've got that sorted out, how's about some lunch?'

She stood up, professional now. 'I'm sorry,' she said, 'the kitchen's closed.'

3

Miller hated Crossmaheart. He hated the people for their narrow minds and streets, for the violence which exuded from every crossed eye, every bricked-up house, for the malevolence which swept the cold, uniformly broken estates day and night. The constant burr of watchful helicopters assaulted and insulted him like an incurable tinnitus.

He had been there before, of course, ten or twelve times. Maybe more. There were good stories to be had in Crossmaheart. Horror stories. It was a place for a fledgling reporter to make his name, but he was long past that.

So when Frank Galvin asked him if he would accept immediate demotion and a transfer to the local paper in Crossmaheart, Miller replied, 'Gladly.'

'You have no problems with that at all?'

'None.'

He was, of course, in a corner. Galvin watched him carefully. He hadn't detected any sarcasm in the voice, so he watched for it in his eyes. None.

'There isn't really any alternative, is there? I'm sorry, Miller. It's the best I can do.'

He wasn't really trying to justify it. He had no need to. He held all the cards, and he could have handed them to Miller and showed him the door. That he was allowing him a foothold, a tenuous foothold, in the organization was much more than his duty. It had been a firing offence, drunk in the office. No, not drunk, more than that: over the top way out pissed as fuck stocious. Where such a state might have produced in others a sullen, meaningless gibber, it had honed and defined Miller's observation, distilled every innocent detail into a barbed comment, loosed in him the demon of honesty. Galvin did have ginger hair. Alec Webb was going bald. Vomit was difficult to get out of a computer keyboard.

Galvin would probably have let it go with a warning but for the fact that the latter part of Miller's performance, an attempted handstand to prove that a blow to the balls had not emasculated him, ended up flattening William J. Deveney, managing director of the newspaper group, as he began one of his rare tours of the newsroom.

Deveney, his pride and his glasses dented, would probably have dismissed it himself as horseplay had he not been accompanied by his wife Pauline, whose beauty was only surpassed by her abhorrence of alcohol.

Now, Miller felt tired. It was a few days since his performance, but there was a weariness about him that was beyond his usual lethargy. He needed a rest. A change. Something different. Later his friends would say to him that he needed Crossmaheart like a hole in the head, indeed that Crossmaheart might mean a hole in the head, but he knew he hadn't the gumption to refuse, to strike out on his own somewhere, somewhere new and hot and challenging, to re-create himself. He needed someone to tell him where to go, to set it up for him, to father him into it.

'I know you've had a hard time lately,' Galvin was saying, 'but we have to draw the line somewhere.'

'I know.'

'You do a good job down there, we'll see about bringing you back up, some time. It's your choice, of course. You can refuse. I'm sure you could pick up plenty of work elsewhere.'

Miller shrugged. 'I'm happy enough. I like the security of it.'

Galvin recognized that as sarcasm. He tutted, but otherwise ignored it. He hadn't expected Miller to go for it. He'd expected Miller to tell him where to go. In fact he hadn't even bothered to formally set up the job. He had put vague feelers out about the transfer, but Miller's placidity, although it fell somewhat short of contrition, had surprised him. 'You know who you're replacing, don't you? Jamie Milburn?'

'I read about him.'

'Yeah.'

'Any word on him?'

'Nothing. Nothing yet.'

'You want me to . . . ?'

'I want you to do nothing.'

'I mean just to . . .'

'Nothing. The last thing we need in Crossmaheart is a reporter nosing around. Something happens, report it, otherwise leave it alone. Crossmaheart's a delicate place. Our paper sits nicely on the fence down there, the last thing we need is someone in there upsetting the body cart.'

'Apple cart.'

'Apple cart, whatever. You write the news like you're a member of the Alliance Party, see both sides, prevaricate. The politics of sitting round a table and having a chat. Nobody's wrong, everyone's right. You know the score.'

'Frank, people who try to kick with both feet usually fall on their skulls. You ever wonder why we don't have an Alliance government?'

'Just because it doesn't work in politics, Miller, doesn't mean it won't work elsewhere. In Crossmaheart, you move slightly to one side, you lose half your market. There is no middle ground in Crossmaheart, that's why our paper has to be that middle ground.'

'You make it sound very noble.'

'Noble fuck, Miller, it's profit. It's a small operation, but it's keeping half the people here in their jobs.'

'Fair enough.' Miller rubbed at the stubble on his chin while Galvin went into the practicalities of his move to Crossmaheart. Galvin appeared to have organized things quite well, although he hadn't, and was mostly making them up as he went along. Miller showed a reluctance to take over Jamie Milburn's room in the boarding house, so Galvin agreed to organize a house or an apartment. And a car.

'I don't need a car.'

'You need to get around.'

'I have my bike.'

'Jesus, have you turned green or something?'

'Only since I went out drinking. The bike's good enough for me. It's healthy. It's good luck.'

'If I had luck like yours, Miller, I'd scrap that bike.'

'Nothing that has happened recently has anything to do with luck, Frank. My dad died of cancer. I got drunk of my own accord and made a fool of myself. And now I'm off to the sticks to practise diplomacy amongst the heathens as a result. It's got nothing to do with luck.'

Galvin shook his head. 'Whatever you say.'

And so to Crossmaheart, arriving on a bright winter afternoon, riding the forty-odd miles from Belfast on the Cycle of Violence, feeling for all the world like the Lone Ranger riding into town.

Along past the grey-brick, single-storey town hall, the burnt-out shell of the Tonic cinema, past the courthouse surrounded by barbed wire and ringed by oil drums filled to the brim with cement to deter car bombers, his hair blown long and dank behind him, his face flushed with the journey, eyes red, a green rucksack on his back carrying his essential possessions. He, and the rest of his belongings, would have come by train, but there was a bomb on the line outside the city and he'd had to leave them back home.

Locking up the house, switching off the power, leaving a home that no longer felt like a home seemed to boost him, to give him that kick up the backside he'd needed since his father's death. It was a mild irritation that the trains were off; he merely redirected the taxi back to the house, spent five minutes unloading his luggage again; then in the headiness of his change-is-as-good-as-a-rest situation set off on two wheels and his own engine for Crossmaheart. He had about five miles under his belt when he realized how seriously unfit he was.

His allegiance to the Cycle of Violence was not entirely based on health, ease of access or the luck, good or otherwise, it brought him. He had managed to keep the fact that he had been banned from driving, following a drunken escapade up on the north-west coast, away from Frank Galvin. It was, like so many other things, a sacking offence to lose your licence. He'd appeared at a local magistrates' court a month later. Representing himself – not having a solicitor meant he had to involve fewer people in the lying process – he had stressed his middle name, which was marginally less silly than his first name, and described himself as unemployed, and thus managed to circumnavigate the attentions of the bright-eyed but dull-witted court reporter who might otherwise have recognized him and sold the story to one of the other Belfast papers, or, indeed, Miller's own. He was, after all, a minor celebrity, ish. A hundred-pound fine and a one-year ban, of which eight months were left to run. Any other part of the UK he would have taken his chances and continued driving, but there were so many police or army checkpoints about the city, and, indeed, in Crossmaheart, that it was pointless. The first thing they asked for was a driving licence, provided you stopped. Otherwise they asked the mortuary attendant for it.

Approaching Main Street the traffic ground to a halt. About two hundred yards up Miller could see a grey police Land Rover. A couple of cops were questioning drivers, while on both footpaths soldiers kept eyes peeled for snipers. Eyes peeled, he thought, a lovely expression. Miller freewheeled up the line of cars towards the checkpoint. It had once been a permanent checkpoint, housed in a sandbagged enclosure, but it had been bombed so frequently that it had given up on any pretence of permanence and now just migrated up and down the Main Street at varying hours of the day.

As Miller approached, one of the officers straightened from speaking through a car window, waved the driver on, then raised his hand towards him.

'Where the fuckin' hell do you think you're going?' he rasped.

Miller drew up a metre in front, brakes whining. 'Crossmaheart,' he said, stepping down from the pedals.

'Ever heard of fuckin' queuing?'

He could feel the steam rising from his body. He wiped his brow and said: 'Sorry, I thought, being a bike . . .'

'Could I see some identification, sir?'

Miller reached inside his jacket, slowly, aware of the increased attention he was getting from the soldiers, rifles raised, and produced his wallet. Normal ID was a driver's licence. Theoretically he could have produced a Cycling Proficiency Test certificate, although he wasn't sure if it would have much pull with anyone over the age of eleven. He showed his press card.

'A journalist?'

'Sure.'

The policeman looked incredulous. 'Who with? With what?'

'The *Chronicle*.'

'Since when?'

41

'Since . . . well, about half an hour from now.'

The policeman nodded his head, then handed Miller's card back. 'Hope you last longer than the last one.'

Miller nodded. 'Hope so.'

'Okay, on you go, Mr Miller. Try and be more careful in future. Jumping queues can get you shot round here.'

'Fair enough, constable . . . ?'

'Yes, constable.'

Miller shrugged and remounted. He looked like a tough one. The kind of cop who would give neither his name, his rank nor his favourite cereal under torture.

He rode on for a couple of minutes, stopped, allowed his breathing to settle down, then wheeled the Cycle of Violence into the *Chronicle* offices. They were situated halfway along the Main Street (halfway up or halfway down? he wondered), sandwiched between an estate agent's and a pub. There was another pub on the other side of the road. Handy, he thought.

Martin O'Hagan, the editor, was a tall, rangy kind of a man. Possibly in his forties, but probably younger, prematurely grey and paunched. He had an earnest handshake and an aura that suggested that he was confident in his own territory, but nervous out of it.

'You're welcome to the *Chronicle*, Miller,' said O'Hagan, then realized the double meaning and laughed. They both laughed. A couple of women in the background laughed as well. Miller turned to them and smiled.

'Hello,' he said.

'Hi,' they said together.

'This is Anne Maguire,' said O'Hagan, indicating a tall girl, maybe twenty-five, with long auburn hair and an earth mother skirt. 'She's a Catholic.'

Miller crocheted his brows.

'And this is Helen Sloan.' A short, weighty girl in a brown leather jacket and ski pants. 'A Protestant.'

42

'Do you always follow someone's name with their religion?'

'In here, yes. With the locals anyway. It reassures them that we are a balanced paper. Since Jamie, ah, went, we have been an unbalanced paper. I myself am a Catholic. That made it two Catholics to one Protestant on the reporting staff. Not good. Your arrival rectifies that. We are once again a balanced paper.'

'It's important,' said Helen.

'To have balance,' added Anne.

'Yin and Yang,' said O'Hagan.

Abbott and Costello, thought Miller.

They found a flat for him about two hundred yards from the newspaper office. It was damp and barely furnished, but he didn't mind that. O'Hagan and Helen Sloan had work to do, but Anne Maguire walked with him down the road to the flat. He took the front wheel, she the back, and they carried the Cycle of Violence up some bare stairs. Anne produced a key from a bulky leather handbag and unlocked the door.

'Thanks,' said Miller, as they set the bike down. 'I'm not as fit as I thought.'

'Which of us is?' said Anne. 'Who of us are?'

He set the rucksack on the floor and paced the room. There was a bed, a writing desk, a chest of drawers. He opened the drawers one at a time. A Bible in one. A coat hanger in the second. A porn mag in the third. He closed each of them. The windows, dirty, looked out over a high-walled concrete yard, bare.

'Is that all you brought with you?' Anne asked, indicating the rucksack.

'Oh, there's much more. There was a bomb on the line. I'll have to get it later.'

She nodded. 'So you're planning on staying for a while.'

Miller nodded. She regarded him silently. It felt uncomfortable. 'You know why I'm here?'

'To take Jamie's job.'

'Temporarily.'

'It's normal practice to wait until a body turns up before giving a man's job away.'

'I'm just filling in until he turns up, one way or the other.'

'Yeah, the way Hitler filled in Poland.'

'That's a bit over the top.'

'So are you.'

Miller shook his head. He walked to the window and stared at the barren yard.

Her voice rose in pitch. 'He could be lying sick somewhere or kidnapped or anything, and all they do up in the city is send someone to fill his boots. I don't care how big a fuckin' star you are up in Belfast, when it comes to Jamie's boots, you're on fuckin' baby sizes.'

He didn't need this. 'You think I wanted to come to this fuckin' open prison?' he snapped. 'You think I volunteered for sticks and stones duty down here? Come off it.'

When he looked round there were tears rolling down her cheeks and her head was moving slowly from side to side.

Miller leant against the window. 'I'm sorry. I'm sure you miss him. I don't know you well enough to put my arms round you.'

'I don't want your soddin' arms round me.' She drew her elbow roughly across her face.

'Listen, I was forced to come here, punishment for a heinous crime. I don't like it, and youse probably don't appreciate me being here, but I'm here to do a job, dull and boring as it might be, and that's all I'm going to do. Mind my own business, keep out of everyone's way, do my time. And I'm not worried if it's in solitary.'

She sighed and sat on the edge of the bed, then produced

a compact from her bag and studied her make-up. 'Jesus,' she said, 'look at the state of me. You'd think I loved the bastard or something.'

'Did you?'

She shook her head. 'Nah. Not me. He was a lovely fella though. Everyone liked him.' She managed a sheepish grin. 'And don't dare say someone didn't.' She snapped the compact shut. 'I'm sorry I had a go at you. We've been a bit rattled ever since he disappeared.'

'Never worry.'

'But you understand our point of view?'

Miller nodded.

'It's nothing personal.'

He shrugged. It felt personal. 'What's all this about, this is Anne and she's a Catholic? Is he serious? It's like a bad chat-up line. Hi, I'm Mike, and I'm a Gemini.'

'Did you never think he might be taking the piss?'

'I thought about it. You mightn't be Catholic.'

'I mightn't be Anne.'

'There's that.'

'Nah. Don't worry about it. Just Martin having a bit of fun.'

She started to rummage through her bag, and after a minute produced two sticks of chewing gum. She held one out to Miller. He crossed from the window. They unwrapped together.

'So,' said Miller.

'So.'

They chewed together, like a couple of cows.

'A Bible, a clothes hanger and a porn mag,' Miller said finally.

'What?'

'A Bible, a clothes hanger and a porn mag. That's what's in the chest of drawers.'

'It sounds like the title of a Peter Greenaway film.'

'I wonder who lived here last?'

'Marty Stevenson lived here last.'

'Who's Marty Stevenson?'

'Poor old Marty. It's always a bit of a shock when you go through someone else's drawers and you find something you shouldn't have. I never would have had Marty down as a Bible man.'

'Maybe that's why he left it behind.'

'Marty didn't leave anything behind, not on purpose.'

'Who's Marty Stevenson? And why didn't he leave anything behind?'

'Marty was one of our printers. Hadn't been with us long. He was in Riley's — that's one of our two pubs — a couple of weeks ago and got into an argument with someone over something stupid. He was asked outside to settle it in gentlemanly fashion and a gang beat him to death with hurley sticks.'

Brilliant, thought Miller, I am fated to walk with death.

'I didn't hear it on the news.'

'It didn't make much impression. It was the day of one of those big bombs in Belfast, it kind of got buried, like Marty. To tell you the truth, he didn't die right away, he kind of lingered for a while. The lingerers rarely make the top of the news.'

Miller took another look at the flat. The dead man's flat. 'Jesus,' he said, shaking his head.

'Marty was only just moving in here, so there wasn't much in the way of personal effects.' Anne nodded at the chest of drawers. 'I suppose he only moved his essentials in at the start.'

'So Riley's is a place to avoid? What's the other place like?'

'Worse.'

'So what is there to do at night?'

'No girlfriend?'

'No girlfriend.'

'Stay in. No one comes to Crossmaheart for the social life. Make use of what you have. Have a wank, get saved and practise hanging your favourite shirt.'

'Thanks.'

'No problem.'

A hundred yards down the road he found the Good Neighbour. A bullet-faced woman served him. She had a fat, ready smile. 'Chilly, isn't it? They say it'll brighten up later,' she said. He nodded.

'Do you have any pasta?' he asked.

Her brow furrowed, but her smile never wavered, which was a difficult thing to do. 'Of course we do. The pasties are down at the back.'

'No, I . . .' But he stopped, for there was something about her manner which suggested that he could spend half an hour explaining what pasta was, and at the end of it she would still say: 'The pasties are down the back.'

He went and got some pasties. They were a pale yellow and as hard as rocks. He bought some tinned foods with familiar labels. A loaf of bread. As she totted up the total she asked cheerily: 'Have you just moved in?'

Miller nodded warily.

'I saw you go past with the bicycle. Lovely bicycle. I'd love a bike. We have a car now. Sold the bike. But I liked the bike. We have a wonderful Christmas Club too.'

He nodded. Again.

'With some excellent bargains.'

'I don't think I'll be here that long.'

'Aw, that's a pity.'

'It is. Oh, well. How much is that?'

He paid up. He glanced back as he left. She was still smiling at him.

* * *

Their coldness unsettled him. He did what he could. He invited them out for lunch, but they were always busy. He asked them for a drink after work, but they always had to go straight home. The office staff weren't much better. When he was on a story, waiting for a call, the telephonist would buzz him. 'Call for you,' she would say. 'Who is it?' 'Don't know.' Click. O'Hagan gave him the shitty work. The jobs at night. Rewriting gibberish. Interviewing the senile and the mad. He'd done it all before. It was what a cub reporter expected to do. But he was an experienced reporter with a national reputation. Then he thought maybe O'Hagan and the rest of them might be being bastardy about it on orders from Belfast. To punish him. To test him. That it wasn't just pig ignorance. Then he had another thought, that it wasn't any of that at all, it was neither the cold shoulder because he was unwanted nor exclusion by design – it was just Crossmaheart.

He made a few trips up to Belfast. He didn't think he'd ever feel nostalgic for the city, but the feeling was unmistakable. His house, his real home, still didn't feel like home. The flat in Crossmaheart certainly didn't feel like home either, but he was able to make it a little bit more home-like now that the trains were running again and he was able to ferry down a lot more of his belongings. He brought his portable CD player and the pick of his collection. Dylan. Van Morrison. Kylie.

On a Tuesday morning he got a call in work. It was Marie. 'Where the fuck were you last night?' she screamed.
'I . . .'
'Where the fuck were you?'
'I . . .'
'Who the fuck do you think you are?'
'I . . .'
'You fuckin' bastard.'

48

'Look, I . . .'

'You fuckin' fucker . . .'

He put the phone down. She rang back within a minute.

'Don't you ever fuckin' do that to me again!' she screamed.

Very quickly he said: 'Now just calm down a minute. I can't talk to you if you're screaming at me. Just calm down.'

'I am calm!' she screamed, and then burst into tears.

'Just take it easy now, Marie. Settle down. Just tell me quietly what's wrong. What's happened.'

He heard her sniff. Then sniff again. Then her voice, quiet, hurt, a spoilt child's voice, but without the knowing calculation. 'You only needed to phone.'

'I didn't . . .'

'All you had to do was let me know. One wee phone call.' The voice grew harder. 'If you weren't interested . . . I mean I knew you weren't interested in the first place, but you had to go through with it . . .'

'Marie, I . . .'

'I won't be used like this! I won't be made a fool of!'

'MARIE!'

Silence. Then the child: 'What?'

'What on earth is all this for? What have I done?'

'As if you didn't know.'

'Marie, I don't know. I swear to God I don't know.'

'Liar.'

'Marie?'

'Why didn't you turn up?'

'Turn up where?'

'Jesus, you don't even remember! You're one smug bastard.'

'Marie . . .'

'I stayed in all last night waiting for you.'

'Marie, Jesus, is that what it's about? Our . . . drink?

Marie, I told you I couldn't see you till next week. Next week. I've been up to my ears. I told you that.'

'You told me last night. You told me Monday night.'

'I said next Monday.'

'Last night was Monday.'

'I said next Monday.'

'Last night was the next Monday.'

'I didn't mean it like that. I meant next Monday. The following Monday. If I'd meant yesterday I would have said, see you Monday. I said next Monday, meaning . . . next Monday.'

'Last night was the next Monday.'

'No, it wasn't . . . I mean, yes, it was Monday, but not the Monday I meant . . .' He tried to work it out precisely in his head. 'I'm confusing myself now. If it's any consolation, I know exactly what I mean. What I mean is, because it was the Friday we arranged this, and the weekend, I said next Monday to mean the Monday of the next week – not the one starting on Sunday, speaking as of Friday, but this coming Sunday, speaking as of today.'

Despite herself, she started to giggle softly. It was a pleasant, nasal giggle, reverberating softly on a bed of tears.

'I hope you write more clearly than you speak,' she said.

'So do I.'

'You ruined my night.'

'I'm sorry, I didn't mean . . .'

'It wasn't on purpose?'

'Of course it wasn't.'

'I don't need to be upset right now.'

'I know that, I wouldn't dream . . .'

'I hadn't seen you in the bar since, and I got to thinking when you didn't turn up that you'd only been messing around.'

'I'm not like that.'

'I hope not.'

'I'm not.'

'I hope not. I don't need that in my life.'

'I know.'

They were silent for a moment. Miller, who'd been speaking with his eyes closed and the thumb and finger of his left hand jammed into the corner of his eyes, glanced up, blinked, and saw O'Hagan watching him from the other end of the office. O'Hagan lifted a finger to his skull and slowly revolved it. His finger, not his skull. Miller shook his head at him.

'My boss thinks I'm talking to a loony.'

'What?'

'The boss, he thinks you're a loony.'

Silence.

'Marie?'

Silence.

'Marie?'

Cold, damp-gravelly-voiced: 'I'm not mad.'

Miller laughed. 'I didn't mean that. I mean, the boss thinks I've someone on the phone complaining about the paper, or something in the town. All papers are the same, they get calls from nuts all the time. It goes with the job.'

'You shouldn't call people loonies.'

'I don't mean anything . . .'

'Then why say it?'

'Marie, I . . .'

'So what are we going to do?'

'Eh?'

'About this going out. For a drink. Do you still want to, or have I scared you off?'

'No, of course, yes, of course I want to.'

'When then?'

'What . . .'

'And don't dare say bloody next anything. Give me a night. A date. A precise date.'

'What about tonight?'

'Tonight? That's tonight-tonight.'

'Yes. Tonight. Tuesday. Out for dinner. To make up for last night.'

Silence.

'Marie?'

Silence.

'Marie? You can't hear nodding over the phone. You actually have to say something.'

'I was just deciding. I really only phoned up to give you a piece of my mind. But if you're sure it was a . . . misunderstanding . . . well, okay. Tonight. As it happens I'm not working. Tonight then.'

When Miller put the phone down, O'Hagan, Anne and Helen were all watching him.

Helen offered him a piece of her KitKat. It was the nicest thing anyone had done for him in the paper yet. O'Hagan and Anne were both out of the office.

'I've been working on this bloody obituary all afternoon,' she said, 'and the only line I've been able to come up with is, Sorry you're dead.'

'Who died?'

'Small-time hard man. No one special.'

'Why do it then?'

'Ach, he was well known locally,' she said glumly. 'Played a lot of sport 'n' that. Dad's a local councillor. His favourite son dropped dead of a heart attack, which is a pleasant change round here.'

'I'm sure he appreciated it.'

He hated that about small-town papers as well. Having to do fawning obituaries for nobodies.

Helen shrugged. 'So,' she said, changing tack with a gossip's polished professionalism, 'I couldn't help overhearing you talking on the phone earlier. I take it that the Marie you referred to was the boul' Marie Young.' Miller nodded. 'Aye, I thought so, she's got a very . . . distinctive manner. How come you know her then?'

Miller shrugged too. 'Met her in the pub.'

'You know she was going out with Jamie?'

He nodded.

'I don't wish to speak ill of her if you're going out with her, like, but you know she's nuts?'

'Certifiably?'

'Well, I don't know if they've got round to presenting her with the certificate, but she's certainly done all the practical work.'

'Like what?'

'Well, it's really not my place to say, but she's got quite a reputation. Martin wouldn't have her in the office. She used to give Jamie hell. Let's just say I wouldn't be surprised if she has him stuffed and showcased in her house somewhere.'

'She seems okay to me.'

'That's the beauty of a real nut. They seem so normal.'

'Well, I'll bear it in mind.' It came out with a hint of hostility. His own tone surprised him, almost involuntarily abrupt.

With matching abruptness Helen stood up and reached for her coat. 'Appointment,' she said sharply, gliding past Miller's desk. She stopped suddenly, wheeled back. 'No offence,' she said softly, 'I just meant it as a friendly warning.'

Miller nodded.

When he got home there was an envelope waiting for him.

He took out a card with a drawing of a Labrador pup on the front, looking sheepish.

Inside it said in minute red writing: 'Sorry I flew off the handle. I promise to be on my best behaviour tonight. Love, Marie. XXX'

Miller smiled.

4

Breakfast they ate together, lunch most everyone was out, and tea you organized by yourself. Sometimes it got a bit hectic in the kitchen, occasionally a fight broke out over who had pan rights or who hadn't cleaned the microwave. Mrs Hardy stayed out of the kitchen at nights. Her work was done. She retired to her own room just off the front door, where you could hear the TV till all hours of the morning. She said her old legs didn't like the stairs any more, but she could move up them with a quare zip when she felt like it. Everyone knew she had that room so that she could monitor the comings and goings. She wasn't strict, but she liked to know. The more you told Mrs Hardy, the more she liked you. That's why she doesn't like me at all, thought Tom O'Hanlon. Tom was a shy man, which didn't help a great deal in his chosen profession. Insurance was a talker's game, and Tom wasn't a talker. That's why I'm stuck in this place still. That's why I'm thirty-five and living in a boarding house in the middle of a battle zone. He had some sales of course. Enough to live on. But he would never be a high flyer, like the smoothies in the sales videos the company sent him from time to time. They don't go red every time they open their mouths. That's what he hated most of all about himself. The redness. The involuntary reddening of his cheeks every time he spoke to someone. No, not every time, he thought. He could understand it if he turned red in the midst of a sales pitch, a sales lie, but he didn't. It happened when he was being honest, happened when he liked someone, happened when he was entirely innocent. If he was trying to warn someone off a particular policy – wham, tomato, and they thought he was trying to rip them off. A girl spoke to him – zap, chameleon, off she goes, embarrassed for him. Someone stole my purse – bam, he looks guilty.

Marie wouldn't have annoyed him so much if she hadn't slept with him twice. Slept was the word. She had been roaring drunk – well, they both had – tumbled into his bed. It had been nice. She hadn't wanted to do anything, but it had been nice. But to look at her you wouldn't think she'd ever met me, ever taken her clothes off and held me. She's like a goldfish, each tour of the bowl a virgin experience. And now I just get embarrassed every time I see her.

Like in the kitchen. Tom was hunched over a bowl of Weight Watchers Chicken Korma when she came in.

'Smells nice,' she said breezily. 'Hot, is it?'

He had started eating a lot of Indian food. It was a good excuse for the redness. He hated Indian food.

Tom grunted, mouth full, and waved a piece of bread at her.

Marie opened the fridge and took out a clingfilmed bowl of fruit salad. There was a little white sticker on top with MINE written on it. She sat down opposite him. He smiled. A mistake. A little squirt of sauce emerged from the corner of his mouth. He chased it back in with the bread. But he knew there'd be a stain there, yellow. Like vomit on a drunk's bake.

She was looking well. Her hair was short, moussed, but not distressingly so. Make-up, but not too much. She doesn't need too much. A brightness in her eyes, a warmth off her. He hoped for a moment she was warming to him, but he knew just as soon as the thought flitted through that it wasn't for him, that she had met someone else. Already – and Jamie not long dead. He cursed himself for the thought – but for the korma he would have reddened deeper than ever on that one.

'Going out?' he asked hurriedly.

Marie swallowed a piece of peach, nodding at the same time.

He meant anywhere nice, he said: 'Anyone nice?'

Marie nodded, took another mouthful.

Bitch, he thought. But he couldn't get up.

'That's a nice blouse,' he said. 'Silk is it?'

'You like it? Yeah, it's silk. Feels nice.'

'They say silk breathes, don't they?'

'Do they?' She examined the material for a moment. 'It cost me £10.99 in Dunnes. If it breathes it's probably asthmatic.'

'Where are you for?'

Marie shrugged. She set her spoon down, lifted her bag onto her knees, and started to rummage.

'Being picked up?'

'In a minute, yeah. Just sneaking something here in case he doesn't take me out for dinner. I'm not going to starve for love.'

He smiled. She got up.

'Forgot me condoms,' she said and hurried from the room. He could hear her thumping up the stairs. Bitch, bitch, bitch, he thought.

There was a knock at the front door. He walked to it quickly. Opened.

'Oh – hello, uh, I'm looking for Marie . . . Marie live here?'

Tom nodded. 'Sure. Come on in. She just popped upstairs. She'll be down in a minute.'

He led the man back into the kitchen. Tom put out his hand: 'Tom O'Hanlon.'

'Miller.' Seeing the quizzical look in Tom's eye, he added, 'But you can call me Miller for short.'

Oddball, thought Tom. Not even very attractive-looking, he thought, though God knows I wouldn't know what was attractive in a man. Pale skin though.

'You from round here?' Tom asked. Better not to use the name at all. Didn't feel right. Miller. Who does he think he is? Wanna buy some insurance?

'Nah, Belfast. I'm here temporarily.'

Good, not a long-term relationship then.

'Oh yeah? How come?'

'I'm working for the *Chronicle*. They were a bit short-handed. I got transferred down.'

'The *Chronicle*? A replacement for Jamie?'

Miller nodded.

Tom was thinking. He had to tell someone. Someone soon, because it was starting to give him nightmares. He couldn't tell the police, of course. And he couldn't tell his minister because God didn't exist. He hadn't thought of a reporter — another reporter. A good idea. Yes, he could tell Miller, get it off his chest.

Marie came thumping back down the stairs. A big smile now lit her face. Miller's too. Tom joined in, feeling foolish.

'Forgot my purse,' Marie said, holding it up for Tom to see. She reached down and picked up her bag and then placed it inside.

Jesus, he thought, how do I tell her about Jamie? It'll kill her.

They had planned on going to Belfast for something to eat, a drink, but there was another bomb on the line, so they found themselves confined to the dubious pleasures of Crossmaheart's night life. They got themselves a table in Riley's.

'A bit of a busman's holiday, really,' said Miller. 'We could always go across the road.'

'You could.'

'Why not? Staff rivalry?'

'Religious rivalry. They'd piss in my beer.'

'Well, I'm Protestant, and I'm in here.'

'That's different.'

'What're you saying, Catholics are more open-minded?'

'No, they pissed in your beer.' Marie shrugged. 'What I mean is, we could go across the road, but I wouldn't feel comfortable. We wouldn't be made to feel comfortable.'

At least in Riley's the food came free, and the drinks at a reduced rate, so they sat and got quietly hammered.

'So what about this book?'

'So what about this name?'

'I'm not that interested in the book.'

'I don't have to know the name.'

'That's what I like, a bit of compromise.'

'It's an encouraging sign.'

Marie laughed, finished her vodka. She went to the bar and got another double. She brought Miller a pint of Harp.

'How's the book coming then?' he asked.

She shook her head slightly. 'Y'know, it's like déjà vu, sitting here with you the way I used to sit with Jamie, and now we're gonna talk about writing, the way I did with him.'

'We don't have to.'

'No – I'm not complaining.'

'You're comparing. That's generally a bad thing.'

'I know. I mean, I want to talk about it, but I'm not so sure how good an idea it is to do it this way, half drunk. That's the way it was with Jamie. I'm not stupid, not stupid at all, I'm just not qualified at anything. I've no exams. Wasn't much cop at school. But I'm bright enough. I'm wasted here. I mean, I can't be a bloody waitress all my life. I can't get a degree in waitressing. I can't go on *University Challenge* reading menus. What Jamie was doing for me, as well as being my lover, was educating me. I'd never wanted to read before, but he schooled me in it, sitting here talking about the great writers. But it was a curious kind of schooling, all done through a drunken haze, a kind of second-hand education in which I picked up on the enthusiasm but only half picked up on all the facts. Half remembered names and titles. There's nothing like walking into a bookshop in Belfast and asking for *Dr Chicago* by Doris Pasterneck.'

'It's easily done, I . . .'

'Or *The Day of the Jack Russell*.'

'Well, I . . .'

'*A Pitcher of Dorian Grey*. The list goes on. What I want to do − what I want to do well is write. Write my book.'

'You've started?'

'A thousand times.'

'It's hard, isn't it?'

'You've tried yourself?'

'Many's a time. I wrote a novel once, sent it off to a publisher. They kept it. Sent me back a copy of the Northern Ireland telephone directory, said it had marginally fewer characters and a better plot. I haven't written much since then.'

'You're taking the piss.'

'Scout's honour.'

'There is no honour in the Scouts. There's too many of them in prison.'

'What about Jamie? Did he write? Was he writing anything before . . . ?'

'Nah. Not really. He was too aware of the really good writers. He was so enthusiastic for them that he couldn't bring himself to attempt anything. He was an enthusiast. Threw himself into everything that way. Into his job. He was a good journalist, Miller. Ambitious. Ambitious to get out of this hole. I mean, he'd only been a reporter for about a year. But he was very good. He knew he was never going to be a great writer, so he threw himself into his journalism, he wanted to be the best at that. The best investigative reporter in the country, that's what he said he wanted to be.'

Miller edged forward. 'Do you happen to know if he was . . . investigating anything when he disappeared?'

'You've got your reporter's hat on now. And a particularly ill-fitting and unfashionable hat it is.'

Miller raised his palms. 'I've sworn on my future career not to do any investigating down here, Marie. It's not my style anyway. I'm only interested from a personal point of view.' He took a sip of beer and added half seriously, 'And if you believe that you'll believe anything.'

'I don't suppose it matters much. I mean, I'm sure everyone's been down that avenue already. Yes, I think he was working on something. No, I don't know what it was. He wouldn't say.'

They drank on after the bar had officially closed. Then he walked her home. She slipped her arm through his as they bent into the wind along Main Street. At the front door of her house she kissed him lightly on the lips and went in. Before the door had shut, he missed her.

Marie went to bed happy, and woke up screaming.

The nightmares did not come often, but when they did the whole house knew about them. Her voice carried the length and breadth of the building, tearing along the passages like shrapnel, affecting all. One by one, as the screaming continued, they would appear at their bedroom doors, then edge slowly towards her room, drawn to the scene of torture like moths to a light. The McCauleys were the closest of all, right next door, but they were generally last to arrive.

Although Mrs Hardy lived at the very bottom of the house she was always the first into Marie's room. Always

61

she closed the door behind her so that they saw nothing of Marie's state, always she emerged saying everything was all right and telling everyone to go to bed. This night, when she turned the light on, she found Marie cowering in the corner of her room. Her pyjamas drenched in sweat. Her eyes wide with fright. Pale, so very pale.

She crossed to her, arms outstretched. 'It's okay, love, it's okay,' she said, bending down. Marie tightened up against the wall. 'It's okay, love, it's only me.'

Slowly, slowly she relaxed, then fell forward into Mrs Hardy's arms, crying. Mrs Hardy held her tight for a moment, then pushed her gently back. She put her hand on Marie's face. 'Another bad one, eh, love?' she asked.

Marie nodded. 'I'm sorry,' she whispered.

'Ach, what've you got to be sorry for, you don't invite them, do you?'

Marie rubbed a hand roughly across her face. 'I'll have eyes like Puffawheats in the morning.'

'Never you mind that, love, you're still the prettiest girl in this house.'

Marie scrunched up her eyes and angled her face up into Mrs Hardy's. It made her look like a twelve-year-old. 'Nicer than Mrs McCauley?'

'I've seen better-looking pieces of liver, love.'

That brought a wee smile to her face. 'I'm really sorry,' she said again.

'Never mind, love. Was it the same one again?'

Marie nodded. Mrs Hardy shook her head. 'All that violence, I don't know where that head of yours gets it all from. Reading too many books, I'll dare say.'

Marie nodded slowly.

'I'll get you a cup of tea.'

Mrs Hardy closed the door and walked down the hall. The McCauleys, Tom O'Hanlon and Mrs Brady stood clustered round the top of the stairs.

'Is she okay?' asked Mrs McCauley.

'She'll be fine.'

'It sounded like someone was killing her,' added Mr McCauley.

'Well, she'll be okay once I get her a wee cup, so away on back to bed.'

Mrs Hardy went on down the stairs.

'If you ask me, it's all alcohol related,' observed Mrs Brady.

'Since when did a drink ever give someone nightmares?' Tom O'Hanlon asked. 'It sends me to sleep.'

'Maybe she's been eating cheese. They say cheese before going to bed gives you nightmares,' said Mrs McCauley.

'Jesus, if cheese could give you nightmares like that they'd have it off the market in no time. It would be outlawed like heroin,' said her husband.

'We'd have to send for the cheese police,' added Tom O'Hanlon. The three of them started sniggering. Mrs Brady remained poker-faced.

'Either way, it's getting to be a bit of a habit,' said Mrs McCauley.

'Once a month at least,' observed Mr McCauley. 'Maybe she's having her period.'

His wife slapped him sharply across the face. 'That's disgusting. Typical male piggery.'

He took a step back. Tom O'Hanlon and Mrs Brady took a step back as well. Mr McCauley rubbed at his face. 'There was no need for that. If I'd been a woman and said that, you wouldn't have said a word.'

'A woman wouldn't have said that.'

'I would,' said Mrs Brady. 'I used to have some very strange periods.'

'Jesus Christ,' said Tom O'Hanlon, 'do you have to?'

'I'm only making the point that periods do affect people in strange ways.'

'See?' said Mr McCauley to his wife.

'See nothing, John, it was a horrible thing to say . . . the poor girl screaming her head off and all you can come up with is it's the wrong time of the month.'

Mrs McCauley spun on her heels and re-entered their room. The door slammed.

'Oh-oh,' said Mr McCauley.

'Maybe she's having her period,' ventured Tom O'Hanlon.

Mr McCauley's face blanched, apart from the red slap mark. 'That's my wife you're talking about.'

He turned and went after her.

Mrs Brady stood shaking her head. 'I can think of better things to do than stand here at three o'clock in the morning waiting for that young girl to pull herself together,' she said. 'It really is ridiculous. It just can't go on.'

'I don't think she's doing it on purpose, Mrs Brady.'

'That's neither here nor there, the fact of the matter is that that girl's got a problem and she should see a doctor about it. Screaming and getting on like that, it isn't normal. I shall have to have a word with Mrs Hardy.'

'Mrs Hardy seems quite taken with her.'

'Well, she's a good woman is Mrs Hardy, but she is liable to be a little too lenient. She let that young girl get away with murder with that Jamie one, for one thing.'

'Metaphorically speaking, of course, Mrs Brady.'

'Whatever.' Mrs Brady began to make her way down the stairs.

Tom O'Hanlon lingered at the top, leaning against the banister. What did the wee bitch have to have nightmares about? She doesn't know the meaning of the word. If she'd seen the half of what I've seen. He shook his head, pushed himself off the banister and started going downstairs. I'll have a nightmare myself now, he thought, I know I will. But I won't scream out.

Tom O'Hanlon was too shy to scream in his nightmares.

Next morning Marie breezed into breakfast as if nothing had happened. The McCauleys, Mrs Brady and Tom O'Hanlon watched in silence. Mrs Hardy fussed about the kitchen, the door wedged open by a Yellow Pages.

'What's it this morning then?' Marie asked chirpily.

'Fry, love,' Mrs Hardy called in.

'Well, I'm glad someone feels cheerful,' said Mrs Brady.

Marie poured some tea for herself. 'I guess I was a little rowdy last night.'

'That's one word for it.'

'Sorry. It wasn't on purpose.'

'Never worry,' said Mrs McCauley. 'It happens to us all.'

Mrs Brady gave her a frosty look. 'Not to me it doesn't. Marie, I don't wish to be inquisitive . . .' Tom O'Hanlon tutted. Mrs Brady switched her frosty look for a moment. '. . . But do you think it might have anything to do with your . . . drinking?'

'There's no need . . .' began Mrs McCauley.

'Well, there is need . . .' Mrs Brady broke in, 'with all that noise, it's not good for any of us . . .'

'Mrs Brady, if you must know, I didn't have a lot to drink last night. I had a nightmare, that's all. I'm sorry if it upset you. I didn't choose to have it.'

'Well, that's as may be, but I don't think working in that bar all hours of the day and night, with all those . . . people . . . it can't be doing you any good, mentally or physically. I thought you had great plans to write a book? Goodness knows you could do with something at least a little cultured in your life.'

'Every time I hear the word culture I reach for my Strongbow,' Marie said quietly. She looked up at an

65

uncomprehending Mrs Brady. Tom O'Hanlon was smiling, so was Mr McCauley. A cider background. 'If you must know, I have started my book.'

'Well, that's something.'

'Mostly research so far.'

'Into what, dear?'

'Male impotency. I'm calling it *Emission Impossible*.'

Tom O'Hanlon choked at the end of the table.

'Very interesting, I'm sure,' said Mrs Brady, nodding.

Marie turned to Mrs McCauley, half shielding her mouth. 'See? It just goes to prove my theory that the old bat doesn't listen to a word anyone says. She just likes to hear her own whiny voice. Speak quietly enough and she'll nod and smile at you all day long.'

Mrs McCauley shook her head. 'You really do have a vicious streak in you, Marie.'

Marie shrugged.

Mrs Hardy came through the doorway with her tray and began dispensing fries. She cast an enquiring eye over Marie, who smiled back at her, gave her a little nod.

She set the tray down and stood back. 'I'm going to try a little experiment tonight, if any of you are interested. For dinner.'

'An experiment?' asked Tom O'Hanlon. 'It sounds chemical.'

'It might as well be, dear. My daughter-in-law, bless her, gave me a book of Indian recipes for Christmas. I've been looking at it for months. The trouble was I wasn't able to get any of the ingredients here, but Colette was down from Belfast yesterday and dropped some in for me. I mean, it just goes against my nature to cook anything without potatoes in it, but I suppose I can't let them all go to waste. We must move with the times. What do you think? Can I tempt any of you?'

Marie nodded enthusiastically. 'Count me in. As long as it's not too late. I'm working tonight.'

'That won't be a problem, Marie.'

'We're in as well,' said Mrs McCauley. 'A change is as good as a rest.'

Mrs Hardy wasn't sure if that was a compliment. Mrs McCauley wasn't sure either. She'd certainly meant it as one.

'Mrs Brady?'

'I don't think so.'

'Aw, why not?'

'It's not really my cup of tea.'

'Have you ever tried Indian food?' Mr McCauley asked.

'No . . .'

'Ach, go on, you might like it.'

'No . . . I really don't think so . . . I mean, no offence to you, Mrs Hardy, but an acquaintance of mine had a rather harrowing experience in an Indian restaurant, and it put me off for life.'

'What way harrowing?' asked Tom O'Hanlon.

'I really don't wish to discuss it. Enough to say, it was disgusting.'

'You can't just leave it at that,' Tom pressed.

'I can and I will. It would put you off your breakfast.'

'Och, go on,' said Mrs McCauley.

'Please,' pleaded Marie.

'May as well,' said Mrs Hardy. 'You're not going to get any peace.'

Mrs Brady rolled her eyes. 'Oh, very well, if I must.'

'Great,' said Tom O'Hanlon, rubbing his hands.

'This friend of mind was in an Indian restaurant in Belfast. She ordered her food, I can't remember what she said it was, something to do with coconuts or something fruity. When the food arrived it was only lukewarm, so she complained about it. They brought it back and she had her meal

67

and went on home. But she was very ill that night. Very sick. Food poisoning. Her husband was so concerned he . . . well, to put it frankly, he saved some of the . . . sick . . . and took it to the health inspectors. They had it analysed.'

'And?' asked Mrs Hardy.

'There were five different types of semen in it.'

The table erupted. Tom banged his head on his side plate. The McCauleys collapsed into each other. Marie hid under the table. Mrs Hardy's face went purple.

'I don't think there's anything very funny about it,' Mrs Brady scolded.

The laughter continued. Mrs Brady started into her fry. To try and defuse the situation Mrs Hardy lifted the pot of tea again and asked if anyone wanted a refill.

'Perhaps,' said Tom O'Hanlon, 'your friend was being unfaithful to her husband.'

'Exceptionally unfaithful,' said Mr McCauley.

'That's disgusting,' said Mrs McCauley.

'There's no need for that at all,' agreed Mrs Brady. 'That's exactly what happened.'

The laughter still circled the table, wild and frothy like horses on a circular course, jumping Mrs Brady with each lap.

Tom O'Hanlon wiped a tear from his eye. 'Mrs Brady, that's one of the oldest stories in the book. Like the Kentucky Fried Mouse and the Chicken Fried Lice. Great urban myths.'

'It's a true story, I tell you,' said Mrs Brady, setting down her knife and fork and wiping her mouth daintily with a napkin. 'Why are people so cynical these days?' She stood up from the table and left for her room.

'I think you can count her out,' Mrs McCauley said.

Mrs Hardy nodded half-heartedly from the kitchen doorway. 'I suppose I could make chips as well,' she said.

*   *   *

Miller was alone in the office when the phone rang. The others had left separately for lunch, but he suspected they were meeting up outside. It didn't bother him unduly. They could do what they wanted. He was thinking about Marie. Beautiful, funny, unpredictable Marie.

He spent most of the one-hour break oiling the chain on the Cycle of Violence. He ate a bacon and coleslaw sandwich and read the Belfast papers. He missed the cut and thrust of daily paper life. Here in Crossmaheart if he got a good story on a Friday, he had to sit on it until the following week when the *Chronicle* came out again; generally someone else had picked up on it by then. He missed it, but he could live without it.

'Hello, editorial?'

'Is that, uh, Mr Miller?'

'Yeah.'

'Ah . . . good. Hello.'

'Hello.'

'Sorry to trouble you, but . . . that's a stupid expression really, isn't it? I'm not really sorry to trouble you, I'm pleased to trouble you, in fact, not to cause you trouble, you understand, but pleased to talk to you, I don't know if it's a trouble to you or not . . . of course you're paid to be troubled by people like me, although of course it's lunch time and . . .'

'Is there something I can do for you?'

'Yes, yes. Uh, you can. I'm sorry. I just find this difficult to . . .'

'You can start by telling me who you are.'

'Yes, yes, I could. In fact, I wasn't going to, at all, but then I thought, why not. Anyway, you probably recognize my voice from the other night.'

'Uh, no – I don't think so . . . from . . . ?'

'Yes, you do, we met . . . you're Marie's boyfriend.'

'Well . . . friend, yes.'

'Not boyfriend?'

'Well, I don't know, it's early days yet . . . is this relevant?'

'Ahm, no, not really. What I mean is, I'm the one who let you into the house . . . we had a brief chat.'

'Ah, yes . . . I remember now . . . John . . . ?'

'Tom, Tom O'Hanlon.'

'Ah, yes, yes, Tom. What can I do for you, Tom?'

'Well . . . this is hard to put really. I couldn't tell Marie — God, no, I couldn't tell Marie. And I couldn't tell the police — I mean, they'd have my guts for garters . . . not the police . . . the others . . . you know how word gets out . . . I mean, look at the confidential telephone . . . someone must trace the calls, otherwise what's the point?'

'Tom, you'll probably find it much easier if you tell me straight out what's on your mind.'

'Yes, well, easier said . . . Miller, I had to tell someone, because I'm having nightmares about it . . . Marie was in an awful state the other night, she knows what they're like . . .'

'Marie was . . . ?'

'Oh . . . nightmares, shouting the house down . . . happens quite a lot, but I . . . what I mean is if I tell you, as a journalist you can do something about it, tell people — the authorities, whoever it has to be . . . but you won't mention my name. I wouldn't be able to work round here if it got out that I told the police, you understand?'

'Yes, Tom. It's off the record. Top secret. Now . . . ?'

'It's about Marie's boyfriend.'

'Jamie? Jamie Milburn?'

'Yeah.'

'What about him?'

'I didn't know who to tell.'

'Tell me, Tom.'

70

'Well . . . look, it's like this. I saw him. I think I saw him. I'm sure I saw him.'

'Where was this, Tom? When?'

'About four days after he disappeared. I saw him out on the Tullycreagh Road. It's out in the country, about two miles out of town.'

'What was he doing?'

'Not very much.'

'Tom?'

'I'm sorry . . . ugh . . . it was at night, not that late, but it was dark. There's not much traffic out there. You know where I'm on about?'

'No, Tom, but . . .'

'It doesn't matter . . . I was out there . . . in the car, like . . . on a job. Picking up a payment on an endowment policy. Some farmer. I was on my way back . . . I, Jesus, I can still see it . . .'

'Take it easy, Tom. Just tell me what you saw.'

'I seen this . . . the lights picked up this fox running along the road . . . blinded it for a moment . . . and God help me . . . it had Jamie Milburn's head in its mouth . . .'

'Jesus Christ.'

'I mean . . . just the head, nothing else . . . I mean, the head, it was battered and all . . . but it was Jamie . . . I mean, I lived with him here . . . I know what he looks like when he's feeling rough . . .'

'Tom, what happened to the fox?'

'It just took off. Disappeared through a hedge.'

'Tom, I think we better meet.'

5

Miller called into Riley's about an hour before the official closing time. Marie was up to her ears, but managed to keep him supplied with free drink. She squeezed in a couple herself. There was a bit of a singsong going on in the bar, mostly traditional stuff, but with a few young bloods singing the Pogues. Miller watched and listened from the back of the bar. It was entertaining, but alien. His own culture, Protestant culture, had no traditional music at all, unless you counted big fat men beating tunelessly on Lambeg drums on the Twelfth. The way it worked everybody got up and did a turn, from the soulful semi-pro to the raggedy-voiced old drunk, but they never asked Miller. They passed over him like a bastard in the Free Presbyterians.

When the last of the stragglers had been coaxed out of the bar, Marie and Miller sat at a table – *the* table, Jamie's table – and had a few more drinks. Pearse Riley and his son Johnny cleaned up around them, raking Marie about this and that as they worked. They didn't mind Miller; they just had nothing to say to him.

Then they said their goodnights, and he walked her home. It was pouring outside and by the time they had scurried along the Main Street to the boarding house they were both soaked. It was after two in the morning.

She kissed him on the cheek, then whispered, 'Do you want to come in?'

'Yes.' He made a habit out of being easy to get. It wasn't a habit he was called on to exercise very often.

'Okay then – but be quiet. The landlady doesn't really approve.'

She opened the door and waved him in. She signalled for him to take his shoes off, then they tiptoed up the stairs. He stubbed his toe twice on the way up, and by the time they got to her room they were on the verge of hysterics.

She opened the door and switched the light on. He closed it softly behind him, then pulled her to him and kissed her on the lips. Their mouths opened and their tongues met briefly, then she drew away.

'Off with your clothes then,' she said.

'Well, that didn't take a lot of persuasion.'

'I mean to dry them. You'll catch your death of cold if you stay in that lot. Stick them over the heater there.'

He started to undress. 'How far do I go?'

'Down to your underpants if you want, but no further.'

She slipped her jacket off and removed her shirt, then pushed down her ski pants. She pointed at her bra and panties. 'These, and this, there's an exclusion zone round this lot. Trespassers will be executed.'

Miller shook his head slowly. Something was starting to happen in his underpants which he had little control over. 'Where do I stand, Marie?'

'Over there, by the heater.'

'No, I mean with you. With this here.'

'We're friends.'

'Like this?' He nodded at her breasts.

'Like this. For the moment.'

'It's . . . like putting the coolest, frothiest pint before an alcoholic and forbidding him to drink it.'

She smiled. 'A nice line, Miller, but it won't get you into my knickers.'

'What will it get me?'

'Into my record collection. Pick something out there, I'll get us a drink.'

It was almost a relief to be able to turn away from her. Almost. Miller and his black y-fronts bent to Marie's record collection.

'Odd socks,' she commented.

'Dressing in the dark,' he replied, flicking through the albums quickly. 'You got me on a good day. I have a pair of Union Jack socks which would just break your heart.'

'Union Jack socks?'

'I inherited them from my brother. A bit of an Orange man. Actually they wouldn't really offend anyone – my dad wasn't a great master of the washing machine, once he'd been at them they were red, blue and grey. Still, I don't suppose they'd be a great hit in Riley's.'

'They'd be a great hit right up to the point you got lynched.'

Miller looked round. 'Haven't you got anything other than Leonard Cohen?'

'Is there anything other than Leonard Cohen?'

'Well, I mean, I've nothing against the man, but he's hardly Mr Happy Party Feet, is he?'

Marie handed him a half-pint glass. It was half full of straight vodka. 'I like him. I get depressed by other people's happiness. Leonard treats me just right.'

Miller took a sip, winced.

'Wimp. There's Coke over there if you want it.'

He shook his head. 'I'll survive.'

'We'll see.'

Eventually he located more fertile ground amongst the monastic depression of her collection, a jangling of Evangelists in the house of doom in the form of Londonderry's Undertones. They sat on the floor, their backs against a small settee, and drank.

'Nice room,' Miller said. It was a nice room, warm, a couple of black-framed art exhibition posters, fluffy bunny slippers, a load of books, a typewriter.

An hour later, feeling hazy, but still nervous, Miller said, 'My clothes are still soppin'.'

'You can stay with me if you like. Sleep with me.'

Miller nodded, smiled.

She put her hand on his arm. 'I mean sleep. Just sleep.' Her voice was clear and fine, unclouded by alcohol, yet she was drinking him under the table. 'Look I'm honestly not trying to give you a hard time, but I really do need to trust someone, trust them a lot, before . . . before I can do anything with them. Anything. So . . . stay, I'd like you to stay, I'd like you to sleep here with me . . . but I understand if you'd prefer to go.'

'I'll stay.'

'And I'm serious.'

'I know. It's okay. I don't mind – for now.'

'One more thing.'

He stifled a tut. 'Mmm?'

'No socks.'

'Ruining my socks life as well.'

'Ha-ha.'

They got into the bed together. They kissed. Then she turned her back and moulded herself into him.

They lay silently in the blackness – save for the reduced hum of the Undertones singing 'Here Comes the Summer'. Then she said: 'Is that what I think it is against my bum?'

'Yes, I'm sorry. I can't help it.'

'I can't help it either.'

'I know. I know. It's okay. It'll go away. Eventually. Maybe I'm too close.' He pulled back into a slightly less fraternal spoon shape. 'Is that better?'

'For me.'

'So, how do I go about earning your trust?'

'Time is what you need.'

'What if I don't have time?'

'No time, no trust.'

75

'Did Jamie have trust?'

'Jamie had trust.'

'How long did you go out with him before trust set in?'

'A few days.'

'That's not long.'

'It depends what you're waiting for. It can go very quickly or it can last for years.'

'And how long do you think it'll take to trust me?'

'Who can tell?'

'Well, do you trust me enough to give me a kiss goodnight?'

She turned in the bed and her lips found his. A long, warm kiss. His hand slipped onto her waist. He moved his groin forward again. Slowly his hand traced the outline of her ribs towards her bra. He cupped his hand over her left breast. He started to work his fingers under the wire. Then her hand was there, pushing his away. He tried to replace it. She pushed him away again. The kiss continued. For the third time he cupped her breast. She pushed her fingers into his chest, her nails hard, penetrating. 'No,' she said.

He rolled away and sighed.

'I'm sorry,' she said.

'Don't worry.'

'You're huffing.'

'No . . . yes, well, what do you expect?'

'I told you.'

'I know. It's just very hard.'

'I noticed.'

He laughed. A sad laugh.

'Can I tell you something, Miller?' He nodded in the dark. 'It's very difficult for me – very difficult to be . . . touched. It's not that I don't like you, I do, I like you a lot. It's not that I don't like men . . . I like them a lot. And I like sex; when I get there I love it . . . but . . . Jesus . . . I hate saying this because I shouldn't have to justify it, and God knows

76

I don't want to think about it . . . but . . . shit . . . right, okay. When I was much younger. When I was thirteen . . . oh fuck, you don't want to hear this.'

He put his arm out, encircled her, pulled her to his chest. She didn't resist. He could feel tears on her cheek. 'It's okay.'

'It's not okay, it's silly and it's childish.'

'Tell me.'

'I'm not looking for sympathy, Miller. I should be over it by now. Shit fuckin' shit.' She rubbed her arm across her face. 'I'm sorry for getting like this.'

'It's okay. It's okay. Tell me.'

'When I was thirteen, on the way home from school, these men offered me a lift home in their car. I was very young, very naïve. Well, they did things to me, y'know? They were caught, put away somewhere. I've always found it very difficult to be . . . touched. Can you understand that?'

'Of course I can.'

'But everyone says that, then they think it doesn't apply to them and they go ahead and try something again and again; they always think they'll be the one who'll break down my defences.'

'I'm sorry. But I had to try. And I did. Now I understand the situation. I'll back off. But I'll be honest with you. I will try again. How else will I know?'

'I could let you know, when I'm ready. Or do you not like me being in the driving seat?'

'I don't know.'

The Undertones record finished. They lay in the silence, her face on his chest. 'I hate saying, be patient with me. It makes me sound like a cripple. But be patient with me.'

He stroked her hair. 'I'll do my best. But I'm not renowned for patience.'

Gradually her breathing steadied into a light snore. His hand remained on her head, gently stroking. He loved this.

He loved the look of her in the daylight, the smell of her in the dark, he loved the closeness and the comfort, the warmth. God, he thought, I feel like this after a second date. He closed his eyes. He knew he shouldn't get involved. He'd been in messy relationships before, and he didn't need another one. How else could it turn out: a lovely girl, but a lovely girl with a murdered boyfriend and a history of sexual abuse. I have sympathy. But I can't build my life around helping other people. I cannot be a father figure to her. I need my own life. Don't let this develop. Get up while you can. Pull your clothes on, go home. Make excuses about having to go to work.

Miller drifted off. He dreamt about a wedding, his own. He couldn't see the bride's face, but his shoes were undone. Every time he bent to tie them somebody kicked him from behind. When he looked round his dad was smiling at him.

Miller came to: throat dry, head throbbing, heart thumping, busting for a piss. He eased himself out from under Marie and sat at the edge of the bed. He felt around for the bedside lamp and switched it on. Blinking, he studied his watch for a few moments until his eyes focused: 5.30 am.

He slipped out of the room. He had no idea where the bathroom was. He knew he couldn't go trying doors at random or he'd blunder into someone's bedroom and cause a panic. He hated the numb-sick feeling of the early-morning hangover. He needed a drink. He needed a pee. In the dark of the hall it came to him that if he stood on his head there and then he could relieve himself and quench his thirst at the same time. He was sober enough to realize he was still drunk.

Miller made his way slowly down the stairs. The kitchen would solve at least one of his problems. When he reached it he opened the fridge door and took out a carton of orange juice. He drained it, then replaced the empty carton.

He thought about the back garden, but when he tried

the back door it was locked, and there was no sign of a key. There was no alternative. Leaving the fridge door open so that its light half-illuminated the room, he went to the sink and lifted a couple of plates out of it and set them to one side. Then he pulled a footstool out from beneath a small two-seater table and placed it below the sink. He stepped onto it and started to urinate into the sink. Ah, heaven. Oh God, yes, heaven.

And then the kitchen was suddenly bright. Miller blinked round to find an elderly woman in a heavy tartan dressing gown and hairnet standing wide-eyed in the doorway.

'What on earth do you think you're doing?' Mrs Brady asked.

Miller blinked at her for a moment more. Then he shook his member, slipped it back into his underpants, and stepped down from the stool. He walked towards Mrs Brady, stopped before her. 'It's okay,' he said quietly, 'you're dreaming.'

He moved past her and walked slowly up the first flight of stairs. Once he was out of her sight he took them three at a time.

Half giggling, half panicked, he slipped back into Marie's room. The bedside lamp he'd left on was now off. He felt for it in the dark again, switched it on. The cover was half turned back. Marie was asleep, but in the time it had taken him to have an adventure downstairs, she had woken, presumed he had left, then removed her underwear before going back to sleep. Marie and her breasts lay exposed.

As gently as possible he climbed back into the bed. He kept the cover turned back and, propping himself up on one elbow, drank in her supine form. Her breasts were larger than he had imagined, and he *had* imagined. The clothes she wore were hardly shapeless, but they were not figure-hugging. Now, naked, he could see how pale her skin was. He realized that the ashen look of her face could not

79

just be blamed on her most recent trauma, but that it was her natural colouring. Her body didn't look as if it had ever been exposed to the intensity of a foreign sun, or even the casual interest of a mildly encouraging break in the clouds above Crossmaheart.

By this stage Miller's erection had radically altered the shape of his underpants. He reached down to rearrange himself, then thought better of it. Too dangerous.

Five minutes, ten minutes went by, during which his eyes did not shift once from Marie's breasts.

He sighed long and loud. He reached over and switched the light off again and pulled the cover back up, right over his head. He sighed again. He resolved to count to five hundred. By the end of it he would be either asleep or flaccid, and he hoped both. He did quite well. He got to three hundred and twenty-six when a vision of Marie's breasts flashed through him and he let out a little squeak of frustration. His erection was still fully conscious. And it could see in the dark.

Miller switched the lamp on again. He slowly peeled the cover back and stared at her breasts again. He moved his left hand across until it hovered over her nearside nipple. Very very softly, he touched her. Beautiful, beautiful, beautiful, he thought, but hand in hand with it, no, no, no. He traced the outline of her nipple with his forefinger, then the shape of her breast. He cupped his hand lightly over it. Then he lifted the cover and looked down at her little triangle of pubic hair. Oh Jesus. He dropped the cover, heavier than he should have and she let out a little blow of air, jiggled her body a bit, then drifted away again.

What am I doing? What the fuck am I doing? Jesus, she's got a real problem because someone abused her in the past, and here I am touching her up in her sleep. He stared at his underpants. It's all your bloody fault, he screamed silently.

Miller switched the lamp off again. He lay back. He

turned to his right – too close. He turned to his left, curled up. He forced himself to think of Jamie, of Jamie's lifeless head being carried by a dead fox.

Tom O'Hanlon had driven him along the road where he'd spotted the fox. When he had spoken to O'Hanlon on the phone Miller had suspected that he knew more than he had let on, but now that he had spent some time with him in the flesh (flesh, he thought, damn, damn, damn – get out of my pants, desist, get anaemic, baby) he thought he was probably mistaken. O'Hanlon was just a naturally nervous man who had been traumatized both by his encounter with the fox and his own inability to pass the information on to the proper authorities.

The road had been all curves and overhanging trees and O'Hanlon had been anxious when Miller insisted on retracing his journey two or three times.

'Them bloody choppers see everything,' he had argued, twisting his neck awkwardly to stare up into the sky. 'They'll have us marked out for gunmen and they'll blow us out of the road.'

Miller didn't bother looking. There were always choppers up there. 'I think they're a bit more discerning than that, Tom. You think any self-respecting terrorist would go on a mission in a yellow 2CV?'

'This is Crossmaheart, Miller. We don't have self-respecting terrorists. They use milk floats. They use prams. They'd try roller skates if they'd anyone balanced enough to use them.'

They had stopped the car at the best approximation of where O'Hanlon thought he'd seen Jamie's head. There were thick hedgerows on either side of the road, no great barrier for a fox but impractical for either of them to plough through.

'There's bound to be a gap further on,' Miller said, starting off down the road.

'I'll wait here.'

'I'd appreciate the company.'

'And I appreciate the car. You don't leave your wagon unattended out here, Miller. Even a 2CV.'

'It is insured, Tom, isn't it?'

O'Hanlon didn't appear to appreciate the sarcasm.

Miller continued on down the road. About a hundred yards along he came to a gap in the hedge. It looked as if it had been made fairly recently. From the state of the ground round about he thought a cow had pushed its way through. Around the shadow of the hedge the grass was long and wet and the bottoms of Miller's trousers were soon soaked as he made his way along the hedge until he was roughly level with the car. He poked about in the grass for a few minutes, but he saw nothing that resembled a human head.

Turning, he began to traverse the field. It sloped gently upwards for a few hundred yards, until the gradient suddenly increased sharply up towards another hedge. He skirted this hedge for another fifty yards until it began to slope downwards again, and where it had just about levelled off he came to a gate. Pulling himself up onto the second bar, he found himself looking down into a small valley. It stank.

Back at the car, he had to rap on the window to get in. O'Hanlon had locked the door and was sitting nervously tapping on the wheel.

'Well?' he snapped as soon as Miller had the door open an inch.

'You didn't tell me the town dump was over there.'

'I didn't know the . . . Jesus, you forget with the twisty roads where the hell it is sometimes. Right enough, I suppose it could be over there . . . I mean, you don't get to it this way. The access road is miles the other way.'

'Yeah, well. I'm no expert on foxes, but if that was a

head your friend had in his mouth, then I expect he got it scavenging over in the dump.'

'And?'

'Well, I'm not about to go shovelling through that shit.'

And now he understood O'Hanlon's dilemma – who to tell. The only friend he had in Crossmaheart lay in bed beside him. Marie, there's something I have to get off my chest. Apparently your boyfriend's head was seen bobbing along the road the other night in a fox's mouth. Yeah, sure.

One alternative was not to tell anyone. He had not been unduly worried about or interested in Jamie's disappearance when he had arrived in Crossmaheart. Galvin's warnings to ignore the story had bounced off him because he had no intention of delving into it; he was more interested in his own physical and mental rejuvenation than chasing a missing journalist. He hadn't exactly come to Crossmaheart to find himself – he hated hippy shit like that – but he'd come to avoid trouble, absorb himself in the tedium of small-town journalism and regain some sort of perspective on his own life. He could just forget about the head. O'Hanlon might have been seeing things anyway. It could have been an animal's head, a tailor's dummy, anything. He could ignore the story completely. It wasn't his concern.

But it was his concern. It was his concern because of the naked woman in the bed beside him. Marie. Mad Marie, Helen in the office had called her. He wondered how that story had started. He could find nothing untoward about her besides a snappy temper and an understandable reticence when it came to sex. What was mad about that? Most women have an understandable reticence about sex when it comes to me, Miller thought.

Stop being hard on yourself, boy. Hard on. Shit – it was still there, laughing at him.

People, women mostly, told him he had a low opinion

of himself for no reason. Usually it was women who wouldn't go out with him who told him this. He was a notoriously easy faller-in-love, but it was with the wrong sort of women. Now, in bed, he wondered how it was that this woman whom he found so attractive, physically, mentally, every way, seemed about to reciprocate this attraction ... not physically yet ... well, yes, physical up to a point, they were in bed together and he was on what they used to call a promise ... but to find her here, in Crossmaheart, by whatever or whoever's design ... Jesus, how can I tell her a fox has probably had Jamie's head for supper? And what if at the end of it all, she'd killed him herself?

Light was beginning to penetrate the room. The curtains were closed tight, but at the top of the window they sagged lazily from the curtain rail and the grey dawn seeped warily in.

He was able to make out the time: 7.30. He had had an erection for two hours.

Then he heard the sound. 'Oo ... ooh ... Oo ... ooh.'

It was close, but could have come from another world. He tried to define it: half ghost, half sensuous, half pleasure ... three halves ... 'Oo ... ooh ... oh ... ooh ...'

Oh God, thought Miller, please no. Not now, not when I'm like this.

Marie had told him that a young couple shared the room next to hers. Now in the first light they were moving together, making slow, sleepy love. Her rhythmic pleasure captured in a faint love song that penetrated wall and glass to pinch chastisingly at him, to tease his erection with visions of orgasm.

Oh shit. Miller sighed. He closed his eyes tight, pulled the cover over him again ... but that was too close to Marie, too bloody close. He pulled it back again and tried putting his fingers in his ears. It worked for a while, until the rush of blood in his head, like the sea in a shell, overwhelmed him and he had to withdraw, and when he withdrew it was to the quiet call of lust from the next room.

'Oh . . . oh . . . oh . . . oh . . .'

His hand began to creep down the bed . . . there was only one relief, only one real relief that he could administer himself . . . but, Jesus, the shame of it . . . if she woke up . . . the mess . . . there were tissues by the bed . . . but what if she too woke up soon and that elusive trust had grown on her during the night and she wanted to make love there and then and he couldn't perform, what pathetic excuse would he dream up? It was getting bright . . . he could leave now . . . go home . . . go to work . . . he looked across at the heater, could see his woollen sports coat now dried, but with its arms pointing in crazy directions . . . Jesus, he knew better than to dry a jacket like that . . . the evils of alcohol, the temptations of the flesh . . . unfulfilled . . . he would have to walk around with his hand in a permanent salute until he could get the jacket to a dry cleaner's for surgery . . . did they have a dry cleaner's in Crossmaheart or did they beat their clothes with stones?

'Oh . . . ooh . . . oh . . . oooh . . .'

He didn't want to go. He didn't want to leave her. He wanted her to wake and fall into his arms . . . maybe if he nudged her lightly awake . . . she would roll over . . . no, she'd feel his erection . . . know he only had one thing in mind . . . the slow building trust would be demolished . . . how could he explain he didn't want the erection, that it had come unbidden in the early hours and would not go away? Come unbidden.

He wondered what she looked like . . . in there, the next room . . . was this teasing, wispy moan of pleasure misleading him . . . was she some gnarled young frump pretending to take pleasure from a hungover husband, moaning in time to some long-prepared script while she thought of career or decoration or worse, real unrequited love? Was he grinding away on top of her, the dutiful husband, hormones leading him on but his thoughts fixed on the day ahead, on the years ahead, stuck with this woman he had once thought he loved . . . or were they simply young and in love, young and in lust, thinking of nothing but the pure pleasure they were giving each other, this fantasy breakfast in bed . . . ?

'Oh . . . oh . . . ooh . . . ooh . . .'

He thought of his own catalogue of love . . . how many? He counted them off on his fingers . . . seven, eight . . . what was that for a twenty-eight-year-old . . . about average? I wish . . . way below, way below . . . but still five years with one girl, that kind of ate in to your mean average . . . he had lost his virginity with that one . . . in Botanic Gardens one summer's night . . . Jesus, stop this . . .

He would think of work. What would happen if Marie did want a permanent relationship with him? Would he be content to stay in Crossmaheart? The hole in the ground that was Crossmaheart. If Jamie didn't return, and the chances of him returning would reduce with each significant body part which turned up, then the job on the paper was probably his for the taking. True, the staff appeared to hate him at the moment, but he presumed that was out of some sort of loyalty to Jamie rather than any real dislike for him. He had not bothered trying to win them over, he had accepted their attitude because it suited him then to do so. But he could make an effort. He had half-heartedly invited them out for lunch, and they had refused. All he really needed to do was break the ice . . . he could go and see Martin O'Hagan, have it out with him.

Or could he entice Marie back to Belfast? He could picture them sharing a house . . . no, not his house, not his father's house, he wanted somewhere new, modern, clean . . . he would return to the paper, cycling merrily off to the bombs and the bullets while she stayed at home and worked

on her book . . . he would come home at night to a nice
meal . . . he wouldn't need to drink . . . unless it was with
her . . . they'd watch the TV and she'd ask him for advice
on her writing and he would go over it with her and later
he'd try writing something himself but he'd come over all
sleepy and she'd put her arms round him and start to kiss
him and they'd go off and make mad, passionate . . .
Jesus.
'Oh . . . ooh . . . oh . . . ooh.'
Jesus, they're Olympian. How long had it been? They'd
been at it since the crack of dawn and now he could see
from the gap below the curtain rail that it was fully bright
outside . . . how long, an hour? Why didn't they get up and
make breakfast and go to work? Jesus . . . he remembered
now that Marie had said they were unemployed . . . God
. . . they couldn't stay in bed and do that all day . . . Jesus, if
I stay erect any longer it'll just snap off the moment anyone
touches it and I'll have to go and join a eunuch farm
. . .Would she go to Belfast? She'd no particular love for
Crossmaheart, he knew that, and yet in some curious way
she seemed tied to it, to her crappy job in a bar . . . but if
he married her it would all be . . . fuck, I'm talking about
marriage and I've had two dates with her . . . you're letting
your dick run away with you, Miller . . . two dates . . . take
it easy, easy . . . build on it slowly . . . she's only getting
over someone . . . she won't want to get involved . . . I
mean, Jamie's dead . . . what sort of an unfeeling, uncaring
woman would throw herself into a new relationship before
they'd even found the whole body . . . exactly, exactly . . .
what sort of a woman is she? Is she just using me to blot
out the despair? Am I nothing but a protective shield? She
just wants someone to hold onto. A Jamie substitute. A
bloody Jamie substitute . . . what other explanation? I do
the same job . . . she just thinks she can slot me in in his
place and there'll be no difference, that life will go on as

normal . . . but I'm not Jamie . . . I'm not Jamie . . . maybe that's why she doesn't want to make love . . . because he was so good, so powerful, so satisfying in bed that it will spoil her fantasy to have me fumbling all round her . . .

'Oh . . . oh . . . oh . . . oh.'

Jesus.

And all the while, her soft, dreamy breathing, lost in another world. Maybe she was using him. Maybe I don't care. She is absolutely beautiful: beautiful in mind and body . . . Jesus, that sounds so trite . . . but she is . . . say it with a straight face . . . say it without an erection, Miller . . . give her all your sympathy and understanding without a hard-on, Miller . . . go and take a cold shower . . . God, he would love one . . .

He could hear the creaks and groans of a waking house now. Of water running somewhere down below him, of pans being moved, doors opening, the mumblings of early morning . . . beside him Marie moved for the first time in hours, twisting, stretching, still asleep but on the verge of consciousness . . . her eyes fluttered . . . she rubbed the palm of one hand into her left eye . . . then the right . . . she turned . . .

'Fuck!'

She reared back, clutching the quilt to her. Eyes wide, teeth bared.

'It's okay . . .'

'I . . .'

'It's okay . . .'

'I thought you'd gone . . .'

'No . . . no . . .'

'You were gone . . .'

'Toilet . . .'

She relaxed, slumping back down into the bed. Then she moved slowly towards him, her hand moved across his chest and she angled her face up to his, her breast touched him

. . . Jesus . . . and kissed him lightly on the mouth . . . 'I'm sorry,' she whispered, 'you gave me a fright . . .'

'It's okay.'

'Is that what I think it is?'

He nodded. 'I'm sorry.'

'He's up early.'

'I suppose.'

She lay with her face on his chest. 'It's too soon.'

'I know.'

'I'm sorry.'

'It's okay.'

'Good.'

'Oh . . . oooh . . . oh . . . ooh,' slipped across the room.

They said nothing.

'Oh . . . oooh . . . oh . . . ooh . . .'

Miller was sweating. And he wasn't getting any softer.

Slowly she drew away from him. She reached over the side of the bed and picked up her underwear. She pulled on knickers under the cover, then clipped on her bra.

She turned to face him. His flushed-with-lust face. 'Those pigeons are really annoying, aren't they?' She pushed herself up off the bed. 'I'm just going for a pish.'

When she had left the room Miller and his erection got up and walked to the window. He pulled one of the curtains back slowly. Two pigeons, common or garden variety. One turned an enquiring beak towards him.

'Oh . . . ooh . . . oh . . . ooh,' it said.

6

Miller was drunk. He knew he was drunk, he knew why he was drunk, and he knew he was drunk for a good reason. He slouched across the bar towards Pearse Riley, all left foot, then all right, like his pockets were heavy with change. Pearse, his eyes already screwed up from reading the paper in the early evening gloom, turned the edges of the *Belfast Telegraph* up protectively. He gave Miller a nod. Miller gave it back.

'Marie here?'

Pearse shook his head. There was no one else in the bar, a combination of the bad weather outside and the lack of liquidity brought on by it being the day before fortnightly dole money was due to the larger part of his clientele. 'Off on her break. Due back at seven. You'll have a drink if you're waiting?' He didn't mean for free, but he knew it had come across that way. Still, one drink. Pearse turned towards the spirit bottles lining the back of the bar. 'A wee whiskey to get you started, eh?'

Miller clambered onto a bar stool. 'Fuck the Pope.'

Pearse turned, whiskey glass in hand. 'I'm sorry?'

'I said, vodka and Coke.'

After a moment Pearse smiled unconvincingly. Miller smiled unconvincingly back. Pearse stuck with the whiskey glass. He reached for the vodka bottle. 'You usually start with a wee whiskey, don't you?'

'I don't want a wee whiskey.'

'I know, I'm just sayin', you usually start with one.'

'Used to. Before you started waterin' it down.'

'I'm sorry?'

'You know. You can tell me, mate. I won't let you down.
But you do, don't you? Run the old tap in it once in a
while? Eh?'

'Miller . . .'

'Ach, don't give me a lot of ould shite, it's fuckin' Mickey
Mouse stuff you sell. Fuckin' Malt Disney.'

'I . . .' Pearse began, and then thought better of it. First
rule of running a bar was not to get involved in arguments
with customers, particularly when you only had one. He
turned and reached for a Coke. Miller dropped his money
onto the floor. He bent to pick it up, mumbling to himself.
Pearse put the drink on the bar. 'Fuck the Pope,' he said.

'Right first time,' Miller said, rising fast and grabbing at
the drink with one hand while depositing dusty change on
the bar. Two pounds too much. Pearse put the excess in the
Trocaire box, just for putting up with the hassle.

'Beautiful girl,' said Miller.

'I'm sorry?'

'She's a beautiful girl.'

'Who? Oh, Marie?'

'Marie, yeah.'

'Yes, I suppose she is.'

'Seven?'

'Seven what?'

'She'll be in around seven.'

'Yes. Seven.'

Miller shuffled across the bar to a table. He sat down,
pushed his drink around the top of the table a couple of
times until he got it in the perfect position, then snorted
twice and fell asleep.

An hour passed. The bar started to fill up, now that those
that worked had been home and had their tea. In one corner
a darts match started up. There was football on the TV.
Marie came in dead on time. She noticed Miller immediately

91

– that table always got her first glance. As she stowed her bag behind the bar, Pearse said, 'Your friend's in.'

'So I see.'

'Pissed.'

'So I see. Any trouble?'

'Nah.'

Marie crossed to him. She shook him gently on the shoulder. 'You okay, sunshine?' she said softly.

Miller woke, eyes wary. 'Uuuuuuugh . . .' he said.

'Hello, sleepyhead.'

'Wha– what?'

'Only me . . .'

He shook his head. 'Jesus . . .'

Marie smiled. 'It's not like you to start this early.'

It was, but she didn't need to know that. He felt the numbness of alcohol fatigue and for a minute he struggled even to remember her name. 'I'm sorry,' he murmured.

'Love means never having to say you're sorry,' Marie said, squeezing his hand, looking into his confused eyes. 'That's from *Love Story*,' she said after a little, 'and personally I think it's a lot of wank.'

Miller pushed himself up from his half-prone position. He yawned, stretched. 'I'm getting too old for this.' He shook his head, laughed.

'What?'

'Nothing.'

'What are you laughing at?'

'Nothing. Just getting old. I was thinking about that book title you got wrong. *A Pitcher of Dorian Grey*. It would be a good name for a beer, wouldn't it? The beer that keeps you young.'

She took his hand again. 'You know I'm working tonight? I won't be finished till late.'

Miller nodded. 'I know. I just felt like a little company, y'know?'

'What's wrong? Bad day at work?'

Miller shrugged.

'Go on, tell me.'

'Nah, nothing really.' He sniggered. 'I actually got threatened. That hasn't happened since I was a cub reporter. It shouldn't annoy me.'

'God . . . who by? How?'

'It's nothing really . . .'

'Out with it, Miller.'

'Look there's . . . okay . . . it was nothing, really . . . I was in court this morning. There was this guy up for theft, a young fella just, nothing very serious . . . he'd stolen half a pound of mincemeat from a butcher's by sticking it down his trousers . . . I mean, it was in a bag 'n' all, it wasn't like running down his legs . . . but he came up to me afterwards and asked me to keep his name and address out of the paper . . . I told him I couldn't do that . . . he told me I could . . . I told him I couldn't . . . he told me he'd break most of the bones in my body if it went in the paper.'

'Most of the bones?'

'That's what he said.'

'A curious way of putting things.'

'That's what I thought . . . however, it doesn't lessen greatly the overall threat . . .'

'And you're worried about it?'

'Ach, not really . . . up in Belfast when I did the courts I never got threatened, it was mostly the big cases, y'know, the murders, and they didn't go in for threats . . . too many reporters involved . . . too much publicity . . . I suppose I should have realized it'd be different down here where I'm the only one covering a case . . . he was an annoying wee bastard though.'

'What'd you call him?'

'Ugh . . . Davie . . . Davie something. Davie Morrow, I think.'

'Davie Morrow. Trust Davie Morrow.'

'You know him?'

'Ish. He's a regular across the road. Thick as shite, like, but as liable to give you a hidin' as look at you. Fuckin' scum, like. Never out of the paper anyway, I'll tell you that.'

'He said he didn't want his mum to see his name in the paper. It would break her heart.'

'Fuck, you couldn't break ol' Ma Morrow's heart with a sledgehammer. She's as bad as he is. You should see her. She's like a fuckin' hot air balloon with legs. The doctor had to wire her jaws shut one time, she ate so fuckin' much. You ever see someone try to eat a Swiss Roll through wire? Not a pretty sight. Davie's hard, I suppose, in his own way . . . but too thick to get into any real trouble . . . too thick to be a terrorist for one thing . . . story has it he couldn't get into the UVF because he wasn't intellectual enough . . . which is fine coming from those noted scholars . . . You know what they're like, they're the military wing of the Presbyterian Church.'

'Marie . . .'

'I'm serious. And they're the ones turned Davie Morrow down. He's just a bully, Miller, he's a vulture, picking on everything, everyone he can.' Marie laughed to herself. Every time I hear the word vulture I reach for my Strong-bow. 'So what're you going to do?'

'Publish and be damned.'

'Just right. Sure I doubt if he can read anyway. He'll probably never know. Chances are he was half cut anyway. He won't remember.'

'Yeah, well. I know I'm being silly. Stupid reason to get drunk.'

'Who needs a reason to get drunk?'

'Who indeed?'

Miller needed a reason to get drunk. Miller had a reason to get drunk, and it was nothing to do with a bloody stupid threat from a cretin like Davie Morrow. It had been the first magistrates' court he'd covered in years, but the style hadn't changed much: first you get the summonses, then you sit through a whole pile of motoring cases, before you eventually get down to the real meat and veg, the criminal cases. Crossmaheart has as much terrorism as anywhere in Northern Ireland, and for the size of it could be described as the murder capital of Europe. But it isn't big enough for its own Crown Court, so the major trials take place up in Belfast. Scheduled offences – anything involving a gun or smacking of terrorism – also get shipped to the city. Crossmaheart's wire-enclosed court has a little old magistrate who listens impatiently to the lame excuses of the thick and fickle, the thugs and mugs, up for theft and assault and intimidation, before finding them guilty. That's his job, to bolster the police. If a defendant is serious about his innocence he can take it up on appeal in the city.

An hour before the court started Miller was handed the summonses by a morose court clerk who didn't even check his ID. He made his way down to the empty court, took his seat at the press table (the only seat) and started noting them down – there were about a hundred different cases up that morning, three quarters of them for minor motoring offences. The rest ranged from shop-lifting to public drunkenness and assault, the kind of cases he had trained on as a cub years before; he didn't mind doing them again; he was out of the office for a change and whipping them down in shorthand still came as second nature.

While he was working through them the door of the court swung open and a policeman came in. Miller nodded at him. The policeman nodded back. He started moving down the aisle between the seats, half bent, looking about him for bombs.

When he got closer, the policeman said: 'Settling in then, Mr Miller?'

'Mmmmm?' Miller looked up. It took a moment for him to recognize the officer who had first spoken to him on his arrival in Crossmaheart. 'Sorry. Yes. Hello. You've a good memory.'

'I never forget a face and rarely a name. Your face was bright red last time I saw it, but I've compensated for that.'

'I wish I'd a memory like that.'

'First rule of survival down here. Know your enemy. Not that you're my enemy, but you know what I mean.'

Miller returned to his work. The policeman sat on the edge of the press table and removed his hat. 'Anything interesting?' he asked, nodding down at the summonses.

'Not so far.'

The policeman nodded. 'Isn't usually.'

Miller nodded and continued with his transcription.

'I'm not disturbing you, am I?'

Miller put his pen down and sat back. 'No. Not at all.'

'Good. I used to come down and share a fag with your predecessor. Nice bloke.'

'You mean Jamie Milburn.'

'Aye, Jamie. Still no word on him?'

'You tell me.'

'No. Haven't heard. Still, no news is good news, eh?'

'Not in my job.'

'Even about one of your own?'

'More so.'

The policeman shrugged.

'You knew Jamie well?'

The constable spread his palms. 'Ish. Mostly from in here. Out on the street a few times . . . that other lot in your paper wouldn't give you the time of day, y'know . . . Jamie always had time for a chat. I mean, it should be their job to cultivate good relations with the police, if for no other reason than to get access to information they wouldn't normally get . . . but they couldn't be arsed . . . just as it should be our role to get on well with the press so that we can pick up on information we wouldn't normally get the public bringing directly to us, but so few of our lot can be bothered making the effort, mostly because you lot won't make the effort to talk to us in the first place. It's a bit of a Catch 2 situation.'

Miller let that one go. 'You have a point, I suppose.'

'No suppose about it, mate. You don't smoke?'

'No bad habits at all.'

The policeman laughed. 'Yeah, sure.' He lit up a cigarette for himself.

'These chats you had with Jamie ... were they, uh, official in any way?'

'No, God, just chats, like.'

'I mean, he wasn't – well, he wasn't an informer?'

'God, no ... well, I suppose in one light you could say that, in that anything you say to a copper down here has you marked out as a tout, but not in any real sense. It was just bits of gossip he might pick up, y'know, like someone's selling bootleg videos, or I hear someone's been threatened if they don't come up with money for the boys. That was the extent of it – he didn't run the terrorists. It was all nickel and dime stuff. Your common or garden crimbo.'

'And in exchange ... ?'

'Not much. I'd let him know about a burglary here or an assault there, maybe a sneaky word on an upcoming visit by a government minister or the occasional royal ... just priming him really ... generally stuff that would be freely available if those buggers at the paper took the trouble to ask us, but they never do.'

'And whatever he told you ... it never got credited to him. It was always off the record, the way a journalist does it, his name never went down in a file anywhere.'

'No one knew. There was never anything important enough exchanged for anyone to want to know where it came from. I mean, the important stuff comes to us on the confidential telephone. That's easy enough to follow up because we can trace all the calls. But Jamie's stuff was just local gossip really – it was more being friendly than anything. It's a rare commodity round here, y'know?'

Miller nodded. 'Just saying . . .' he began, decision made, 'that I had something a bit more important to tell you than Jamie ever managed, could I be left absolutely out of it? I mean all I'd want would be to tell you a simple yarn and leave it like that, no follow-up questioning, no carting me down to the station for a session under the disco lights. How would that be?'

'Try me.'

'I don't want to try you. I want promised.'

'The word of a cop?'

'The word of a cop.'

The policeman giggled and put out his hand. 'Shake on it.'

They shook.

'Okay,' said Miller.

'One born every minute.'

Miller told him about the fox.

It was a relief, but a disturbing one. A betrayal, really, of his profession. Yet though he still considered himself a journalist, he felt no loyalty to the profession in Crossmaheart. The only loyalty he felt was to Marie, and through her, however tenuously, to Jamie. It was time for Jamie to be gathered together.

He breezed through the court on autopilot. More than half of the cases were adjourned, the others dealt with in a matter of seconds by way of fines. Davie Morrow's case was the only vaguely interesting one – mincemeat down your trousers is always a good story – and the threat afterwards only made him more determined to make a bigger issue of it.

The court was over by lunch time and he returned to the office. As usual, his editorial colleagues had made other arrangements for eating. After gnawing through a sandwich, Miller asked one of the girls in the front office to direct him to the old newspaper files. She sent him to a dusty stationery store at the rear of the building where he sought out the file for 1977. The year of the Queen's Silver Jubilee and punk rock. The year Marie had been abused, as far as he could work out.

Back in the office, he said: 'The files only seem to go as far back as 1980.'

The girl, her fingers deep inside a packet of cheese and onion crisps, spat crumbs at him. 'We had a clear-out a few years ago. Didn't seem much point in keeping them here.'

'What happened to them?'

'I'm fucked if I know,' she cackled.

Another girl said: 'I think they're up at the library.'

Miller nodded, gave his helper a half-smile. 'Thanks. I'll go up there then. If O'Hagan makes it back from lunch, tell him I'm out on a story, will you?'

As he went out the door, he heard the crisp-eater ask: 'Is he allowed out?'

They were more helpful up at the library. They practically fought over him. Reading wasn't a big pastime in Crossmaheart. He was set down before a microfiche, and tapes of the relevant year lined up for him. He thanked his helpers profusely, then gazed at them until they grew embarrassed and left him in peace.

After about an hour he located what he was looking for. He was hindered by the unfamiliar style of the paper – O'Hagan's reign as editor was relatively recent. Back in 1977 might as well have been back in 1877: no garish headlines, no fancy type; adverts covered the front pages; news items were all over the place; one lead story was 'Our Local Graduates'. It was the style of having no style; O'Hagan's style was nothing to write home about, but at least he made the effort.

The story was on page three of a September paper.

Prison for 'Disgraceful' Sex Attack

Three Crossmaheart men have been sent to prison for what has been described as a 'disgraceful' sexual assault on a member of the Girls' Brigade. Magistrate J.D. Raphael Mills heard on Monday that the men offered the girl a lift home in a stolen car, then took her to a secluded country lane before subjecting her to a series of sexual assaults.

Michael Rainey of Sommerton Heights, Tom Callaghan of Meadow Way and Tyrone Blair of Shackleton Walk each admitted the charge of indecent assault when they appeared at Crossmaheart Magistrates' Court.

Inspector Michael McCourt, RUC, prosecuting, told the court that the girl, who cannot be named for legal reasons, was returning from a meeting of the Girls' Brigade on Thursday, 16 April, when the car stopped beside her. One of the men told her that they'd been sent by her dad to pick her up as it was very wet.

'The girl,' said Inspector McCourt, 'an innocent thirteen-year-old, took these men at their word and as a result was made to suffer a disgraceful sexual assault.

'The men,' continued the Inspector, 'took her to Cairnmarten Wood Road where they forced her to remove her clothes. All three then interfered with her and forced her to perform acts of a sexual nature.

'When they had finished with her, she was taken back to the GB hall and let out of the car. She was told that if she reported what had happened her father would be killed by the UVF.'

Inspector McCourt explained that the girl kept the incident secret for several months, but eventually broke down

100

and confessed to a teacher at school, who informed the police. When the girl was interviewed she was able to recall her experience in detail. Subsequent enquiries led to the arrest of Rainey, Callaghan and Blair. All three made statements to the police, admitting their part.

Mr Sam Annette, representing all three defendants, described them as young men – all three are eighteen – who came from difficult backgrounds in Crossmaheart.

Rainey's parents, he said, had split up the previous year. Rainey now lived with his father; both were unemployed. Callaghan's father had been murdered by the IRA. Blair, he said, had been kneecapped on two occasions for joyriding and petty criminal activity.

'On the night in question,' said Mr Annette, 'all three had been drinking for an extended period. What started out as a bit of good-natured fun with the girl got out of hand and the offences were committed. All three are thoroughly ashamed of themselves. I ask you to give them credit for the fact that these three young men admitted the offence immediately to the police, and did not seek to put this young lady through a harrowing ordeal in the witness box.'

A medical report was handed in to court.

In sentencing the defendants, Mr Mills described the indecent assaults as particularly cruel as they were against an innocent, naïve young girl, whose innocence was now lost for ever. 'Thankfully,' he added, 'there was only some slight physical injury, and there does not appear to have been any lasting psychological damage.'

Blair, who had a previous criminal record, was sentenced to four years in prison. Rainey and Callaghan each received two-year sentences, one year of which was suspended for twelve months. A one-month sentence for the theft of the car, which was returned to its owner, was imposed on each defendant, suspended for one year.

When he had finished, Miller ran off a copy of the story from the microfiche. Outside, he unlocked the Cycle of

Violence and rode along Main Street until he came to an off-licence. He bought half a bottle of Smirnoff and rode back to his flat and started to drink.

He sat on the bed, sipping steadily, staring out the window at nothing (there was nothing there besides a wall anyway) and from time to time slipped in a different CD on the player. Everything sounded too raucous. Even Smokey Robinson. Even 'Tears of a Clown'. He knew what he needed: he needed Leonard Cohen.

At about 5 pm the phone rang.

It was Martin O'Hagan from work. He said: 'Do you mind telling me where you are?'

'Well, that's a stupid fuckin' question. You phoned me.'

'I mean, why aren't you in work, Miller?'

'Just.'

'Just why?'

'Just because.'

'Miller, I'm not running a bloody holiday camp down here.'

'I'm aware of that.'

'So where the hell were you?'

'I left a message. I went to the library. Didn't you get it?'

'Yes, I got it.'

'Well then?'

'Miller, when you want to go somewhere, when you want to disappear for the afternoon, you come to me, you ask me. I'm the editor. I assign the work. I want you to go to the library, I send you there. You don't just go off by yourself.'

'Listen, Martin, no offence like, but I've been a reporter since before you learnt to write and sometimes you've got to follow . . .'

'Don't spout that crap with me, Miller. You work for me, or you don't work at all. I had jobs set aside for this afternoon.'

'Don't tell me, subbing the Women's Institute notes, was it? Proofreading?'

'I don't like your tone very much, Miller.'

'Tough.'

'You're not making this very easy.'

'It's not meant to be easy.'

O'Hagan was silent for twenty-six seconds. Miller counted them off. Then he said: 'Come and see me first thing tomorrow, Miller, when you sober up.'

Miller said, 'You can stick your fuckin' job up your fuckin' hole,' just after he put the phone down.

He continued drinking. He didn't remember a lot else for a while. He woke up in the pub, Marie was there, looking great. While she sat there, talking, he tried to picture her in a GB uniform. He couldn't even think of what a GB uniform might look like. Vaguely military, with girlie bits, he supposed. From thirteen to this beauty in the bar – look at her. What must it have been like? Three men. Three boys, really, eighteen only, but they would have seemed like men. All drunken. There's nothing worse to a sober person than getting stuck in a conversation with a drunk; multiplied how many thousands of times for a girl, barely a teenager, to be assaulted by three drunks? He felt sick. He had felt sick then, in the library, he felt as bad now. The alcohol did not dilute it, it made him worse. Mad. Mad Marie. No wonder.

Miller felt a tear in his eye. He wiped at it. Marie's hand was on his shoulder.

'Are you okay, love?'

He shrugged it off, physically, mentally. 'Sorry, I'm just tired. Here, you, on with your work anyway. You're not paid to stand and slabber to me all night.'

'Aye, right, boss.'

'And geddis a drink while you're there.'

'Dorian Grey, is it?'

'I think not. Make it a Coke.'

She brought him a Coke. Two or three, as the night passed. The bar really busied up as the hours ticked by, and by not much before eleven it was jam-packed. There was singing going on, but it came from two or three different directions and all Miller could make out was an occasional Gaelic cry and cheering.

Bringing him another, Marie said: 'Someone's got their rellies in from the States – this'll be a laugh. They've ordered Flaming Samboucas. That's a first in here.'

Marie and her tray pushed back through the crowd. She leant on the bar and shouted her order across to Pearse. He lost her in the crush for a couple of minutes, then he saw her again, from behind, still at the bar, with four Flaming Samboucas on her tray. As she started to turn someone bumped into her from behind. One of the glasses fell over and a little lick of flame lapped at her blouse. She dropped the tray onto the bar as she slapped, panicked, at her shirt. The other glasses rattled against the bar, spilling their contents into a small but expanding pool of fire.

Marie leant forward and tried to blow the flames out, but instead of quenching them she encouraged them into an advance along the bar. It just took a few seconds: the flames along the bar, the shouts, the crush, the pub doors being pushed out, the smoke, the loud mix of laughter and fear. Miller pushed against the crowd to get to Marie and they pushed back. A smoke detector buzzed from the ceiling, for all the good of it. He shouted at them, but his cry was lost in the excited roar. Pushing, pulling, he advanced slowly, inch by inch, then most of them were gone out into the night air and there was only Marie and Pearse at the bar beating at the fire with damp towels. Miller reached across the far end of the bar and picked up the ice bucket. The cubes were half melted. He threw them along the bar and the flames threw up a last lick in surrender and then died.

'Well done, that man!' said Pearse, laughing.

'Jesus,' said Marie, running a hand across her brow, 'that was a close one. I knew Samboucas were trouble. Samboucas and me, anyway. Jesus, Pearse, me and fire just don't mix, do we?'

'Ach, it was an accident. Could happen to anyone.'

'Aye, but it happens to me. Last time it was those fuckin' sausage rolls got stuck in the oven nearly burnt us down. Time before, the toaster.'

'Miller,' said Pearse, 'you ever marry this girl, keep her away from matches, eh? She's murder.'

'Pearse!'

'Oh, don't come all embarrassed with me, girlie.'

'Aw, fuck up.'

Miller nodded back to the doors. 'You lettin' that lot back in again?'

Pearse came round from behind the bar. 'They're only hanging round on the off-chance there'll be something to loot. Customer loyalty is so touching.' He closed and barred the door, then turned to the pair of them. 'A drink, fire-fighters?'

Marie nodded enthusiastically.

'Shouldn't we, uh, phone the Fire Brigade, or something?' Miller asked. 'I mean, these things have a habit of flaring up again, don't they?'

'Nah,' said Pearse, shaking his head, 'it's out. No point. Anyway, last time the firemen came here they were stoned.'

'Jesus.'

'He doesn't mean they were on drugs, Miller. Everyone threw stones at them.'

'Jesus.'

'Then the police arrived. They joined in too. Wasn't a pretty sight. They closed our own fire station down years ago – government cuts, y'know. Now when there's a fire they have to be brought over from Ballyblack – and everyone hates those bastards.'

'Jesus. Is it, like, a religious thing?'

'Nah, they join in from across the road as well. It's a loyalty thing. We hate Crossmaheart as much as anyone, but we have a right to. Those wankers from Ballyblack look down their noses at us, so we don't mind breaking them.'

'Fair enough.'

Pearse rapped his knuckles on the bar. 'Now, youse had better take a drink or I'm going to huff. A wee whiskey, Miller?'

'Uh . . .'

'What is it you like . . . oh yeah . . . Malt Disney, isn't it?'

'What?'

Pearse looked at Marie. 'Memory is a wonderful thing, isn't it?'

7

Their talk was of perfection. They lay in her room, he sober now from drinking too much, she drunk, a late starter. Their clothes, bundled in the corner, stank of smoke. She remained in her underwear. He remained in his. The Erection Which Would Not Go Away, which had eventually, had returned. Leonard Cohen was singing mournfully in the background. On the record player. Actually, inside the record player. Miller was getting quite used to him, although he didn't fancy taking him to a party.

'Who's your perfect man, Marie? What are you striving for?' he asked. It sounded like he was fishing for compliments, but he didn't mean it that way. Her cheek rested on his chest. He could feel her breath – warm.

'Dunno,' she said. Her voice was light, far away almost, but there was no hint of sleep in it. Thoughtful.

'Was Jamie perfect?'

'No.'

'How come?'

'Dunno.'

'Am I perfect?'

'Not yet.'

'Meaning I might be one day?'

'Maybe.'

'You'll let me know?'

'You'll know.' She scratched lightly at the hairs on his chest. She knew one thing. She didn't want to sleep. The flames had unsettled her. She didn't want the nightmare to return. It was nightmare weather. Close. Rain falling steadily, pattering against the window like a thousand bony fingers chastising her. Thunder rumbling around like a death rattle in a starved stomach. 'There's perfection out there somewhere, Miller. There must be.'

It didn't hurt, exactly, but it was hardly cheering. Still, he was in her bed, again. They were close. It was only a matter of time.

'And what happens when you achieve this perfection? Do you exist in a state of perpetual nirvana for the rest of your life?'

Jesus. I want to spit love words into her ear. I want to touch every part of her, slowly, for a long time. And I'm talking about states of perpetual nirvana.

'No. I don't think so. It will be fleeting.'

'You think so?'

'I know so.'

'What does that do to your life? Make the rest of it an anticlimax?'

Climax, now there's a word.

She nodded against his chest.

'That's a bit sad,' he said.

'I know. Better to go out on top, eh?'

'Meaning?'

'I don't know. Kill myself, I suppose. Achieve this elusive perfection and then have done with it all.'

He stroked her hair. 'Tomorrow it's meltdown for your Leonard Cohen collection, madame. I'm investing in some Kylie for you. That's as close as you can get to pop perfection without killing yourself.'

She dug her fingers into his ribs. He let out a groan.

'I'll have you for sexual harassment,' he said.

'Since when were your ribs sexual?'

He tutted. 'Obviously nobody's ever played the spoons on your ribs while making love to you.'

She shushed him with a finger to his lips. Then she kissed

him. A good long kiss. The Erection Which Would Not Go Away prodded her. Her hand touched it fleetingly. She turned away.

'It's okay,' he said, before she could say anything.

Is it? Am I being the martyr? What if she's just winding me up? What if she never intends to let me make love to her? Does it matter? I'm not just here for sex. Or am I? Am I in love with her or with the idea of making love with her? Is it one and the same thing? Who wants to go to bed with their sister? I'd get a better night's sleep by myself. There's less chance of me getting murdered. God, mustn't ever think that. I just want to make love to her so much. I know how good it would be. But it doesn't matter now. It really doesn't. I am content to be here. Better here with someone I'm falling in love with than home in bed with a Swedish porn mag, a Bible and a coat hanger.

'Teachinina,' he said softly, stroking her hair again.

'Mmmmm?' she said, turning back, her head once again settling on his chest. When the word had sunk in for a few moments, she said: 'What?'

'Teachinina. It was a word my mother used when I was a wee lad. I thought it was something pretty profound. Latin or something. Of course I'd never heard of Latin back then, but you know what I mean, something otherworldly. It took me years to find out what she'd meant. When I was little she'd stroke my hair like this. She'd say, "I wouldn't give you away for all the teachinina."'

'Tea in China,' murmured Marie.

'Tea in China, yeah.'

'Ach, that's nice. Mum used to say that as well. Funny. I never knew what it meant either. Tea didn't come from China. It came from Punjana.'

'The Punjana factory in Belfast.'

'Yeah, Pink Punjana. That's what it always said on the

109

advertisement on TV. "Pink Punjana tea." I could never work it out, I mean, all tea's the same colour.'

'It wasn't "Pink". It was "Pick". "Pick Punjana tea."'

'Oh.'

'Oh indeed.'

'Well, it's not as bad as teachinina.'

'Granted.'

She squeezed him, nestled closer, but not so close that the Erection Which Would Not Go Away was in any further danger of being interfered with, however innocently.

'I love you to bits,' she said.

'Good.'

They were silent for a minute. 'Reciprocate,' she said eventually.

'I love you to bits too.'

She nodded and kissed his chest.

'Did you love Jamie to bits?' He didn't quite mean it that way, but it was out before he could do anything about it.

He felt her tense up. She rolled off him. 'You have to go and spoil it,' she said quietly.

'I'm sorry,' he said, reaching out to her. He tried to lighten it. 'Love means never having . . .'

'Oh, fuck up.'

'Okay. But I am sorry. Maybe I'm just jealous.'

'How can you be jealous of a dead man?'

'You don't know he's a dead man, Marie.'

'Of course he's a dead man. You don't disappear like that in Crossmaheart and turn up alive. Jesus, Miller, for someone who's such a big . . . git up in the city you're bloody naïve. Even the Women's Institute kidnaps people down here. They torture them for days, then throw them in the lake wearing concrete boots and a crocheted life jacket.'

'I was only . . .'

'You were only trying to patronize me.'

110

'Okay.'
'Okay.'
'Do we kiss and make up now?'
'No.'
And they didn't. They huffed, back to back. Miller tried to work out an apology that didn't involve losing face, and had almost cracked it when he fell asleep. Marie slipped into a doze.

It wasn't quite the nightmare she was used to – although you never got used to it – but it had the same cast of characters: her father screaming, screaming, 'Didn't you learn anything? Didn't you learn anything? Nothing? Nothing at all? Nothing? Didn't you learn? Didn't you? Didn't you learn?' Screaming, screaming. It was the sound she thought a pig would make if it was put on a spit alive. His face, all pinched, mouth spitting, stench of sweat and beer. 'Didn't you? Didn't you? Didn't you? Didn't you learn anything, you stupid little bitch?' And then the pain. Her pain. Her mother's pain, cowering helpless in the background. And distant, outside in the garden, on the swing, her sister. Her face so sad.

She woke, slick with sweat, with a start. Her shoulder was being shaken. The room was bright.

'Marie?'

Softly. The bright-blindness faded, she homed in on Mrs Hardy. Panicked, she spread her arm under the cover. Miller was gone.

'What time is it?' she mumbled.

'Gone ten, love.'

'Oh . . . I'm sorry . . . was I screaming . . . ?'

'No . . . love . . . will you come down to the kitchen?'

'What . . . what's the matter?'

'I have the pot on . . . come on down, love.'

Mrs Hardy nodded to her, gave her a little smile and left. Marie pushed the dank hair out of her face and tumbled

111

from the bed. She pulled a dressing gown on over her underwear and followed her landlady.

Downstairs, the kitchen was empty save for Mrs Hardy. The breakfast table was spotless. 'Everyone been and gone?' she asked.

'Everyone bar Mrs Brady. She hasn't been down for a couple of days. I don't think she's too well. She's been complaining about hallucinations.'

'Maybe she has the DTs.'

'That'll be the day.'

'I'll say.'

Mrs Hardy set a cup of tea down on the table. 'There you go,' she said.

Marie sat. She took a sip. 'What is it?'

Mrs Hardy bit her lip. 'I just heard it on the wireless, love. I thought you should know first. It's about Jamie.'

The news that the police, having sealed off Crossmaheart dump, were now beginning to recover body parts, cast the office into a black depression. Ninety per cent of it was, of course, due to the fact that Jamie had been an esteemed colleague and friend to most of them; even Miller felt like he knew him; indeed, he was better acquainted with Jamie than he was with O'Hagan or either of the girls. Even though they had presumed him dead, while there was no body there was still some little hope. Ten per cent of it was, however, caused by professional despair, that, even though they had been positively – negatively? – discouraged from searching for Jamie, the story of his apparent discovery had broken early on Friday morning, just after the paper was published. They would have to wait another week before they could carry the morbid details, and by then it would be very old news.

Miller apart, of course. He could hardly have been depressed about other media scooping the story. In fact,

Jamie's discovery had its plus side as his argument with O'Hagan on the phone seemed to have been forgotten. The editor, ashen-faced, smoking one after the other, sat at the front of the office, staring into space, occasionally mumbling, 'Poor guy, poor guy.'

Helen Sloan and Anne Maguire, between bouts of tears, spent the morning lost in memories, recalling apparently humorous incidents from Jamie's short career with the paper. Miller really didn't have anything to say. Occasionally he nodded, once or twice he politely laughed at an anecdote, but for the most part he sat glum-faced, thinking as much about Marie as about Jamie. He hated leaving her on an argument. He shouldn't have sneaked away so early. They should have made up before he left.

About noon, with no work done, O'Hagan said: 'Let's go to the pub.'

Helen and Anne stood up immediately and pulled their coats on. Miller sat where he was.

'Aren't you coming?' Helen asked.

'Me?' replied Miller, genuinely surprised.

'Of course.'

'Uh . . . yeah . . . okay.' He stood up. He sat down. 'In a minute. I've something to sort out first. Uh, can I join you?'

'Sure. Where are we going, Martin?'

Martin shrugged.

'Ulster Arms,' suggested Anne, 'it'll be quieter.'

'Who needs quiet?' asked Helen.

'Better food,' said Martin.

'Who needs food?' asked Helen.

'Cheaper drink,' suggested Martin.

'Ulster Arms,' said Helen.

'I'll see you over there then. I won't be long.'

They filed out of the office. They love me really, thought Miller, reaching for the phone book. He called Riley's, but Marie hadn't started work yet. Then he tried her lodgings.

113

When she came to the phone she was all sniffle-voiced.

'Miller? I'm sorry. I'm sorry.'

'Nothing to be sorry for. It was just a silly argument. You've heard the news, I take it?'

'Yeah.'

'I'm sorry.'

'It was bound to happen sooner or later. Why him? Why wee Jamie? What did he ever do to hurt anyone?'

Something. 'I know.'

'And to end up . . . like that . . . Jesus . . . who could do that?'

'I don't know.'

'I mean, the UVF, the IRA, whatever, I mean, they don't cut people up, do they? They murder people, but they're not . . . beastly about it . . .'

'It's a fine line, Marie . . .'

'I'm not justifying them . . . I mean . . . I don't know what I mean . . . but to be cut up in little bits . . .'

'Maybe he wasn't killed like that at all.'

'Oh, he just fell to bits, did he? What're you saying, he committed suicide?'

'No . . . I mean it could have happened a different way . . . just as . . . beastly . . . but different . . .'

'Like how? You're just trying to make me feel better.'

'I'm not . . . I am . . . but I'm journalist enough to know it's better to wait for an autopsy than to speculate.'

'Have you not got that the wrong way round? Surely you speculate first, report the facts, if there's room, later?'

'You're so cynical.'

'I'm so lonely.'

'I know. Marie, you were his girlfriend. Let's not even think about dismemberment.'

'I'd just prefer to know.'

'Curiosity killed the cat. Killers who chop up their

114

victims, that's all very American, or at the very least English. In Ireland it would only happen by accident, like most things.'

'Miller, I've had an awful thought.'

'Suppress awful thoughts. There's enough awfulness about already.'

'I can't.'

'Try.'

'I can't. What if he wasn't dead at all, just injured, or knocked unconscious or was drunk or something? And then he was chopped up while still alive . . . what if . . .'

'Marie, don't . . . there's no point . . .'

'But what . . .'

'Marie! Stop it. We'll never know. There's no point in dwelling on it.'

'I know.' She was crying. Half-strangled sobs. He wanted to reach out and hold her.

'Do you want me to come and see you?'

'No . . . no . . . I'll be okay . . . I'm going to go back to bed for a while . . . sleep a bit . . .'

'I could be there in a few minutes . . .'

'No . . . no, thanks . . . honestly . . . I want to . . . I need to think for a while, that's all . . .'

'And we're friends again?'

'Of course.'

'Can I see you tonight? You're not working, are you?'

'No, not tonight. Yes . . . come round and see me. That would be nice.'

After he put the phone down Miller slipped on his jacket and left the office. The Ulster Arms was only up the street a few yards. It was half empty. Or was it half full? Miller could hardly tell the difference between it and Riley's, the same aura of barely suppressed violence, the same whiff of desperation brought on by poverty laced with alcoholism. Where Riley's was decorated with Gaelic insignia, hurling pennants, Glasgow Celtic team photos and throbbed to the beat of a Rebel Rebel juke box, the Ulster Arms had its Glasgow Rangers Supporters Club flags, its Loyalist Prisoners of War banner and a juke box full of Protestant out-of-work ethic interpretations of country classics. Nobody smiled very much in either bar, save the staff, who smiled because it was the done thing, but resignation dulled their eyes.

Anne and Helen were sitting at a table. O'Hagan was getting drinks at the bar. Miller nodded at his editor and joined the girls. He heard O'Hagan asking for an extra pint.

'You still seeing Marie then?' Helen asked.

'Ish.'

'Ha. Told you you'd have trouble.'

'Nah . . . we're okay . . . we made up . . .'

'You make the first move?'

'No. She did. She answered the phone.'

'She'll have you twisted round her little finger. She had Jamie. Still, I'm sure she's pretty cut up about him. If you'll excuse the expression. As cut up as you can be, if you're a nut . . .'

'Look, I really don't think there's any need . . .'

'Hey, lay off him, Helen, will ya?' Anne broke in. 'Each onto their own, eh?'

Helen tutted. 'Yeah. I suppose so. There's no accounting for taste.'

'Helen!'

'I'm only joking . . . for God's sake . . . I've nothing against the girl . . .' She stood up and crossed to the bar to help O'Hagan carry the drinks.

Anne tapped Miller on the knee. 'Never worry about her. She took an instant dislike to Marie when Jamie fell for her. I think Helen here had a bit of a soft spot for him herself, if you get my drift.'

'You mean all this stuff about Marie being . . . well, a bit strange . . . is just her way of . . .'

'Well, I wouldn't say that . . . Marie is a bit . . . odd . . . but she's harmless.'

O'Hagan and Helen arrived. O'Hagan handed Miller a drink. 'I got you a pint of Harp, okay?'

'Yeah, great, cheers.'

'Well,' said O'Hagan, sitting, then raising his pint, 'here's to Jamie.'

They clinked glasses and repeated the name of their dead colleague.

The drink flowed, the hours passed, they all got pretty drunk. Helen was the first to leave, citing a boyfriend. Anne followed half an hour later, citing a dog. There was nothing left to be said about Jamie. O'Hagan got them another drink.

'Settling in okay then?' he asked. It was the nearest he'd come to small talk with Miller.

'Fine, yeah.'

'Jamie's a hard act to follow.'

'Yeah.'

'But you're doing okay.'

'Thanks.'

'And I hear you've got a girlfriend.'

'Yeah.'

'Good. There's not much else by way of distraction in Crossmaheart.'

'No. There's not.' It was hardly flowing, thought Miller, but at least we're talking. 'Without being unduly mawkish,' he said, 'it's a pity Jamie didn't turn up before we went to press. It's a shame missing it.'

'The wee bugger probably did it on purpose.'

Miller laughed. 'Yeah, sure. Still, now he's been found and we're not putting anyone in danger, we can maybe look ourselves at the whys and wherefores of it all. See if we can find out what happened.'

O'Hagan sipped at his drink. 'Yes, well, we'll see about that.'

'Why on earth not?'

'Let sleeping dogs lie, Miller. Always good advice down here. He got topped for one reason or another. If there's a reason, it'll turn up soon enough.'

'Do you think there was a reason?'

'I don't know. Nothing I can think of. Half the ones disappear down here there's no reason for, just your common or garden random sectarian killing.'

'Well, was he working on anything specific when he disappeared?'

'Stop interviewing me. As far as I'm aware he was out for a quiet pint, and that's the extent of it. If he was working on something, it wasn't for me, okay? Anyway, it's time I was off too. I've a wife to argue with.'

O'Hagan drained his pint and stood up. His hand lingered by his jacket pocket for a moment, as if he was about to reach over and shake Miller's hand, but then he thrust it into his coat, smiled and said goodbye.

Miller sat on. He got another few drinks. As the afternoon turned into evening the bar began to fill. The customers, save for their religious and political views, graphically depicted in a bewildering display of tattoos, were the dead spit of those in Riley's. The moneyed poor. Miller scratched absentmindedly at his arm. He'd been in Crossmaheart so long he felt like he was starting to grow a tattoo.

He knew it was getting near time to go and see Marie, to console her, to love her, to lie with her. He got another drink. Just one before hitting the road. A couple of couples, unable to find an empty table in the bar, joined him at his. They got talking. They were already drunk. The talk flowed. The drink flowed. Time wore on. The singsongs started right across the bar: 'The Sash', 'The Green Grassy Slopes of the Boyne', 'Follow, Follow'. The heritage of his youth he had not delved into for years, the rabble-rousing tunes he had disdained for so long now crowded back into his memory and he found himself singing disjointedly along with the rest of them.

The couples at the table started including him in their rounds. He protested that he couldn't reciprocate because his funds were low – they were, honest – but they said never mind, sure it's Christmas or Charity Week or one of the two, but they were drinking brandy and he could never manage brandy at the best of times, let alone on top of a skinful. One round, he tried to get them to get him a Coke, because the table was starting to spin, but they got him a brandy and Coke. It stilled the table, but his head started to spin.

Miller was holding onto his seat, head down, eyes up, looking at the world through the jumble of glasses on his table. The conversation around him had turned to jabber by the time it permeated his brain. He thought of Marie. He slept.

He wasn't out for that long, but when he woke the bar was a lot emptier. The female half of the quartet at his table had left. In fact, most of the women in the bar had left. The singing continued, but it was different, harsher, vicious. Three men at the bar broke into one he hadn't heard before about the IRA hunger striker, Bobby Sands.

> 'Would you go a pasty supper, Bobby Sands?
> Would you go a pasty supper, Bobby Sands?
> Would you go a pasty supper,
> You dirty fenian fucker?
> Would you go a pasty supper, Bobby Sands?'

Half a dozen others joined in, stamping their feet and clapping their hands. The boys with him banged the table in time. Miller mumbled along. He felt sick. He would have to go.

As they came to the end of the third rendition of it a new voice broke in sharply.

'No! No! No!'

The singing stopped immediately. Miller looked up, round. The voice came from the end of the bar. A tall man, mid-thirties maybe, in a grey suit. And a dog collar.

'Fuck,' said one of the boys at the table in a whisper, 'Rev. Rainey's sticking his oar in again.'

'Fuck,' said the other, 'who rowed his fuckin' boat ashore again?'

The Rev. Rainey put down his half-pint of beer and strode purposefully to the end of the bar, opposite Miller's table, where the three who'd instigated the latest bout of singing stood, grinning stupidly.

'Aw, Rev.,' said one, 'we were just getting into the swing.'

'Never mind that,' said the Rev. in a raspy voice, waving a finger in front of them.

'Aw, Rev.'

'Don't you know there's no need for language like that? No need at all.'

'Aw, Rev.'

'Christ didn't die on the cross so that you could fill your mouths and my ears with barbaric language like that.'

'It was only a song.'

'It was only a sin. As you well know, I'm the last person would want to stop you all having a good time, a bit of a singalong, but there's no need for language like that. I suggest if you wish to sing, you sing this . . .' He put his hand on his chest, took a deep breath . . . then stopped. 'Excuse me while I wet my whistle.' He lifted one of the pints off the bar, took a deep swallow, set it down. 'Right, then . . .' His voice rang out, deep, beautiful, emotive:

120

'Would you go a pasty supper, Bobby Sands?
Would you go a pasty supper, Bobby Sands?
Would you go a pasty supper?
Would you like some bread and butter?
Would you go a pasty supper, Bobby Sands?'

He finished to wild cheers and laughter. 'There you go,' he said, lifting someone's drink from the bar again, 'perfectly clean and not a soul offended.'

Draining the pint, he turned and left the bar, a broad grin on his fat red face. As the door swung shut behind him laughter filled the bar again.

'What a wanker,' said one of the boys beside Miller.

'But a Protestant wanker, and that's what counts,' said the other.

'Exactly. One of us.'

Miller's head turned at another new voice. This time it was the barman. 'Ladies and . . . sorry, gentlemen, we seem to be lacking on the ladies front . . .'

'Aren't we always!'

'Fuck up there, Andy . . .'

'I'm telling Michael Rainey about you!'

'Try it! Now, gentlemen, will you all be upstanding for the National Anthem . . . it's gone one and I'm knackered.'

Everyone stood. Except Miller. He tried. God knows he tried. But he had lost the power of his legs. Brandy legs to Bambi legs.

Everyone looked at him. Waited.

'Will you all be upstanding . . .' the barman repeated.

'I'm shorry . . .'

It was getting cloudy.

One voice: 'Who the fuck is he anyway?'

'Fucked if I know, he was here when we came in.'

'He's not from round here.'

'He's a bloody drunk.'

121

'Lemme see . . .' It came from the other end of the bar
again. He heard footsteps, then his head, contemplating the
floor, was yanked up. It took a second for his eyes to focus.
'I know this fucker. He works for that fenian paper . . .
he was in court yesterday . . . did you see all that shite he
wrote about me?'

'Hey, Davie, you did have that meat down your
trunks . . .'

'Aye, but he didn't have to go and make such a fuck'n'
song 'n' dance about it, did he?'

'What'd your ma say?'

'Fuck her.'

Miller was pulled up out of his seat by the hair. It wasn't
a good idea. He was sick down his front.

'Get that bastard out of here,' the barman screamed.

'My pleasure.'

He was lifted by more than one person and propelled
through the doors, his feet off the ground. It was pouring
outside. Refreshing, if he hadn't been thrown head first
into a water-filled pothole. He lay there, coughing into the
puddle. Then the boots started to pound in. Six or seven
people he reckoned as he lay there, soaked, curled up as best
he could. Painless. Too well anaesthetized. Except round the
head when the odd pointed toe found its way between his
gravelled fingers to his nose, his eye. He didn't cry out. It
was pleasantly quiet – no cars, the gentle hiss of the rain
on the tarmac, damp thump of the feet into his body, the
street lights and neon sign from Riley's. If he could have
seen it from above, disembodied, the rhythm of the feet, he
might have described it as almost balletic.

'He's had enough, Davie.'

The kicking stopped.

'Do you want a hidin'?'

'No.'

'Okay.'

The kicking started again. He tried to play dead, but every time a boot landed he was forced to give a little sigh. It wasn't intentional, because it really didn't hurt, but his body was insisting.

In the bloody gap between his fingers, in the glistening gap between their legs, he saw a police Land Rover cruise slowly by. It entered his vision, it left his vision. The purr of its engine grew, faded, disappeared.

The beating continued. He grew bored with it. His eyes closed. It was time to sleep.

The last words he heard were youthful, enthusiastic: 'Aren't you gonna hang him?'

8

Marie was in bed. A white bed. A hospital bed, he realized. Antiseptic smell. She looked well. Pale, of course, but well for what she had been through. She smiled when he came in. A smile of love. A smile of pride. She was sitting up with a tray across her lap, eating.

'Where is she?' Miller asked. He regretted it immediately. His first thought should have been for his wife.

'In the incubator.' No admonishment.

'Can I see?'

'They'll bring her in in a minute.'

He kissed her, then sat on the edge of the bed. The warmth in him was . . . warm. He couldn't think of any other way to describe it.

'Didn't take you long to get your appetite back.'

'It's not food, exactly.' She poked at the plate with a fork. 'It's placenta.'

'Jesus.'

'It's good for her.' A voice from behind. Authoritative, healing . . . familiar. He turned. A man in a white coat. Pinched face. His father.

'Dad . . . you're . . .'

'A gynaecologist, and all those years you thought I was a civil servant.'

'But you're . . .'

'Also an expert on diet, that's why I have Marie eating her own placenta.' He glided up to Marie and put an emaciated hand on her shoulder. 'Most doctors believe it's a very good cure for postnatal depression, in fact eighty placenta them do. So we fried it up and gave it back to her, although I suppose in these health-conscious days we should have grilled it. So, away with all those nasty post-natal symptoms, Marie, even if it does mean a bit of cannibalism . . .'

They were both laughing, his dad and Marie, louder and louder and louder and he didn't know whether they were taking the piss or not, then suddenly there was a hand on his shoulder . . .

'Uuuuuuh . . .' he said, shaking his head.

'Hey there, sleepyhead . . . it's okay.'

He opened his eyes, blinked, shook his head. 'Dad?'

'Do I look like yer da?'

A nurse, blue uniform. White bed. Hospital.
'Where . . . ?'

'Well, it's not Butlin's . . . you've been unconscious for a couple of days now . . . I'll let the doctor fill you in now that you're back in the land of the living . . . he'll just be a moment . . .'

Miller lay back. His head throbbed. His side ached. He pulled the covers down. He was heavily bandaged across his chest. He was in a small ward, six beds in all. The other five patients were elderly men attached to a bewildering variety of machines. Those that could turned red-rimmed eyes towards him and gurgled, little globes of moisture puffing at their yellow lips like air bubbles in a boiling custard. It didn't smell like a hospital. It smelt of death, like a whiff of the grave had followed his father through the ward and now lingered beyond the dissipation of the dream.

The doctor appeared. He was young . . . Miller's age, anyway . . . youngish. Jaundiced face, hardly much better than the patients on their deathbeds . . . worse in someone so young, ish. Glasses. Thinning, danky hair. He lifted Miller's chart from the end of the bed and studied it intensely, nodding to himself, lips pursed . . .

'Doctor, I . . .'

'Professor . . .'

'Professor . . .'

'How are you keeping?' He peered at Miller over his horn rims. 'That was a long old sleep, wasn't it? I like to keep a close eye on the head cases myself. I don't mean head cases, of course. Bit of a double meaning there, eh? Still, I'm sure you know what I mean? So let's see how the old nut is, eh?'

Miller, whose mouth had been sagging impatiently, asked quickly: 'What's wrong with me, doctor?'

'Well, now . . . concussion for a start . . . we'll take another X-ray of you shortly, but I expect that little sleep you had has allowed you plenty of time to recover, and there certainly didn't seem anything to worry about on the initial X-ray. Besides that, you have a few cracked ribs, bruising . . . just exactly how close to the bomb were you?'

'Uh . . . I think I was beaten up, Professor . . .'

'Hardly . . .'

'No, I think I was . . .'

'No, my name's Hardly, Professor Hardly . . . not a very common name, I'll grant you, but then where's the harm in that . . . well, it says bomb on here . . . still, there was a bomb the night you were brought in, so a little mix-up is understandable in all the confusion.'

'Will I be in for long?'

'No, not at all, now that you're conscious, I don't see any reason why you shouldn't be up and on your way tomorrow . . . in fact I have several reasons why you shouldn't be up and on your way tomorrow, but the fact of the matter is that we need the bed . . . you know this is a terrible government, not happy unless it's closing us down . . . closed another two wards just last week . . . what do they expect us to do? . . . you know, I bought a house in town just the other week and I half expect to have a government

126

inspector round to close two of the bedrooms and discover
legionnaire's disease in the roof space any day now . . . still,
that's life . . . sooner that than a United Ireland, eh? No,
you'll be okay if you take it easy . . . take a week or two
off work . . . try not to move your head a lot . . . and keep
an eye on those ribs . . . I wouldn't let anyone tickle you
for a while . . . I'll come and discharge you tomorrow, Mr
Miller. I'll maybe see what I can do about stitching those
legs back on as well.'

'Professor . . . ?'

'Take it easy, son, you're a big boy now.'

Professor Hardly clipped the chart back onto the end of
the bed and moved off along the ward. Miller slowly moved
his hands down the bed, patting the covers carefully, trying
to trace the non-existent outline of his legs.

'Uuuuuuuuuuuh . . .'

Miller opened his eyes. A coloured quilt. His coloured
quilt. His bare room. His lack of furniture – save for the
seat by the bed. Occupied. The new face was familiar. The
moustache was familiar. The body was familiar, but subtly
different – not so cocksure, out of uniform. His friend . . .
his acquaintance . . . the policeman with no name. They
watched each other for a while.

'You're looking better,' his visitor said finally. 'Ish.'

Blinking. Dark room, but brighter than his dreams.
'Thanks.' His voice was thick, slurry. He coughed. The cop
passed him a glass of water. He swallowed it greedily. He
wiped his mouth with the sleeve of . . . 'Who put me into
these pyjamas?'

'One of the least pleasurable aspects of my job, I can
assure you.'

Miller shook his head. A mistake. He counted his
legs. Both present and correct. His chest was sore. 'What
brings you, or me, for that matter, to this neck of the
woods?'

'Seemed the best idea. There's no hospital for miles, so I thought it was best to bring you here and get a doctor to look at you. You've a bit of a bang on the head and a couple of cracked ribs, but he said you'd sleep off the worst of the damage.'

'God,' said Miller, touching his forehead tenderly, 'it doesn't feel like it. How'd you come to bring me? Last thing I remember . . . I don't remember . . .'

'You don't remember getting blood all over the car?'

'I do have vague memories of a police wagon . . .'

'Fuck the police wagon, I'm talking my brand-new Ford Escort. It has one red seat now, thanks to you.'

'I only remember a wagon . . . I remember it driving away . . .'

'Well, yes, it would. We tend to ignore most of the rumbles outside Riley's or the Arms . . . but I happened to be driving past and I recognized you . . . part of you, despite the blood and guts. I fired a couple of shots into the air and they scattered for a couple of minutes while I got you into the car . . . they were soon back kicking the doors, so you can pay to have the panels beaten out again as well as the seat dyed back to normal . . .'

'I suppose I should thank you.'

'Damn right.'

'Thank you.'

'No problem.'

'And you've been here babysitting me ever since? That's kind of you.'

'Ever since I arrived back about five minutes ago, yeah. I've better things to do than watch sleeping beauty. I let myself in. I hope you don't mind – I left the door on the snib. Safe enough. We've few enough regular burglars to worry about in Crossmaheart. They've all been kneecapped by the IRA and now they can't get their crutches up the stairs to apartments like this.' The policeman took a notebook out of his pocket. 'This is the official bit. Are you making an official complaint?'

Miller nodded. It hurt.

'You are?'

'Yes.'

'Oh. Well, in that case, did you recognize any of your assailants?'

'Yes.'

'But you don't want to name them? Fair enough.' He snapped his notebook shut.

'Yes, I do.'

'You do? Why?'

'So they might be brought to justice.'

'Are you serious?'

'Very.'

The policeman shook his head. 'Well, there's a turn-up for the books. Still.' He opened his book again.

'Davie Morrow.'

'Davie . . . Morrow . . .' the policeman repeated, noting down the name. 'Would you like him arrested or beaten up?'

'Are you serious?'

'Very.'

'Arrested.'

The policeman looked at him for a moment, then tutted and made another note. 'Anyone else?'

'No. Yes. I don't know. I was a bit pissed. I remember . . . I seem to remember a minister . . . a Rev. . . . I don't know . . . Rainey? A Rev. Rainey mean anything to you? I don't know if he was involved or not . . . I remember him in the pub . . .

'That figures . . . sure . . . Rev. . . . Rainey . . .' He made another note. 'I'll take a full statement later. Now, I understand that you have no close relatives living locally.'

'No.'

'But you have a girlfriend.'

'Yes.'

'One Marie Young.'

'Yes.'

'Has she been to see you?'

'I've been unconscious.'

'Yes, of course, stupid of me.'

'I doubt if she even knows what happened to me.'

'And you have no idea where she might be?'

. . . Something about his tone . . . 'Why do you ask?'

'I'd like to talk to her.'

'For why?'

'Besides being concerned about your well being, I'm also concerned about her whereabouts.'

'She wasn't with me when I was beaten up. I don't see the connection.'

'It's an unrelated matter, Mr Miller. At least we believe it to be unrelated at this stage. Miss Young, besides being your girlfriend, is . . . was also the girlfriend of your predecessor on the newspaper, Mr Jamie Milburn.'

'Yes.'

'As you may or may not know, Jamie Milburn's body was discovered yesterday, and some of it this morning, at Crossmaheart dump . . .'

'Yes, but I . . .'

'And we would seek to locate Miss Young in order to further question her about the disappearance and death of Mr Milburn. Unfortunately we cannot locate her. She's not at her normal place of residence, neither is she at her parents' house. Can you shed any light on her whereabouts, Mr Miller?'

He could picture her − beautiful, in bed, a mother. 'Placenta,' he mumbled absently.

'I'm sorry?'

'Nothing . . . I'm sorry . . . I don't know, this has come as quite a surprise to me . . .'

'I'm sure,' said the policeman, writing down PLACENTA in his notebook.

The cop, for all his questioning, seemed a decent spud. He heated up some soup for Miller and chatted about the injuries he had suffered over the course of two decades in Crossmaheart. Miller tried to sound interested but his body was too sore and his mind was too full of images of Marie to do much more than grunt. Finally he fell asleep.

It was a dreamless sleep. He woke with a start in total darkness. He reached over and switched on the bedside lamp. The policeman was gone. He checked his watch. It was still there. 6.30 am. He threw back the covers and limped slowly round the apartment. His head wasn't quite as sore, but his legs and arms ached. The bandages on his chest weren't heavy, but they were still constricting and when he breathed he snatched at the air as if the Red Cross was doling it out in welcome but insufficient pockets.

He was thirsty. He went to the fridge for a pint of semi-conscious milk. He shook his head blearily. Semi-skimmed. He drank it straight from the carton. Refreshed, somewhat, he returned to his bed and sat on the edge. His thoughts returned to Marie, of what she had said about people who disappeared in Crossmaheart, that they never turned up alive.

He phoned her. A gruff female voice answered.

'Hello . . . my name's Miller, I'm a friend of . . .'

The voice was immediately softer. 'Yes. I know who you are.'

'Oh . . .'

'I'm Mrs Hardy. It's my house. She told me quite a lot about you.'

'Oh, well . . . I'm sorry to trouble you so early . . .'

'Not at all, not at all. I'm up. I can't sleep with all this going on . . .'

'I'm sorry . . . I've been . . . away . . . there's no word on her then?'

'No. Nothing at all.'

'Have the police said nothing?'

'Not a word. God, I don't know, I hope the wee love's okay.'

'Have you any idea what might have happened?'

'None, none at all. Listen, love, she was there one .minute, gone the next. Her clothes are all here. Her medicine's all here. It's like she just popped out to the shop and disappeared off the face of the earth.'

'What sort of medicine?'

'I can't really say.'

'Can't or won't?'

'No need to get cheeky, son.'

'I'm sorry. I don't mean to be. I'm just worried.'

'I know, love. It's okay. She just wouldn't like me to say.'

'I understand that . . . but, I mean, she's not going to, like, die without it or anything, is she?'

'No. Of course not. She'll just be . . . well, less well balanced without it. Oh dear, I don't know, to lose one guest is unfortunate, to lose two is sheer carelessness.'

'Quite an analogy.'

'I'm sorry?'

'The paraphrase from Wilde.'

'What?'

'It's from his play, *The Importance of Being Earnest.*'

'Marty Wilde has written a play?'

Word of Marie Young's disappearance had evidently not yet filtered through to the newsroom at the *Crossmaheart Chronicle.* When he phoned in sick on the Monday morning they were sympathetic and shocked about his own experiences, but they had no questions waiting for him about his missing girlfriend. When he put the phone down he was relieved that he felt no sense of betrayal this time – he had deprived them of their second scoop in a week and damned his journalist's soul once and for all, but he was beyond caring.

It had been a long, empty Saturday, lying on the bed, his stomach hollow, his head full only of Marie and her fate, his body aching for her, his body aching. He wondered about the significance of his dream of her in hospital with their baby: how his mind had jumped so far ahead of his real achievements, bypassing sex and marriage – marriage and sex? – to the birth of their child. His dad would have had a phrase for him an owl romantic, lacking the wit to woo. He'd have been right too, thought Miller, my last time with her, maybe my last time ever, and I argued and sulked with her. What did his dad always say? Never go to sleep on an argument. Quite right. Quite right. My dad. The gynaecologist.

He hardly felt better on the Sunday, but he forced himself up and out of the apartment and went out walking, moving stiffly along the Main Street past the darkened shops and pubs. There weren't many people about. It was grey and cold and a light drizzle pattered off the rumpled tarmac. He found a paper shop and bought a *Sunday Times*, then continued with his forced exercise on up the road. After a while, when what passes for a commercial district in Crossmaheart had fallen behind, he came across a Presbyterian church. The name on the board caught his eye – the Rev. M. Rainey BD. He laughed at the thought of the minister, supposedly pious, downing a pint and singing about Bobby Sands. The droning horror of organ music leaked from the church. Miller shook his head and limped on.

Then he stopped. Perplexed. Something tugged at his memory. He turned back towards the church, entered the gate and eased himself up half a dozen steps. He was hardly dressed for it – tracksuit bottoms, trainers, an ancient Harrington jacket – but he slipped as slippily as a virtual cripple can into the back row.

The church was about half full. Rev. Rainey was in the front bit, sermonizing . . . What did you call it? The font? The soapbox? The pontificating table? He had no idea. He had no interest. His eyes were on the minister. He looked different. Perhaps it had something to do with the fact that he wasn't looking at him through an alcoholic gauze, but Miller fancied that the minister, though still tall, looked smaller, stooped, kind of, and sounded less eloquent, than he remembered him. He realized that to compare properly he would need to drink an awful lot of brandy and Coke, but he ruled this idea out. He was never drinking again.

The minister talked of Sodom and Gomorrah. Monotonously. A very difficult thing to do. Miller took none of it in: he watched the minister's face intently and wondered. Was it possible?

At the end of the service, Rev. Rainey stood at the door, shaking hands with his flock. Miller managed to snake past him, sheltered by an enormous woman in a bright-red coat.

'Are you well, Mrs Morrow?'

He fancied she replied, 'Never been fatter,' but he couldn't be sure.

As he moved down the street an idea began to form in his head. It wasn't a plan, as such, in that he had no result in mind, but there was something compelling about it, something practical for him to do in Marie's continuing absence, something that might at an outside chance tell him more about her, and perhaps a little about himself and his reactions to her situation. Thus far, and Marie aside, Crossmaheart had been a stultifying experience, at the opposite end of the spectrum from rejuvenating. He had hoped for a new challenge, but it was an old challenge, tarted up; the fresh perspectives on life he had sought were as stale as beer slops. This could be his new aim. Instead of looking for impossible answers in the future, he could look for attainable answers from the past. Also, he felt like stirring things. It wasn't for badness as such, more of a reaction to the helplessness he felt over Marie, and before her Jamie and even, perhaps, his father.

That evening he arranged the appointment. The minister was only too keen to be profiled in the *Crossmaheart Chronicle*.

On Monday afternoon Miller ate a subdued lunch in Riley's. In fact he was subdued, the lunch was pretty lively, a peppery concoction he felt obliged to cool down with a couple of pints. Normally, professionally, he wouldn't have gone out on an interview with a few pints on him, especially with the clergy, but Rev. Rainey was different.

His house was about half a mile from the church, a smallish bungalow, painted red. There was a well-tended garden. The minister answered the door himself. He wore his dog collar above casual clothes and carried a child's plastic tricycle in his arms.

'Come on in,' he said, indicating the way with the toy. Inside, the house was bright, well decorated to Miller's eye, orderly. He turned left into the lounge. Big leather settee. Two matching armchairs. Small colour TV. Picture of Rev. Rainey, his wife, two toddlers.

Miller sat in one of the armchairs. 'Good of you to see me,' he said.

'My pleasure entirely — though goodness knows what you want with me. I would have thought the priest up the road would have been of much more interest to your paper — you know he had a heart transplant?'

'Yes, yes, we will get to him, Reverend, but we like to cover all the denominations.'

'Quite right, sir, quite right. Does that include the

135

Mormons? They seem to be seeping into town lately, you know?'

'Well, it would have, Reverend, but they haven't been quite as keen on publicity since Little Jimmy reached puberty, y'know?'

It was a one-of-the-boys flippancy he should have immediately regretted, blaming it on the drinks, but Rev. Rainey sniggered along with him. There was a smiley mateyness about his demeanour Miller didn't like. He knew he was prejudging him on the strength of what he knew, or what he thought he knew. But tough.

Miller took out a mini-recorder and placed it on the arm of Rev. Rainey's chair. 'Just forget that's there,' he said.

'Do you want a cup of tea, or a drink before we start?'

'No, thank you.'

The minister sat back in his chair and clasped his hands before him. 'Shoot,' he said, smiling.

'Could you tell me a little about your day-to-day work in your parish?'

A little was a lot. Miller nodded once in a while, checked the tape on a couple of occasions, let him get on with it for twenty minutes. It was the sort of bland, patronizing stuff ministers always rolled out for the press. Eventually he got round to the problems of a dwindling congregation. These were difficult times for God everywhere. He saw hope for the future, particularly in Crossmaheart, where he was continually working to bridge the gap between the communities.

Miller perked up. His cue: 'Would some of that work include singing songs about Bobby Sands in the Ulster Arms?'

The smile faded. The eyes darkened. 'Excuse me?'

'I was in the bar the other night when you sang that song about Bobby Sands.'

'And?'

'I was just wondering how that might affect your work to unite the communities?'

Rev. Rainey placed a hand on the mini-cassette and switched it off. 'I'm not sure I like the way this conversation is developing.'

'It was you in the pub, wasn't it?'

'Yes.'

'And you were singing.'

'Yes.'

'I was asking how . . .'

He snapped: 'Yes, I know what you're asking. I'm just wondering why.'

'I thought it might add an interesting dimension to your profile.'

'You're trying to cause trouble, aren't you?'

'No. No. Honestly. I'm not. I just happened to see you.'

Rev. Rainey stood up. 'I don't see the point in this . . .'

'I thought our readers . . .'

'You are trying to cause trouble!' He ran his fingers through his hair.

Miller put out his hands, palm downwards. 'I'm not, I'm not,' he said, placatingly. 'Honestly. I just thought you might explain . . .'

Rev. Rainey sat down again suddenly. He scratched at his brow. 'You're not from this town, are you, Miller?'

Miller shook his head.

'You have no comprehension of what pressures there are on a minister here. Sometimes you have to be seen to be agreeing with one particular point of view in order to gain a certain influence, in order to change that point of view. Do you understand?'

'So you go drinking with Loyalists so that you can change them?'

'I don't go drinking with Loyalists. If I'm passing I might

137

call in for a drink – there's nothing wrong with that, Miller, it's the Free Presbyterians who promote prohibition, not our lot.'

'But you sing along with them. Sectarian songs.'

'Just because I'm a man of the cloth doesn't mean I'm not entitled to my views. I'm a Protestant and proud of it. I'm British, and proud of it. I'll defend this country to the last drop of blood in my body. But don't go making me out to be some sort of fascist just because I sometimes have to keep bad company. Jesus kept some pretty dodgy company in his time.'

'Okay. All right. No offence meant.'

'Yes. Well.' He clasped his hands again. 'No offence taken, but you can't go writing stuff like that in the paper. It would upset everyone, and it would give an entirely incorrect representation of my attitudes to the minority community.'

'They're a majority down here.'

'For now. I mean, we're always converting, it's part of my mission. There is, after all, only one true way.'

'You would say that.'

Rev. Rainey smiled. 'That's what I'm paid for.'

Miller smiled too. He reached over and switched the tape recorder on again. 'I didn't mean to upset you, Reverend. You have my assurance that none of that will appear in the paper. May I continue?'

'Yes, of course.'

'Thank you. Tell me, have you ever been convicted of a sexual offence?'

'Jesus Christ!'

Rev. Rainey sprang from his seat. Miller thrust himself back in the armchair, tensing up ready for an assault, but the minister veered off to stand with his back to the window. His face was extremely white.

'You are Michael Rainey, formerly of Sommerton

Heights, aren't you? You were sent to a young offenders' centre for a year for sexually abusing a young girl?'

Rev. Rainey stared at him.

'I thought it might make an interesting angle to my story. How a child abuser becomes a Presbyterian minister whose responsibilities include teaching young girls in Sunday school.'

'Who are you, Miller?'

'No one. Just a reporter trying to do a job.'

'So why are you trying to crucify me?'

'I'm not.'

'Why bring this up then? Who's going to gain by it?'

'Well, hopefully I will. It should bring in some cash, shouldn't it?'

Rainey was shaking his head. He started biting at a fingernail. 'I don't understand this.'

'Nothing to understand, Reverend. What perplexes me is how, fifteen years after sticking your fingers into a young girl's knickers, you come to be a reverend in the same bloody town.'

'My . . . my past isn't unknown to the church elders . . . I . . . it was so long ago . . . I took my punishment, I acknowledged the wrong . . . I was only a wee lad . . . we were all drunk . . . we were only having a bit of fun with a fenian . . . it just got out of hand . . .'

'She was thirteen!'

'It's not that young when you consider how old we . . .'

'Thirteen . . .'

'It's what you think of at that age, but you can't get any . . .'

'Thirteen . . .'

'We were only messing around . . . she was okay at first . . . then she just got hysterical . . .'

'Thirteen . . .'

'Will you stop saying that! I know what age she was!

Don't you think I haven't thought about it from that day to this?'

'Have you touched your own daughter yet?'

'Jesus Christ!'

'Does your wife even know?'

Rev. Rainey threw his head back. Tears were rolling down his cheek. 'Holy God . . .' he whispered. 'You are the cruellest man I have ever met. I took my punishment. I found God. I started over. I have rebuilt my life. Have you no compassion?'

'Would it surprise you to learn I'm an atheist?'

Miller reached over and lifted the cassette. He slipped it into his pocket.

Rev. Rainey pulled at his upper lip. His own upper lip. 'You know,' he said quietly, 'with my connections, I could have you killed.'

Miller shook his head. 'Well, aren't you just the rebuilt man of God.'

He wanted to hit him. He wanted to take his head and bang it repeatedly against the wall, and then stamp on it for good measure. He saw this man before him, he saw that he had rebuilt his life, won a wife, created a family, from adverse beginnings he had created respect and prosperity . . . and he saw Marie . . . this man, this reverend, had seen parts of Marie he himself had never seen, he had torn her clothes off and touched her in places Miller had not dared approach, out of love, out of respect, out of fear . . . he had turned her off the one turn-on in life . . . condemned her to fear and suspicion and, for all he could imagine, medicine . . . and now she was gone, in all probability murdered, lying in a ditch or dump, her short life shaped by one disgusting incident after another, all started by this man and his accomplices . . . and he was God's representative on earth. It was even hard for an atheist to stomach.

He wanted to hit him. But he wouldn't. He walked to

the front door. Rev. Rainey remained by the window, tears on his cheeks, eyes closed.

'Read all about it, Reverend,' Miller said, and left.

9

Darkness. Complete. Absolute. But not silence, not quite. The dozing insect hum of fluorescent lighting. The occasional shallow padding of feet. Soft breath. More than one person. Circling him. He tried to move his hands, but they were strapped to the chair. A big chair. Long — down to his feet. Bent back. Felt like leather. A dentist's chair? His head was sore. He had been struck, he knew that, but he didn't know who by or where or when. But there was an oddness beyond the soreness, a tightness of scalp that felt like his skin was melting into his skull. The material against his face smelt of . . . hairspray.

Whoever they were, they wouldn't be aware that he was awake. So he sat on, listening, but he heard nothing above a murmur. He waited for what felt like twenty minutes, but might have been only five. Several times he heard matches being struck.

Eventually, he said: 'Hello?'

'Tell the boss.'

Footsteps. A door opened, a door closed. Footsteps receding: change in tone from lino to concrete. Footsteps approaching: two sets, concrete to lino, door opens, door closes.

'He is awake?' Thick German accent.

'Yes, boss.'

'Has he said anything?'

'No, boss. Yes, boss. Just "hello".'

'Very well.'

Miller felt the chair being turned, angled further back, a

142

slight brightening as he took the full glare of the fluorescent light.

He felt a presence at his left ear. The voice, sharp, military: 'Is it safe?'

'. . . Hello?'

'Is it safe?'

'Is what safe?'

'Is it safe?'

'Is what safe?'

'Is it safe!'

'Yes . . . yes, it's safe.'

The man at his ear burst suddenly into laughter. Two others joined in. The same man, same voice, Crossmaheart accent. 'I can't keep this up . . .'

Another voice. 'You're Oscar material, Curly, Oscar material.'

A third: 'Excellent. Excellent. Should have kept it going longer.'

'I couldn't, I was bursting.'

'Shame.'

'Listen, Curly, it's been good fun, but we'll need to pop back to work. What do you say, we give you another half-hour with him, then pop back? It's only a wee job, but the boss'll kill us if we don't get it finished.'

'Ach, what're yees runnin' off for? I've only just started.'

'We'll be back in a wee while. Give us a break, eh?'

'There's nothing to it. We'll be back by three.'

'Aye, okay, sure I'll see yees later. Make sure the door's locked after ye, would ye?'

Footsteps, door open, snib off, closed. A shallow breath, then heart-thumping silence.

Miller knew he was there, but the silence dragged into minutes. Finally he said tremulously: 'Hello? Hello?'

'Hello, hello?'

143

'What's going on? What do you want with me? Where am I?'

Movement. Slight tug at the ears.

'And let there be light!'

Blinding. Miller screwed his eyes up, dying to rub at them, then slowly opened them. Blinking. The man who stood before him was perhaps six foot tall, well built, very receding hairline, a dull, hammerhead, lost-in-a-crowd face, but sharp, predatory eyes. He wore a white button-down shirt, no tie, mauve waistcoat. He nodded at Miller.

'I wouldn't like to be you when the fashion police get hold of you.'

Miller shook his head. 'I don't understand.'

'You will.'

'Is this some kind of joke?'

'To me, yes.'

'I don't understand . . .'

'Do you know who I am?'

'No. Uh, Curly?'

'On one level, yes. You don't recognize my shop?'

Miller looked about him for the first time. He faced a wall decorated with framed photographs of handsome young men, head and shoulder shots. There were four ordinary plastic chairs, then three soft leather ones with hair-dryers attached. On either side of him there were big leather seats. He caught a slight reflective glare off what he took to be a lengthy mirror behind him.

'No.'

'Curly Bap's.'

Miller shook his head.

'I'm a hairdresser.'

Miller nodded. 'I take it that's not your real name.'

'No.'

'What am I doing here?'

'You should be able to work it out for yourself. What do you remember about coming here?'

'Nothing.'

'Well, where were you earlier today?'

'I . . . was at a funeral.'

'Whose funeral?'

'Rev. Rainey's.'

'And how did he die?'

'He committed suicide.'

'Why?'

'I don't know.'

'How did he do it?'

'He took a whole heap of sleeping pills then tied a Dunnes Stores Better Value bag round his head.'

'And who found him?'

'His wife and children.'

'His children found him. They didn't realize he was dead. They were playing with him for ten minutes until their mum came in.'

'If you know all this why are you asking?'

'Because.'

'Because why?'

'Who's tied to the chair?'

Miller nodded.

'Who's got a sore cheek?' He slapped Miller hard across the face. When the stinging faded, Miller nodded. His captor slapped him again. 'I don't like people who nod, usually it means whatever you say to them goes in one ear and out the other. Well?'

'Well what?'

'Who's tied to the chair?'

'I am.'

'Who's got a sore face?'

'I have.'

'Okay. Good boy. So why were you at the funeral?'

'I was reporting on it.'

'And what did you do after the funeral?'

'I was on the Cycle of . . . I was riding home . . . a car stopped in front of me . . . somebody hit me, knocked me off . . .'

'And here you are.'

'Yeah.'

'But you had met the good reverend before, Mr Miller, had you not?'

'I saw him in a pub.'

'And you went to his house.'

'Yes. To interview him.'

'To blackmail him.'

'No.'

'Yes. To blackmail him.'

'I went to interview him. About his past.'

'You went to dredge up some minor indiscretion from his past.'

'He was a child abuser.'

'Was he?'

'He got a wee girl down in the back seat of the car and interfered with her.'

'Yes, now that you mention it, I do recall the incident.'

'So?'

'As I recall it, those seats were quite hard. And the girl was quite soft.'

'Oh.'

'Oh, indeed.'

'The old boys' network.'

'In a manner of speaking. Michael phoned me the other night. Now you've got to understand, Michael never phoned me; we've operated on different sides ever since . . . then . . . but he phoned me out of desperation . . . some guy had tried to blackmail him over this thing he'd done when he was a wee boy . . . and he was so shaken up by it he broke ten years of silence to see if I could do anything about it. Like something violent.'

'You . . . you're a . . . hairdresser.'

'You've never heard of the Demon Barber?' He laughed. 'I don't wish to boast about it, but Curly Bap by day, commander of the Provisional IRA's active service unit in Crossmaheart by night. You come to me for one of two things, a tight curly perm, or you want someone removed. In Michael's case, I obliged with both.'

Curly suddenly grabbed hold of the chair and swung it round until Miller faced the mirror full-on.

Miller shook his head. 'You complete bastard,' he said.

'You were unconscious for so long, I had to do something to put the time in. Look on the bright side, it's not everyone can say they've had their hair permed by one of the world's leading assassins.'

Miller was aghast. On one level he could see just how funny it was. On another he could already see his own body, lying shot in a country lane, his hair permed. It was the Ulster version of getting run over by a bus and being found to have on dirty underwear and holey socks.

'Will it grow out?'

'Yes. Into an Afro.'

'This is surreal.'

'Possibly. But deserved.'

'Nothing deserves this.'

'You caused the death of someone who used to be a friend.'

'I didn't kill him.'

'Yes, you did, you threatened to expose him – no pun intended – in the paper. I assured him the *Chronicle* wouldn't print a story like that. He knew for a fact that they wouldn't. But he thought you'd take it elsewhere. He did his checking. Found you were a blow-in from Belfast; he feared it getting that far, and from there to the nationals. He was frightened, frightened of losing his wife and family, his job, the public disgrace over something so innocent . . .'

'Innocent! Abusing . . .'

'She was a wee tart, she was asking for it . . .'

'She was thirteen!'

'Ach, dry your eyes, she had tits and she had hair, what more of an invitation is there? I don't care what age you are, you get into a car with a gang of fellas been drinking, you've every right to expect to get touched up. Where do you think wee girls learn these things, Miller, in finishing school? Girls get to that age, they have a healthy interest in sex, they want to experiment, they just don't know how to go about it. Just say we gave her a helping hand along. She wasn't the first and she won't be the last. Not even particularly memorable though, save for the fact that we went to prison for her. As I recall, her mouth wasn't big enough, if you get my drift.'

Miller strained forward in the chair, trying to get at him, but his bindings were secure. 'You're sick! You're fuckin' sick!' He tried again, twice, but he couldn't budge. He threw himself back in the chair, breathing hard. 'Jesus,' he said, 'you talk about Rainey's life being ruined. What about hers?'

'Fuck her!' Curly pushed his face into Miller's. He smelt of bootleg Chanel and chips. 'Wish I had,' he said, leerily, 'wish I had.' And then he hit him. Hard. Into the side of the face. Somewhere that wouldn't bleed. Miller let out a little groan and slumped, then watched himself come back into focus in the mirror. He noted the discoloration already setting in.

'Thanks,' he said. It hurt.

'Don't mention it.'

'What now?'

'What do you think?'

'You let me go?'

148

'Try again.'

'You kill me.'

'Correct.'

'In revenge for Rainey, or to cover up your own sordid little secret?'

'Revenge, of course. I don't give a flying fuck who knows about the wee whore. The only thing I regret is not killing her there and then and shutting her bake before she had the chance to squeal on us. With maturity, I know it's better to cut the throat there and then.'

'Charming.'

'Your lot started it.'

'Childish.'

'Yes, you did. Your fuckin' Shankill Butchers, cutting up innocent Catholics for fun.'

'What the hell are you, the Crossmaheart Hairdressers?'

'You're very funny, Miller, for a dead man.'

'Is that what you did to Marie? Cut her throat?'

'Marie who?'

'The girl in the car.'

'The girl in the car died years ago.'

'Part of her did.'

A sudden knocking turned Curly round. He strode to a door behind and to the right of Miller and opened it a few inches and peered out. Immediately Miller felt a draught of fresh air, and he thought of Marie, of lying beside her in a graveyard. The pair of them united in death as they couldn't be in life, because of bastards like Rainey and Curly. But it would never happen like that. They would be buried separately. In different graveyards, their services conducted by ministers of different faiths. Did it matter? Was God a Protestant? Did She exist at all?

Curly strode down the hall, satisfied that there was no threat. A door opened, closed. He reappeared in the doorway with, Miller presumed, the pair from earlier.

'The pall bearers have arrived,' Curly said, slapping the back of the chair, jolting Miller.

He looked at the new arrivals in the mirror. They wore blue overalls, both stained with oil. Their faces were red, their hair shaggy, long straight noses. Brothers. Twins, perhaps. They stood in the doorway, grinning.

'Do it here, Curly?' one asked.

'Nah, too messy, I've a cut 'n' blow later. It's a bugger getting blood out of the curling tongs.'

'Fair enough.'

Curly unstrapped Miller from the chair. His mates pulled him up from it and held him firm.

'Time for a run in the country, eh?' said Curly and smiled.

Miller smiled back. A nervous smile, and then some.

As they walked Miller to the door, doom was approaching. After a fashion.

The plot to kill Curly was planned by some of the finest terrorist brains in Crossmaheart. Seasoned UVF commanders had taken the decision months previously to eliminate their chief rival in Crossmaheart. There had been an uneasy peace between the upper echelons of the town's rival terrorist communities; it was taken for granted that it was okay to snipe at the enemy's minions – thugs and wastrels for the most part – but the leaders had remained above the violence, content to maximize the war against either the police and army (in the case of the IRA) or innocent Catholics (in the case of the UVF). But times change. Police crackdowns in Belfast on racketeering were starting to filter through to Crossmaheart. The cops hadn't taken any action, as yet, but it would come. Businessmen were beginning to object to their payments; some had even refused. Soon there would be less money to divide up between the warring factions. Something had to be done. The UVF never quite said it in those words; to the troops it was a redoubling of the military campaign against those who would seek to destroy Ulster's Protestant heritage, but actually it was to keep bread on the table, and champagne in the fridge.

Watch was kept on Curly over the course of several weeks. Times were recorded. Associates were noted. The bomb was assembled in the store room of a children's creche in Meadow Way. The ingredients, innocuous enough when kept separately, were not blended together until three hours before the planned attack. A car was hijacked in Belfast, repainted, number plates changed, new documentation acquired, fluffy dice attached. It was driven to Meadow Way, parked in a garage, and the bomb loaded. Five hundred pounds' worth. A few pounds of Semtex might have done the same trick, but the UVF didn't have access to international markets. Fertilizer, chemicals, batteries, wire, a detonator, a clock.

Unfortunately, after such meticulous planning, they chose two potatoes to carry out the mission. Two potatoes.

One potato was Davie Morrow, the thug with the threat and the ma with the jaws wired shut. Davie had plagued the UVF for so long over getting something decent to do for them that they finally overcame their well-rooted reluctance to give him his big chance.

The other potato was Tom O'Hanlon. They all felt sorry for Tom because his heart was in the right place and he was obviously fairly intelligent, but he was as shy as they come and had a worrying tendency to go red under pressure. He was, in fact, a roast potato. He was also saddled with a Catholic surname, although that was construed as being a bit of a plus when it came to alibis.

Tom O'Hanlon was the driver. Davie Morrow went along for immoral support. Though Curly Bap's shop was less than half a mile from Meadow Way, Tom, unfamiliar as he was with engines more powerful than a hairdryer, managed to flood the Volvo before he was three hundred yards from base. With the clock ticking, Davie pushed and Tom steered. Two hundred yards further on they were stopped by a police patrol. Their documents were checked and found to be in order, and the police joined in the pushing. The engine finally fired and they took off.

Tom, however, was practically in convulsions by this stage and turned into an unfamiliar corner of the housing estate and immediately lost himself in the labyrinthine complexities of its interior.

'Fuckin' bomb, fuckin' bomb,' he said over and over to himself, his voice all squeaky and squeezing out from between clenched teeth like escaping gas.

'Will you quit whining? For Jesus' sake! Take a left here. A left!'

'I know where I'm going . . .'

'Do ya fuck . . .'

'Just round . . . oh . . .'

'Jesus Christ!'

'This is ridiculous. We'll call it off. We'll go back.'

'Oh, certainly. You think they're all waiting for us back at the house? They've disappeared, Tom. You know how to defuse that fucker?'

'We could just leave it here.'

'Oh, certainly. That would go down well. Bombing our own people.'

'Everyone would think it was the IRA.'

'Everyone but the boys. And they'd kill us. Wise up, Tom. Come on, you're a bit spooked by the police, that's all. Drive on up here, right to the top. We should hit the back road eventually, then we'll have a straight run down to Main Street, and Curly's.'

'That wasn't the plan. We were to go straight along Main Street.'

'We've fucked the plan, Tom. Besides, maybe they'll appreciate us showing a little bit of initiative.'

'Yeah, sure. Initiative, certainly. Fuck it' – he slapped the steering wheel – 'what sort of initiation is this? They should be making us take an oath or roll a flag or sing all the verses of "The Sash" or something. You think this is what they did to Lee Harvey first day at the CIA office – away out and shoot Kennedy there, see if you're good enough to join us?'

'Calm down, Tom. It's only a bomb.'

'Yeah. Like you've done it before.'

'I have. Petrol bombs.'

'Not quite the same really, Davie. As I recall you threw the only unleaded petrol bomb in the history of terrorism.'

'Funny-ha, Tom, it makes a big difference.'

Tom drove on. In a couple of minutes they came to the back road, and then began winding down towards the town again. Half a mile in the distance Tom, when he wasn't wiping sweat from his forehead, could see the vague outline of Curly's shop. He had sold Curly an insurance policy only a few weeks before. It seemed ridiculous at the time, selling a policy to a man who specialized in collecting protection money, and hardly less ridiculous now that he was about to be instrumental in flattening that shop and its owner.

It had all seemed so clear in his head. The wanting to do something for his people – that had always been there, but he'd never known how. Removing one of the biggest murderers in the land would elevate him from his humble life to something bigger and better; he would be a man amongst men, a hero of Ulster, a Red Hand Commando. In reality, he thought ruefully, as he drove ever closer to his date with destiny, a Red-Faced Commando. Oh Jesus, he thought, dreams, dreams, dreams, I'm not a terrorist, I'm an insurance man, a bloody insurance man.

'Why don't we just bloody shoot him?' he wailed.

'Use your brains, Tom.' Davie's voice was high, excited – but not scared, Tom thought, not scared at all. He's enjoying this. 'If you use a gun, first you have to get into the place, and it's locked up tight most of the time. Then if you do, the gun can jam, or you can miss, and we've a habit of doing that . . .' We've, thought Tom. 'With a bomb, all that can happen is it doesn't go off, and no one knows the difference. When it goes off, bang, flattens the building and flattens that fenian bastard with it. Relax, Tom, what can go wrong?'

A lot. The bombers' route into town had been picked for a reason – not just the safest approach, in terms of eluding possible security patrols, but the smoothest, in the interests of keeping the notoriously volatile explosive steady. The back road was largely fine, apart from a section about two hundred yards from the junction opposite Curly's shop. Here a tiny brook was prone to flooding in the winter, which in turn had undermined the tarmac surface, which had cracked and crumbled over the years and not been fixed because the government didn't recognize it as an important enough road.

The Volvo crunched into a two-foot-wide pothole. Davie Morrow cursed. Tom O'Hanlon thumped the wheel. The Volvo exploded.

They didn't suffer. In fact, they probably did suffer – being blown into a thousand pieces can't be entirely painless. The pothole expanded, a rounded steaming chasm. The car, shrapnel, peppered a radius of half a mile. The shock wave rolled up to the junction, hit the far side of Main Street then ricocheted from building to building along the street. Every window shattered. Roofs lifted, masonry fell, road signs, shop signs buckled, those on the street were flattened, roofs descended again.

Curly, Miller and the two in overalls were thrown backwards as they reached the front door. It was a narrow passageway to the door – one of the twins had led, then Miller, the other twin holding him, and Curly at the back. The door, half glass, half wood, shattered, spraying the leading twin in shards of glass that seemed to float around him in slow motion like Satanic confetti; propelled backwards, he crashed into Miller, who hit the others, and all four dominoed to the floor. Immediately the top twin rolled off, his face in his hands, then he pulled his hands away, looked at them, and the pain arrived in the same instant. He screamed. It was a few seconds before Miller realized that he'd been unintentionally released by his captors. He grabbed hold of the screaming twin's shoulder and hoisted himself up. The twin turned round, his face a crumpled sheet of blood, as if it had been forced along a cheese grater. 'Help,' he said.

As Miller rose, Curly grabbed at his leg and he crashed down again. But Curly's hold was weak and Miller yanked free, pulling himself up to his knees. Curly used the twin's shoulder to lever himself up as well, but fell back when the bloody face turned to him.

Miller launched himself for the door, the remains of the door. Curly went with him and caught the back of his jacket just as Miller caught his first glimpse of the scene of devastation outside. Alarms were sounding, but they were neither as loud nor as scary as the human screams. The twin's cry was joined by others along the length of the Main Street, a horrific, discordant choir.

As he was pulled back, Miller turned suddenly and grabbed at Curly. The hairdresser's eyes widened in surprise, as if Miller was breaking one of the rules of the game. Grabbing his shirt, popping two buttons, Miller used all his strength to heave the unbalanced Curly past him, banging his head off one wall and then flinging him towards the door. Curly, dazed, felt his feet slip from under him in the glass and he pitched forward. The other twin was starting to rise. Miller swiftly planted a foot in his face and he fell back. The first twin, the bloody twin, remained on the ground, screaming, one hand on his face, the other stretched out in front of him, palm up, fingers stretched wide, louder in its own way in its appeal for help than the terror that emanated from his throat.

Miller, gasping for breath, his legs shaking now, turned again towards his avenue of escape and found it blocked by Curly. The terrorist had fallen across the shattered door, and was now doubled up like a drunken ploughman floundering over a farm gate. Beyond him was freedom. Miller ran for it. It was only half a dozen steps along the bomb-dusted passageway, then he put one foot on Curly's curved back and pushed himself up and over and out into the street.

He landed amongst glass and debris on the pavement. Ahead he could see the crater where the bomb must have exploded. People were beginning to pour out of the shops and houses; a few lay on the ground. Someone was shouting: 'Get out! Get out! There might be another one!' He started to turn left, back into town, when a groan, hollow, rattly, turned him. He looked into Curly's dead eyes.

Immediately he knew what had happened. It didn't take a great detective to work it out. The great rip in Curly's stomach and the copious amount of blood kind of indicated that Miller's step up on the hairdresser's back had rather helped along the impaling process which had begun with his landing on the shattered door.

Miller started to walk quickly away. He breathed deeply as he moved, rejoicing in the air, in the freedom, in the life, while all around him lay the injured and dying. He wanted to help, wanted to stop, but the rush of adrenaline propelled him forward. The helpless gaze of those on the ground couldn't stop him. What could he do? He had once kissed the head of a pineapple in a compulsory life-saving class, but that was the extent of his medical training; that was no use to anyone. He needed to run, to gallop off down the Main Street, to go to work, to write about the bomb, to recapture his journalistic soul, to mend the savagery of the terrorists with dashing words and . . . and he stumbled, his legs gave way, he rolled onto the ground . . . and . . . and . . .

'It's . . .'

'It's not . . .'

'I'm telling you it is . . .'

'But . . .'

'I know . . . you think it's possible?'

'I mean, I've heard of people's hair turning white after a shock, even a bit curly, but . . .'

Miller opened his eyes. He saw dark, near-dusk clouds. Two heads looking down at him, blue lights flashing to left and right.

'Uuuuuuh . . .'

He focused on . . . the Rileys, father and son, the Riley's pub Rileys, kneeling beside him.

He tried to get up.

'Easy there, fella . . .' said Pearse.

'Am I . . . ?'

'You're okay,' said Johnny.

'You've a few cuts on the face, son, but that's it, nothing to worry about.'

'Is he okay?' Another voice. Familiar as well. Martin O'Hagan, standing over him.

'He's fine. I think he just fainted. Can't see anything wrong.'

'I think he has a few busted ribs anyway,' said his editor.

'What about the rest of them?' asked Johnny.

'I think there's maybe two dead back there, the rest are a bit cut up with the glass,' said O'Hagan, thumbing back down the street. 'What's the story over there?' He nodded at Curly's.

Johnny shook his head. O'Hagan walked back the twenty-odd yards to Curly's shop. Curly's body was now lying face down on the footpath. The twins sat side by side on the kerb, the bloody one slumped forward, his brother with his arm round him, cradling him. O'Hagan knelt down beside them. He reached up and drew the injured one's hands away from his face, then replaced them. He said a few words, then looked down the street towards two ambulances about a hundred yards away and, from the crowds surging around them, clearly busy. He stood up, crossed to Curly and slowly turned him onto his back. He spent a minute just looking at him, then stood again and crossed back to Miller.

'What happened to you anyway?' he asked, kneeling beside the Rileys, his face ashen.

'Bloody obvious,' Miller croaked.

'You were meant to be off sick.'

'Jesus, don't give me a hard time. I went to get a haircut to cheer myself up, and the fucker went off.'

'No harm to you, Miller, but that style went out with . . . Jesus, I wouldn't even call it a style . . .'

'Thanks for your sympathy.'

Miller pulled himself up into a sitting position. 'I'm okay, I'm okay,' he said, his heart racing, his head revolving. 'Come on then, Martin, we've work to do.' He stood up.

O'Hagan gave a slight nod. 'You're an old hand at this, of course. I forgot.'

'Of course,' said Miller, and slipped to the ground.

10

And the people had a fine time.

When you exist on the First World poverty line – you can only afford to hire out two video cassettes each week and you take your summer holidays within a hundred miles of home – looting is less of a crime and more of a signal from God that he's busy elsewhere but here's an early Christmas present just to keep your interest. Almost before the injured and dying were ferried off to hospital, and certainly before the police and army could clear the shops and cordon off the street, the road was filled with people anxious to make a killing from a killing.

The shop owners weren't that fussed either, as the government would pay them compensation for everything they lost. They realized there wasn't that much they could do when a horde of spitting, cursing heathens came plundering through their wrecked shops in a twenty-minute surge before Her Majesty's Forces decided that it wasn't all an elaborate ambush and cleared them out.

Once the looters had gone – there would be a rush the next day for accessories missed in the mêlée: plugs, fuses, bulbs, left shoes – the tidying up began. Most of the Main Street had merely suffered glass damage, so it was a case of sweeping up and boarding the windows. By next day they were nearly all back in business, doing a booming trade, so to speak. Just about the only place that didn't have a bomb damage sale was Riley's, which, by some magnificent trick of physics, had missed out on the shock wave. It was packed all day, nevertheless. The same could not be said of the

159

Ulster Arms, which, by some malignant trick of physics, had not only lost all of its windows but had been condemned by a Health Department official to dispose of its entire stock of alcohol. Although the stocks appeared intact, the inspector was concerned that slivers of glass might have shot off the inside of bottles and other containers and rendered them dangerous to drink. The owners had protested that this could hardly apply to the beer supplies in metallic kegs, but the official had muttered something about upset chemicals and insisted that the lot be thrown out. It would be three days before they could get restocked. Johnny and Pearse Riley were magnanimous in their good fortune, opening their doors to the customers of their erstwhile rivals, irrespective of religious or political differences. The people were united for a few short days. It was playing football across the trenches of No-Man's Land. It was the Blitz spirit, or at least the getting blitzed spirit. It was bloody annoying for the hard-core Loyalists who refused to budge from their shadowy corner of the Ulster Arms, refused to darken the Republican stronghold that was Riley's. They sat drinking purloined bottles of Harp, sieving it with their teeth for particles of glass, cheered only by the fact that although they had lost two brave volunteers, the potatoes, they had also managed, by some God-given means, to remove Curly Bap from this mortal coil.

Miller was back on his feet that day. This time the news story had fallen at a better time of the week for the *Chronicle*, and all hands were required to give the bombing the fullest coverage. Although Miller could have taken some more time off – the beating and bomb had taken their toll – he preferred to get back to work. He had spent enough time over the past week moping about Marie. He didn't begrudge her the time, of course he didn't, but he was frightened by how much she was in his thoughts when he was by himself. Getting back to work, forcing himself to talk to people, alleviated it a little. He didn't know what to make of Rev. Rainey's suicide. Certainly it had come as a shock. Certainly it had been his fault. He knew it had been a bad thing to do, to approach him like that. But try as he might, he couldn't feel regret over it. He felt sorry for the family, of course, the wife, the toddlers, but not for Rainey. Not when he thought of Marie. Now he had Curly Bap's death to think about as well. Just as he had killed Rainey through a verbal assault, he had physically killed Curly. Accidentally, of course. In fleeing for his life. What would they call it, manslaughter? The word intrigued him. Man's laughter. So apt.

Curly was an even smaller loss to mankind than Rainey. This he knew. He also knew better than to acknowledge any knowledge at all of the true circumstances of his death. The police questioned him, of course, but he could remember nothing of value. He wrote a detailed account of his experiences as a bomb victim for the paper, which everyone seemed to appreciate.

'Much better than your hair,' said Helen.

'The farming page is much better than your hair,' said Anne.

And they all laughed, even Martin O'Hagan, who had been looking worried all week. The work was hard, frantic, but enjoyable. Miller even thought at one stage that there might be a team spirit developing, but he tried not to get carried away with that idea. He was pleased that at last his colleagues seemed to be accepting him. He put it down to the fact that Jamie was definitely dead and definitely buried and there was no chance of him coming back. Miller was no longer the interloper.

Then, late in the week, the thought occurred to him. It came unbidden, as he was stumbling out of a dream about Marie. He woke, sweat-soaked. He went to the bathroom and dried himself off with a towel, then went to the fridge and got a Diet Caffeine-Free Pepsi. They'd had a few drinks after they'd finished the paper and his throat was thick. He sat on the edge of the bed sipping at his can of rusty water, his eyes focused on far away.

He sat for ten minutes, then clicked himself back into reality. He reached for the side of the bed and lifted his notebook. He read over the names: Michael Rainey, Sommerton Heights. Tom Callaghan, Meadow Way. Tyrone Blair, Shackleton Walk. Michael Rainey was dead. Tyrone Blair, known widely and bizarrely as Curly Bap, was dead. What of Tom Callaghan? What of the third man? What did he know of him besides the fact that his father had been killed by the IRA and that he had spent a year in prison for his assault on Marie? Had he gone on to respectability, like Rainey, or had he plumbed the depths like Curly? Did he have a wife and family, love and respect, peace of mind? Did he even know that his two accomplices on that spring evening so many years before were now dead?

Try as he might, he could not rid himself of these thoughts, and, seeking to quell his curiosity by making a few discreet enquiries, he succeeded only in inflaming it.

There was no Callaghan listed in the telephone directory for Meadow Way, but there were three others listed for other parts of Crossmaheart. He called them one by one, but none of them had heard of the Tom he was after. At lunch time he unchained the Cycle of Violence and pedalled up to Meadow Way and began knocking on doors. Most of the houses were occupied by very young couples who had only lately moved into the estate. Their gardens were uniformly overgrown. Each house had at least one cracked window. Once he had convinced them that he wasn't a policeman or a debt collector they opened their doors to him, but they weren't much help. One couple directed him to a house right at the end of the Way. Compared to the others, it was a little palace. The window frames were freshly painted. The garden was a lawn, rather than a

162

wilderness. It was bordered with flowers. A card sat in the front window. It said: There is only One Way, the Way of the Lord.

Miller wheeled his bike up the short path to the door. He rang the doorbell. It played 'All Things Bright and Beautiful'.

A little old lady answered. She couldn't have been more than four and a half feet tall. Her face was small, angular, wise. She wore a hat, and what looked like her Sunday best.

'Oh. Hello,' she said. 'I was just going out to the Mission.'

'Sorry to trouble you,' said Miller.

'Not at all. What can I do for you?' She smiled widely. Good teeth. False, but good. 'I'd invite you in, but the last time I invited a stranger in he stole my TV. Isn't it terrible you can't trust anyone these days?'

'You can trust the Lord,' said Miller.

'That you can, that you can.'

She stepped out and closed the door behind her. 'I'm very sorry to rush you, but I am in a hurry, I'm afraid I've left it rather late.'

'May I walk with you?'

'Yes, of course,' she beamed. 'You're not going to the Mission yourself?'

'No, no, I'm not.'

'It's a wonderful service. The pastor is a very good speaker. And an excellent singer.'

'It sounds very nice.'

'It is, it's lovely.'

They turned left and began walking back up the Way, Miller wheeling the Cycle of Violence very slowly as the woman shuffled along at a snail's pace, tapping her way ahead with a blackthorn cane. He was aware of curtains moving as he passed each house.

'I'm told you've lived here for quite a few years,' he said.

163

'Oh, my, yes, indeed – quite a few.'

'As many as ten, or fifteen?'

'Oh, I'm sure it is. Since the estate was first built. There's not many can say that now, you know.'

'I'm sure.'

'How old do you think I am?'

'Oh . . . sixty maybe?'

'Sixty! My, no, good heavens . . . I'm eighty-five years this June. Eighty-five! And I can still spell!'

'You don't look it at all.'

'You're too kind. And a fibber, I think.'

Miller smiled. She smiled back.

'I'm trying to find someone who lived here a few years back. One of your neighbours said you used to know everyone round here.'

'Most everyone . . . I don't remember them all, of course, there have been so many, and my memory isn't what it was.'

'Do you remember a family called the Callaghans?'

'Callaghan? I'm not . . .'

'There was a young fella, about eighteen, Tom.'

'Tom? I don't know. When was this?'

'A long time. 1977.'

'Was he a tall fella?'

'I'm not sure. I never met him. I'm just trying to find him. He's come into some money.'

'Well for some . . .'

'You might remember he got into some trouble. I think he went to prison for a bit . . .'

'Ah . . . now there's a thought. You might mean Wee Tommy. Yes, maybe you're talking about Wee Tommy. He was a big tall fella, I never knew his second name, but I remember there was some talk about him going to prison . . . I don't know what for. Between you and me, son, there's not many of them round here don't end up in prison at one time or another. Wee Tommy, yes. He was a nice big fella, always helpful, always polite, not like most of them . . . he used to give me a hand with the shopping once in a while. I was very surprised that he ended up like that. I didn't know his parents, but I think they moved out very soon after. Went back up to Belfast.'

They came to the end of Meadow Way. Ahead of them, on the other side of the road, a large circus tent had been pitched in an open field. A hand-written sign taped to the side of it proclaimed: Pastor William Grant's Mission from God, Ye Shall Be Saved!

'Well, here we are, dear, I must rush.'

'Thank you, you've been very helpful.'

'No trouble at all, dear. You're sure you won't come with me? It's a wonderful service.'

'No, honestly.'

'He's a fine speaker, and his message is very important.'

'No, I can't, I've to get back to work.'

'There are so many souls to be saved. Just come in for a little while?'

'No, I can't.'

'It could change your life.'

'I can't, really, you see, I'm a Catholic.'

She lifted her stick and whacked him once across the shins. 'Papist, get back to Rome,' she said, and whacked him again.

Miller hopped backwards, swinging the bike round in front of him for protection. 'Whatever you say,' he said, 'and praise the Lord.'

He climbed onto his bike and pushed off towards the town centre again as the little old lady started shuffling across the road, muttering.

The days dragged. The work grew even more monotonous. He was a better and more experienced writer than O'Hagan would ever be, but his editor still insisted on checking every bit of copy he subbed, running his eyes over it like he was some wee cub reporter, tutting when he found a comma missing or a heading that didn't quite fit. Miller kept his silence. Hung onto his patience by counting to 130 every time he wanted to say: 'Fuck you, you supercilious bastard.'

He found the office unique in one respect. When O'Hagan was out of it, nobody stabbed him in the back. Helen and Anne would work away quite happily, would let their small talk truffle-hunt through every subject under the sun, but never once did either of them say: 'That Martin O'Hagan, he's a bit of a cunt, isn't he?' Okay, maybe not the 'c' word, but not even a mild barb or a subtle rebuke. It was certainly beyond the range of his experience. It was like a family, and he was the foster child from the wrong side of the tracks.

One day, just for effect, he said 'Bastard' under his breath as O'Hagan went for an early lunch.

Anne and Helen just tee-heed.

It gave him a sore head. He went into the Good Neighbour for some pills. She sold him some Anadin, but warned him not to take too many.

'I'm not a child,' he said, then added the cheeky grin just a little late.

'Oh, I know,' she beamed. 'I'm sorry, but I just worry about everyone. Do you know what I do when I get a sore head?'

'No,' Miller said flatly.

'I just smile my way out of it.'

Miller smiled his way out of the shop. It took him a while to push his lips back into a snarl, but the wind and the rain and the clatter of a helicopter racing overhead helped.

He went home to Belfast for the weekend, ostensibly to check on the house and get an operation on his serious head injury. Hairdressing in Crossmaheart had not progressed as it had nationally and for the most part was subject to a kind of follicle apartheid. Men largely got their hair cut in barbershops with names like Sammy's and Billy's. Women got theirs done in hairdressers with names like Vicky's and Hair Do. There was no crossover, no unisex. Lately there had been some small movement, in that a couple of the barbers had progressed beyond simple sheep shearing to offering a limited choice of styles. They even called themselves hairdressers now. But women were still not welcome. It didn't matter much to Miller. If he stayed in Crossmaheart for another twenty years, he wouldn't have his hair cut there again.

This time he took the train home, leaving the Cycle of Violence secured inside his apartment. There were no delays. Within forty minutes he was striding down the centre of Belfast, feeling pleasantly relaxed in the swell of shoppers.

At the earliest opportunity he took himself into a unisex salon and asked them for some advice. After the three young ladies had stopped laughing, they suggested he let the perm grow out, and then try to do something with it, but he wasn't prepared to look like a fool for three or four months and insisted that they went to work on it there and then.

There wasn't a lot of styling to be done, it was shorn short and shocking. Taken with his grey, baggy eyes and sallow complexion, it made him look like someone being weaned off hard drugs.

His house, his father's house, smelt musty. There was a pile of bills waiting for him, a few postcards from friends abroad who didn't know he'd moved. He called a couple of people and went out for a drink with them in the afternoon, downed three or four, but his heart wasn't in it and he returned to the cold house in the early evening. He slept for an hour, then popped out to get some chips. He bumped into another old friend on the way home, and by the time he finally got to eat the chips they were half cold. One of his friends had asked him if he had any women on the go and he'd said no, and the fella had laughed and said, 'Sure who'd go out with a woman from Crossmaheart anyway?' Later, he picked up the telephone directory and started checking for Callaghans.

There were about twenty listed in the greater Belfast area. He tried four T. Callaghans first, but had no luck. It took him about an hour to get through thirteen more variously prefixed Callaghans. On the fourteenth a woman answered, her voice working-class Belfast tinged with slightly vertical mobility. The address was off the Malone Road, a poor person's idea of a genteel area.

'Hi,' he said, 'sorry to trouble you so late . . . I'm looking for a Mr Tommy Callaghan?'

'He's not here right now. Can I take a message?'

'Ahm . . . sorry, that wouldn't be the Tommy Callaghan that used to live in Crossmaheart, would it?'

'Well, yes . . . who is this?'

'Oh, God, sorry, yes . . . I used to go to school with Tommy in Crossmaheart years ago . . . I've just moved up to town and I thought I'd look him up, y'know . . . are you his wife? I didn't know Wee Tommy was married.'

'I'm his sister, Flo.'

'Flo, yes, Flo, I'm not sure if I remember you . . . I wasn't round the house much . . . Meadow Way was a bit of a walk, wasn't it? God, it's been so long. It's been such a long time since Tommy's seen me, he probably wouldn't recognize me.'

'No, probably not.' There was a coolness in her voice now, an impatience. Maybe he wasn't a very convincing liar.

'Listen, sure I'll maybe phone back tomorrow. He'll be in in the morning?'

'He goes to church.'

'Okay. Sure. Later then. Thanks. Bye.'

Miller sat for a while, cradling the receiver under his chin, trying to picture what this third abuser might be like. He was out at the moment, probably out on the town getting drunk. Unmarried, obviously, sponging off his spinster sister, unwilling to sacrifice the Protestant drink ethic for domestic bliss. Yet the next day he would get up and swap the breath of hangover for the breath of the Lord in a spartan Presbyterian church, a hypocrite from his Temperance Lodge badge, shiny and proudly displayed on a too-wide lapel, to the faded Kick the Pope tattoo on his left arm, the one he kept hidden all year round save for the three-day binge round the Twelfth.

He fell asleep in the chair. He came awake again during the night and in the darkness fancied that he could make out dimly the shape of his father sitting in the opposite chair. He turned the light on quickly, but there was no one there. He kept the room lit and spent the rest of the night slipping in and out of consciousness.

When he finally roused himself it had gone eight. He put the immersion heater on, fooled about the house for half an hour while the water heated, then took a long bath. In the steam he reached his arms out and pretended to hold her. He kissed the back of his hand as if it was her lips. He missed her more than he dared think. He was a journalist, a trained investigator, but instead of investigating her whereabouts, he was looking into the abuse she had suffered many years before. He knew why, really: because, horrible as it was, he could cope with her past. It was printed in black and white, an historical document. But he couldn't cope with her present: the manic vibrancy of her personality, the anger that was so compelling, the undoubted

169

madness that was fascinating and frightening at the same time. He didn't want to investigate her present because he feared he might come to the conclusion that he couldn't live without her, and then find her head in another fox's mouth.

With the heat in the house off for so long, most of the clothes he had left behind felt damp to him, so he made do with dressing in the same outfit again, which kind of defeated the purpose of the bath. But he felt fresh, wide awake, not befuddled by alcohol: he would deal with Tommy Callaghan better, wouldn't sink to playground abuse. He would get to the bottom of him. Delve into his psyche. Tommy Callaghan, you sexually abused my girl-friend – explain yourself.

He walked for a while, then as the skies let loose with a sudden shower, he whistled down a taxi which took him up past the university onto the Malone Road. Fletcher Ter-race was off on the left, a cul-de-sac about a hundred yards long. He paid off the cab then dandered down to the Cal-laghan residence, number 34. No garden, but a couple of smart window boxes. Miller pressed the bell. After a few moments the door opened and a middle-aged lady poked her head out. She didn't say anything, although her eyes said a lot about his hair. She didn't know how much it had improved.

'Hi. I was looking for Mr Callaghan.'

'And who might you be?'

'My name's Ronson, I . . .'

'And what do you want?'

A man's voice broke in from behind her: 'Is that him?'

Miss Callaghan looked back briefly, but kept the door mostly closed. 'I don't know.'

'Well, ask him.'

'Were you on the phone last night?' she asked quietly. Miller nodded. She bent forward, lowered her voice. 'What do you want with him?'

'Just a chat . . .'

'He's not well,' she hissed, 'I don't want him dis . . .'

The door was pulled back behind her. A tall man in a dark ulster looked out. Or, rather, didn't look out. His eyes were yellowed-white, spare, vacant, blind.

'Tommy, there's no need . . .'

'Flo, it's okay . . .'

'But, Tommy . . .'

'Flo . . . stop worrying . . . I was going out for my walk anyway . . . sorry about this, but she's an old fuss-pot . . . she never even thought to ask your name last night . . .'

'John. Johnny Ronson.'

Callaghan nodded. 'Johnny. Johnny, how are ya?'

'I'm fine.'

'Good. Good old Johnny. We'll go for a walk then Johnny, will we? Catch up on old times?'

'Sure, Tommy, that would be nice.'

'Hold on there a minute. I'll get Sheila.'

Callaghan turned from the door. Flo stepped forward again. 'What do you want with him?' she demanded.

'Nothing, just a chat.'

'He was up to high doh last night when I told him some-one from the old town had called. He doesn't need to be upset. He's not a well man.'

'We're just going for a walk.'

'I don't like the look of you.'

'Don't judge a book by its cover,' Callaghan said, re-appearing at the door with an elderly-looking Labrador on a lead and harness. 'I don't.'

'Very funny, Tommy.'

'Lighten up, Flo, will ya? Does he have pockmarks on his gob?' He held up his free hand. 'Maybe I could read his face, tell you what he's really like?'

'Oh, stop it, Tommy. Put your collar up.'

'Listen, dear, if a collar up could stop you from dying you not think you could get a prescription for it?'

'Och, Tommy . . .'

'Yeah, yeah . . .'

Callaghan and the Labrador, Sheila, stepped out onto the footpath. 'Shall we walk, Johnny?'

'Sure.'

Miller stepped in beside him and they started to move up the Terrace towards the Malone Road. When Miller looked back, Flo was still watching.

They walked the first fifty yards in silence. Then Callaghan reached into his coat pocket and produced a pair of sunglasses. 'A bit cold, I know,' he said, slipping them on, 'but it stops people staring.'

'How can you tell?' Miller asked.

'Couldn't you?'

Miller shrugged.

'Couldn't you?' asked Callaghan again.

'I suppose.'

There was a crossing at the top of the road. Callaghan found the button, and in a second the green man was up and bleeping. Sheila led them across. 'We campaigned for this crossing, y'know? Me and Flo. All this for one blind man. Marvellous.'

On the other side of the road they turned right and started walking back towards the university.

'I know who you are,' Callaghan said presently.

'You do?'

'You're the angel of death.'

'I've never been called that before.'

'I've been expecting you. Ever since I read about the others I've been expecting you. I may be blind, but Flo reads me everything, everything. I read about Michael. I read about Tyrone. I always get the Crossmaheart paper sent up. Flo thought I was mad, getting nostalgic for a hole like that.

But I knew. I knew you'd come for me, knew you'd come soon.'

'You knew more than me then.'

'I knew. I've been waiting. Waiting for a long time. A lot of years.'

The voice was sad. Resigned. It was the voice of an old man in a relatively young man's body. It threw Miller. Put him off the inquisition.

'I just came to talk to you,' he said.

'About the girl.'

'Yeah. The girl.'

'And what I did to her.'

'And what you did to her.'

'You know what I did to her?'

'I've read about it.'

'What, in the paper?' Miller nodded. 'In the paper?'

'Yeah, the paper.'

'I thought you might be a brother, or a cousin, family anyway.'

'No. My girlfriend.'

'Teenage sweethearts.'

'Not quite.'

They crossed the road again and turned into the university itself, crossing through the main hall and out into the crisp air again. Callaghan stopped by a seat on the edge of the central quadrangle.

'Do you mind?'

'Not at all.'

'I usually sit here for a while, and let Sheila have a run round. To tell you the truth I've walked this way so often I really don't need Sheila's help at all.'

He reached down and expertly unclipped Sheila, and she sauntered off, sniffing at the grass. Then they sat side by side.

'Before you kill me,' Callaghan began, 'I should tell you

about it. I've never told anyone else – who can you tell, really? I mean, I was eighteen, theoretically responsible for my actions, and I was there. In the car. You've got to expect to be tarred with the same brush, don't you? You can't make excuses.'

'Am I about to hear an excuse?'

'No. God, no. I accept it all, always have. My own fault. Look – Tyrone had the car, he'd stolen it, of course, from somewhere. He was a bad wee rip, even then. Didn't get much better, did he? We all knew each other through Macy's shop – we'd all done paper rounds for years from it. We shouldn't really have been knocking about together, different religions 'n' all, but we just seemed to click. Tyrone had started us drinking as well, just a couple of weeks before really, and you know what it's like when you first start drinking, the first year or so you get drunk really easily. That night we'd been on the cider, driving about, then Tyrone produced a bottle of Bacardi as well, and we all had a go at that. I had a couple of slugs. That, mixed with the cider, mixed with the driving around, my head was away. I had the spins. I think I was sick somewhere. I was half asleep in the front seat. Next thing I knew there was a girl in the car. I don't remember picking her up. I was only half focused on her. She was chatty, laughing, then Tyrone took something off her, a badge or something and she tried grabbing for it and he threw it on the floor. She bent down to get it and he was on top of her, touching her. She was stuck down there and he started pulling her clothes off and she was shouting and screaming and crying but we were parked out in the country by then, so it didn't matter, and after a while she was just lying there letting them do whatever they wanted, just lying there with her eyes closed. I was there, I was leaning over the front seat, watching, I mean, I couldn't do anything, my head was spinning. That was my crime. Watching. I couldn't help her, because I couldn't

174

help myself, I was incapable, physically incapable. I knew it was wrong, I knew it then, I knew it after, I know it now. And God punished me for it.'

'He sent you to prison for a year.'

'A life sentence. A death sentence. Would that I could go back and change things, but who can? That poor young girl. Sometimes I think of her every minute of every day, what we did to her. Ruined her life.'

'So what happened to the eyes?' He couldn't think of a subtler way to ask.

'Blind drunk to blind sober. Prison did for them. Borstal, anyway. I was eighteen, my dad had been murdered by the IRA, so I was expected to fall in with the Loyalists in the borstal. I didn't want anything to do with them. I've never been political. And in my own wee way I found a bit of peace in the borstal. I know it's a bit of a cliché, but I did discover God when I was in there. I worshipped him in my own wee way, but that didn't go down too well with the boys; they expected me to fight for God's own country, and when I wouldn't go along with them they had a go at me. Gave me a proper hiding. Lost my sight through it.'

'That must have been rough.'

'Well, it wasn't much fun. I hate people who say God's will whenever things go wrong, but I suppose it must have been. Punishment, y'know? I got out a few weeks early on the strength of it. Yippee. Then my mum upped and died a couple of months later, so me and my sister got this house up in town and I've been here ever since. I got Sheila, of course, but she's getting on. I have my work too. I go down to the YMCA, work with a group of blind kids there. I work with the church a lot, I do what I can, sit on a lot of committees, go and visit the old folk, though goodness knows I'm probably a bigger danger to them than they are to themselves, the way I stumble about, but they seem to appreciate it – sometimes it's good for them to concentrate on someone

175

else's problems, they realize they mightn't be so badly off themselves. I mean, just because you're old and confined to bed doesn't mean you're useless, that's what casters were invented for. So I keep myself busy, but at the back of it all, always, is the girl. I try not to be selfish about it, because I know that whatever happens to me, she was always the victim, but sometimes I think what might have happened if I'd not been in the car that night. If I'd have gone on to university instead of borstal, if I'd kept my sight, got a good job, met a good woman, been . . . well, happy. And now here I am, riddled with the cancer too.'

'If it's God's will, he's having a good time with you.'

'Oh, I don't blame Him. I blame myself. For being in the car.'

'According to what you say, you couldn't have known.'

'I knew I was running with a bad lot. I wasn't stupid. Just a bit naïve. You know, I've never had a girlfriend. Never a one. I'm virgin territory. I'll go to heaven and be stamped, returned unused.'

'You think you'll go to heaven?'

Callaghan laughed. 'You never can tell. I'll know soon enough.'

'Have they told you how long?'

Callaghan shook his head. 'I think maybe they told Flo, but I haven't asked.'

'My dad died of cancer last month.'

'I'm sorry.'

And from nowhere, tears were rolling down Miller's face. He wiped at his cheek and sniffed up. Callaghan heard it and reached out to him, his fingers touching his face, his head nodding slightly. He moved his hand down to Miller's shoulder and squeezed it lightly.

'I'm sorry,' Miller whispered. 'Jesus, what am I like?' He shifted his shoulder and Callaghan removed his hand. 'Sorry. I . . . just talking to you reminds me . . . I never had

176

a chance to say goodbye to him, y'know? By the time he was diagnosed, he was gaga.'

'Sure if I see him up there, I'll tell him you were asking for him, is that a deal?'

'Yeah. Sure.'

'You're a lot more sensitive than I would expect an angel of death to be. Of course, you're a personal assassin, not political or religious, so you can maybe get away with shedding a tear or two. Anyway, what's it to be, the preferred method of execution?'

Miller laughed. 'I'm no assassin.'

'But you killed those people, then you came looking for me.'

'I only ever wanted to find out more. I just wanted to talk. Those deaths were an unforeseen by-product of those talks. I've no desire to kill anyone, Tom, least of all you.'

'But do you have it in your heart to forgive me for what happened all those years ago?'

Miller looked at his own reflection in Callaghan's sunglasses for a moment, at the vague outline of those sightless eyes. Sightless eyes which had once looked upon Marie, naked, helpless, and done nothing.

'No,' he said.

Callaghan stood up. 'I understand,' he said quietly. Miller rose too. 'Now where's that dog got to?' Callaghan asked.

Miller surveyed the quadrangle, but could see no sign of her. 'She's wandered off somewhere,' he said.

'I hope she's not out on that road again. You'd think a guide dog would know better. I'm convinced she flunked her finals. But I wouldn't change her for the world.'

Callaghan turned back towards the main hall, crossing the grass and mounting the three steps to the entrance with a pace and easy familiarity which belied his condition. Miller hurried after him, catching him as he exited on the other side. They crossed the car park together, Callaghan calling the dog's name, Miller scanning for the wandering animal.

Miller spotted her emerging from behind a bin on the far side of the road, nose to the ground. He took Callaghan by the elbow. 'She's on the other side,' he said.

'More trouble than she's worth sometimes,' said Callaghan, stepping towards the road.

Miller stopped him. 'I'll go on from here. You're all right getting home from here?'

'I know the way like the back of my hand,' said Callaghan, and looked down at his hand. Then he put it out to Miller. 'Will you shake my hand, even if you can't forgive me?'

'I'm sorry. I can't. I know you weren't to blame . . . but . . .'

'Don't worry about it. I just want it to be clear in your mind what my role in it was. I'm not a bad man, I'm a victim of circumstance and inebriation, and if I could have helped that little girl I would have. But I couldn't.'

Miller knew Callaghan wasn't a bad man. You could sense that off a person, and he had sensed it off Callaghan from the beginning.

'Is it clear?' asked Callaghan.

It was clear to him, but he had been there, he had witnessed, and he was forever tarnished.

'It's clear,' said Miller.

'See,' said Callaghan nodding, 'don't need the dog.'

He stepped out.

And was almost flattened by a lorry.

The shock of the horn and the blast of wind knocked him back and as he stumbled up the kerb Miller took a firm hold of him. 'Are you okay?'

Flustered, blowing big gulps of air out of his sallow cheeks, Callaghan spluttered: 'Yes, yes, of course . . . I . . . well, that seemed close. Did it look close?'

'It looked close.' Miller shook his head and scanned the

other side for the dog again. She had wandered a further twenty yards up. Miller whistled. The dog's ears pricked up, she peered at them for a few moments and then darted across the road, impervious to the traffic.

Callaghan made a great show of affection as he clipped the lead on again. 'Where've you been, you old stop-out, eh?' he said, rubbing at the floppy ears.

'I'll see you around,' said Miller, turning away at last.

'I won't,' said Callaghan, grinning.

As Miller crossed the road the rain began again, heavier. He pulled up his collar, but his hair was so short that the rain felt heavy on his scalp. He didn't relish walking the whole way with it pit-pattering on him like a woodpecker come calling. A hundred yards up the road he stopped and waved for a taxi, but he was ignored: once, twice. The third one was just about past him when he let out a shrill whistle. As it braked, Callaghan's faithful dog answered the same call and pulled her master out into the road, where both were flattened by a lorry.

11

Paul McKeown, manager of the Joyce Hotel in central Dublin, had a problem. In fact, as he stood in the foyer watching a clutch of German tourists struggle with their bags, he realized that he had a lot of problems – the Guards were giving him hassle over his entertainment licence because of repeated complaints from near neighbours about the noise of the disco, the Irish Writers Circle was refusing to pay for its annual dinner because the chef in a drunken fit had included a first course called Salmon Rushdie on their menu and because the battling Maguire sisters had managed to break thirty-eight plates during a punch-up in the kitchens. He was fed up to the teeth with the Germans and their constant catalogue of complaints. And he was growing increasingly exasperated at the continuing hassle his four-year-old son Rory was giving him as he careered round the foyer like a headless chicken, toppling suitcases and stepping on elderly German feet with the determination of a zealot. But the problem which perplexed him most was the woman in 78.

The hotel was dowdy enough to suggest something of a literary background, but the fact of the matter was that it was less than twenty years old, and Joyce had been dead for that long already by the time its conversion from tea warehouse to middle-priced hotel had got under way. Its only tangible connection with Joyce was that the great man had probably drunk tea once or twice in his life. There were a couple of photographs of the author hanging cock-eyed in the foyer, a half-hearted attempt to imbue the hotel with some literary tradition which fooled no one, not even the Germans.

The Germans had a problem with their bill. There were eight of them, two sets of grandparents, two daughters and a pair of gangly teenagers. Their English was good, but they had a habit of dropping their voices and arguing viciously in German before smiling sweetly and reverting to polite English again which didn't endear them very much to the portly hotel manager. Their problem lay with the telephone bill. They were being charged for several phone calls to Paris, which they denied all knowledge of. McKeown thought they were probably right, that someone must have sneaked into their room while they were out and availed himself of their phones, but he had to go through the rigmarole of a polite inquisition.

'And you say you have no relatives or acquaintances in Paris?'

'Not in Paris, not in France,' one of the grandfathers said, staring down at the computer printout, as if it might change there in front of him.

'We made no calls at all,' said the other grandfather, 'but one to Berlin . . . and that is accounted for here . . .' He pointed at the printout. McKeown nodded. A sharp yell diverted his attention. One of the younger German ladies was hopping around, holding her foot. Rory was chasing her, stabbing at her other foot with one of his own.

'Rory!' McKeown snapped. 'Stop that now!' Rory veered off towards the swing doors. 'And keep away from those doors!'

The youngster turned again, stuck his tongue out at his father, then raced towards the bar.

McKeown shook his head and returned to his computer. 'Sorry about that,' he said to the Germans. 'Now, let's see if the computer can tell us anything else . . . now, these calls were all made last night . . . between eight and nine . . .'

'Impossible, we were having dinner last night, all of us, at that time . . .'

Bernie Campbell, his assistant manager, appeared at his elbow, and whispered, 'No luck with 78.'

McKeown tutted. 'Excuse me,' he said to the Germans, then whispered, 'What did she say?'

'She didn't say anything.'

'Did you go in?'

'I didn't like to.'

'Jesus, Bernie, it's yer job.'

'Ach, I know, but she's been so nice to us 'n' all.'

'Bernie, it's not her place to be nice to us, it's her place to pay us . . .'

'She's only a few days . . .'

'Bernie, I want her out, or I want some money, now go back up there and if she doesn't let you in, use your key, this can't go on . . .'

Another yelp snapped McKeown's head round. This time one of the grandmothers was holding her foot. Rory was circling menacingly. The grandfathers turned from the reception desk to offer assistance, but McKeown was out like a shot from behind the computer. He crossed the dark-carpeted foyer, grabbed Rory by the arm and slapped him sharply across the back of the legs. The boy immediately emitted a high-pitched scream and burst into tears.

'Please,' said the uninjured grandmother, reaching for the child, 'in Germany we do not strike our children.'

'And in Ireland we don't gas our Jews,' snapped McKeown, pulling the child forcefully round behind the desk. The manager's face was already bright red, his mind racing scared at his appalling retort.

'What did you say?' demanded the grandmother.

'Shoes,' said Bernie rapidly, slapping his hand on the desk, shaking his finger at the wailing child, 'in Ireland we don't step on shoes. You naughty wee boy!'

'Shoes,' rejoined McKeown, 'shoes indeed. Never step on them! In Ireland a man's shoes are his . . .'

'Shoes,' said Bernie, 'never come between an Irishman and his shoes! Now, Paul, about this bill . . .'

'Ah, yes, the bill, the bill. My apologies, sir, these calls seem to have been incorrectly added to your account . . . now, with a flick of a switch . . . there they go. Plus a further five per cent discount for any inconvenience caused . . .'

After the Germans had regrouped and departed, and Rory had been reclaimed by his mother, McKeown sat with his head on the reception desk. 'God, I don't know what came over me,' he moaned. 'Thanks for stepping in like that.'

'Ach, sure never worry,' said Bernie, 'no harm done. Just one of those days.'

'Well, it's appreciated. Is your wee one as much of a menace as that?'

'Sure they're all the same, Paul.'

'And would you give yours a slap once in a while?'

'Don't we all? Never did us any harm when we were nippers, did it? Me da used to whack me every day on God's earth, and what harm did it to me? Apart from the limp.'

'Ach, quit it, Bernie,' McKeown laughed. 'Still, one good turn deserves another − you want me to go and see 78?'

'Nah. I don't mind. It is my job, I should stop pussyfootin' around.'

Bernie turned towards the lift.

'If I'm not mistaken, Bernie, you're a bit taken with her.'

Bernie smiled back. 'Who isn't?'

He had a point, thought McKeown. She had breezed into the Joyce a week and a half before, splashed down a pile of cash on the desk, and asked for the best room in the house. The best room was taken, but she settled for 78; it was a bit smaller but had a better view of the city. She was young, attractive, had sparkly eyes, a less moany than usual northern accent, and before she'd been there three days she was on first-name terms with just about every member of staff, including himself. On her fourth night she'd held a party in her room for all the maids, and when Bernie had gone to warn her that it was against the rules for the staff to drink on the premises she had challenged him to a game of poker to decide the fate of the party. Bernie had refused. She had refused to abandon the party, and Paul had been brought in to give his opinion. Two hours and a bottle of vodka later, Paul and Bernie had been comprehensively beaten at poker and were dancing with the rest of the maids to Van Morrison's 'Brown Eyed Girl'.

And then the money had run out, and she'd stopped answering the door. Paul had stopped room service immediately, in an attempt to flush her out, but it hadn't worked yet. Either she was starving, or, as he suspected, food was being smuggled into her by her many allies amongst the lower staff. He hadn't told Bernie yet of his suspicions.

Up at 78, Bernie knocked gingerly at the door. 'Marie,' he whispered, 'are you there?'

He had heard her moving about earlier, so he knew at least that something awful hadn't happened. That was his big fear, finding someone dead in bed – or, worse, someone decomposing. That would really be neglect of duty. Guests had a right to privacy, of course, but the Joyce's policy of allowing rooms to go unserviced for up to three days at a guest's request could only lead to trouble.

'Marie . . . it's me, Bernie, are you awake?'

Silence. Bernie fished out the master key and opened the door. The room was in darkness. In the dull light from the corridor he could just make her out lying on the bed surrounded by . . . he crossed the room and opened the curtains . . . shoe boxes, a dozen of them, lined up six on each side of her, the tops scattered on the floor, the room heavy with the smell of leather and something else . . .

'Marie?'

There was no response. She lay, fully-clad, face up on top of the sheets. He bent over her, wincing slightly at the fetid smell of stale alcohol that enveloped her. Her face was pale but her breathing was strong and steady. An empty bottle of whiskey lay on the floor beside her. He shook her gently by the shoulder. Nothing. He shook her harder, but still it had no effect.

Bernie lifted one or two of the shoes – they were all newly bought and carried labels from some of Dublin's finest shops. There were six pairs of ladies' shoes, six pairs of men's. As he moved along the bed inspecting them his foot caught on something. He looked down, then dragged his foot back, revealing a strap, and then the black leather handbag it was attached to. Cautiously he lifted it and peered inside. With one eye half on Marie he fingered the contents: although he didn't know what he expected to find of an unusual nature, he was nevertheless disappointed to discover that there was nothing inside that he wouldn't have found in his own wife's bag. Make-up, tissues, an empty purse, cinema stubs . . . He set it down on the floor again and pushed it under the bed. There were clothes strewn about the rest of the room, on the writing table a half-eaten, putrefying apple. He was reaching for the waste bin to scoop it in when he noticed a half-written letter on the table. The address, neatly printed in the top left corner, was that of a Mr Miller at a newspaper office up north. He pushed the apple off the edge with the side of a Gideon Bible, then set the bin down and lifted the letter . . .

And was whacked round the back of the head with a stiletto. He pitched forward over the table then rolled off sideways, crumpling into the corner, one hand stretched protectively before him, the other already reaching back to check for blood.

'What do you want?' Marie screamed. 'What do you want?' She swiped again and again, but he was hedged in between the table and the wall radiator and she missed his head, her heel pounding instead into his less vulnerable, fleshy back.

'What do you want? What do you want?'

Her voice was high, hysterical, frightening.

'Marie,' he squealed, 'don't, don't, it's me, it's me, Bernie, Bernie, Marie.'

'What do you want?' She was still screaming, but she pulled back from the assault. Bernie carefully turned and then raised himself cautiously onto one knee. Marie was shaking her head, tears in her eyes, but the shoe was still levelled menacingly at him. He could see a smear of blood on the heel. The sight of that, rather than his own pain, made him feel dizzy. He put his hand out towards her, and she stepped back.

'What do you want?' she asked falteringly.

'It's okay, love,' he said.

'What do you want?' Pained.

'I just came to see if you were okay.'

'I'm okay.'

'Are you sure?'

'Yes, I'm sure.'

She turned wearily, dropping the shoe, and returned to the bed. She cleared the remaining boxes off the quilt and lay down.

'Close the door after you, Bernie, would you? There's a dear.'

'Okay, love, whatever you say.'

Bernie hurried to the door. He closed it after him and locked it, then leant against it for a minute, getting his breath back. Crumpled in his left hand, he held the letter Marie had been writing. He reached back and gingerly touched his head. When he looked at his fingers, they were smeared with blood. 'Fuck,' he said aloud, then made for the lift.

The call came through shortly after lunch time, not that he had eaten. He didn't have much of an appetite. Three murders in one week tended to do that to him.

Miller had been staring listlessly into his computer screen. There were words there, but they didn't make sense to him; instead of little green letters he saw little green decomposing faces. He had set out to kill them, he knew that now. There had been no master plan, but the idea must have been there somewhere. There had been a rupture in that dark recess of the mind where human nature is kept in check, where the barbarity inherent in every man is shackled to a feminine advocate for the defence. He could admit to himself that he had killed Marie's three tormentors, but to no one else. There was no justification for their deaths, and although legally he was sure that he couldn't be touched – one suicide, one accident and a bomb victim – he did not claim any moral high ground from it, nor did he wish to.

They noticed it in work, his staring, his paleness and distraction. They blamed it on the bomb, on the beating, on the disappearance of his girlfriend. The girls made sympathetic noises, of course, but he held back from them, denied anything was wrong, seemed cheery for a moment before lapsing back into his dreamy lethargy. O'Hagan just worked quietly on, occasionally glancing at Miller; his contribution was not pushing any work Miller's way, unless he specifically asked for it.

'Hey, Miller.'

'Huh?'

He looked up into Helen's eyes. She gave him a little smile. 'Your phone.'

'Mmmm?' His head shifted lazily to the phone. It was a

couple of moments before he heard the soft trill. 'Oh, right, okay,' he said, and lifted the receiver.

'Editorial,' he said.

'Ahm – Mr Miller?'

'Well, yes.'

'Good, ahm, Mr Miller, I have something of a delicate problem and you just might be able to help.'

A lilty southern brogue. Miller tutted.

The man paused. 'Ahm, yes. Well, my name is Paul McKeown, I'm the manager of the Joyce Hotel in Dublin.'

'Uh-huh.'

'We have a guest here who . . . well, who is . . . confused, and I understand she may be a . . . relative, or an acquaintance of yours.'

Miller snapped out of his coma. 'She . . . who is it?'

'Ahm, her name is Marie, Marie Young, she . . .'

'How is she?' Miller demanded sharply. Sweat broke across his brow like a wave on a virgin beach.

'She's . . . well, drunk.'

'Brilliant!'

'Well, I don't think . . .'

'No, no, I mean . . . she's healthy?'

'She has attacked one of my employees, Mr Miller . . .'

'Brilliant! I mean, I'm sorry, but she's been missing and . . .'

'She hasn't paid her account for several days . . .'

'Never mind about that, man, I can cover that, but she's okay . . . ?'

'We don't like to call the Guards, Mr Miller, but eventually . . . I hope you don't mind that my assistant manager took the liberty of entering her room and removing a letter she was writing . . . it had your name and address on it . . .'

'Not at all, of course not . . . what did it say?'

'Ahm, well, let me see, ahm . . . Dear . . .'

'Yes?'

'Ahm, that would appear to be it. She didn't get very far.'

'That's okay, that's okay. I'll come right down and get her, Mr ... uh ... McKeown. Will you just ... uh ... keep her there until I arrive?'

'The difficulty, Mr Miller,' McKeown said testily, 'has been in getting rid of her.'

He hated asking Martin O'Hagan for a favour. Hated it more than shaving cold with a blunt blade. Hated it more than elderly women running their nails down a blackboard. But it had to be done. It wasn't that he wasn't owed the time. It was the timing of the time he was owed. He swallowed his pride and his bile and explained it as succinctly as he could. He needed the rest of the day off. His girlfriend was safe but had to be collected from Dublin. He knew there was work to be finished on the paper, but, really, he had to go. O'Hagan looked at him for a long time. Miller was just about to turn on his heel and head south when the editor nodded his head slowly and said okay.

'You can ask me these things, you know,' he said. 'I'm not the big bad wolf.'

'I never said you were.'

'But you watch me, and your eyes are like thunder.'

Miller tried to imagine eyes like thunder. He couldn't. He needed to go. 'Sorry,' he said, 'for my strange eyes. Maybe you read too much into them.'

O'Hagan shook his head, slightly. 'I think not.'

Miller turned for the door. As he reached it O'Hagan called after him.

'What?' Miller snapped.

'Good luck.'

'Oh. Right. Thanks.'

*   *   *

189

Elated, deaths forgotten, Miller made tracks for Dublin. He stopped first at Marie's lodgings to pick up her medicine. Mrs Hardy handed it over with a smile and a flourish once he had told her that Marie was alive. 'After all this trouble she's put us through I hope they're not just bloody contraceptive pills,' he quipped.

Mrs Hardy lost her smile. 'They're not, no,' she said sadly.

Miller grimaced apologetically. 'I know,' he said.

From there to the train. His timing was good. Five minutes after he arrived at Belfast Central he was aboard the Dublin express. He dozed off with his head vibrating gently against the window. Two and a half hours later he was racing through the drabness of Connolly Station. He emerged into the darkness and jogged easily through the damp streets, drawn by the polluted air of the Liffey towards the Joyce. He knew the city well; the mixture of tourist trap and easy drinking bohemia made it a relaxing place to be.

The Joyce loomed out of the darkness, a great boxy intrusion amongst the squalid but characterful stores around it. He mounted the steps three at a time and approached the reception desk, his heart pounding, his face an odd mixture of hope and exhaustion.

Paul McKeown looked up. He reviewed Miller, and his hair, quickly. 'I'm sorry,' he began with polished condescension, 'we don't . . .'

'Marie Young,' Miller said breathlessly.

'Ah. Yes.'

'What room?'

'First there's the small matter . . .'

'Of course, of course.' Miller fumbled for his wallet, then slapped a card down on the desk. McKeown picked it up, then turned it over.

'It's kosher,' said Miller.

McKeown smiled. 'It's a kosher kidney donor card.'

'Sorry. Jesus.' He took the card back. 'Sorry,' he said

again, handing over the real thing. 'I'm puffed. I've been running. I'm not fit.'

'Not all the way from Belfast, I trust.'

'No,' Miller smiled. 'Of course not. How is she?'

McKeown stopped himself mid shrug – not very professional that, not quite that caring hotel manager he was striving for. 'Ahm – well – I honestly couldn't say. Since Miss Young saw fit to inflict a head injury, requiring some six stitches, on my assistant manager, none of us have been of a mind to ask after her health.'

The manager ran the card through and handed it back.

'Thanks. I appreciate the call. I'm sorry she's been such trouble.'

'Well, these things happen. She's a nice girl, but she seems to have some problems.' He handed a key across the desk to Miller. 'Seventy-eight,' he said, 'and good luck.'

Miller nodded and turned for the lift. Upstairs, he knocked lightly on 78. When there was no response, he knocked harder, waited for half a minute then slipped the key into the lock and opened the door slowly.

As he entered, Marie rose menacingly from the bed, a stiletto in either hand, like a B-movie gunslinger. Her eyes, red-rimmed, crossed in confusion when she saw him. She dropped the shoes and sat back on the bed.

Miller closed the door and leant against it. 'Hello, Imelda,' he said quietly.

Marie looked to the shoe-strewn floor. 'Half of them are yours,' she said wearily.

'They look nice.'

She picked an Oxford brogue up and ran a finger along the sole. 'I hope they fit,' she said, dropping it lightly back to the floor. 'How did you know?'

'Hey, I'm a journalist. Besides, you shouldn't write letters to me . . .'

191

'Oh . . .' She looked to the writing table. Marie nodded slowly. 'I'm sorry . . . I'm so glad to see you . . .'

He crossed to her. She flung her arms round him and held him tight, tight enough to take his breath away. She sobbed. He started to sob. The relief flooded out of him.

After a couple of minutes he extricated himself gently. He wiped at her face. She wiped at his. 'I brought your medicine,' he said.

'I don't need it.'

'Yes, you do.'

'I don't want it. I can't take it. Not all my life. I thought if I got away for a while, got used to being without it, I'd be okay . . .'

'But you're not.'

She shook her head sadly. 'No.'

'It doesn't work like that.'

'I know.'

'I came to take you home. And your shoes.'

'No. Not yet. I can't.'

He took her in his arms again. 'Will you talk to me?' he whispered in her ear. She held him tightly again, he felt her head nod against his chest. He led her to the bed and they lay down together.

'I'm sorry,' she said.

'Don't be sorry. Tell me why you're here.'

'I . . . God, I don't know. I wanted . . . when I heard about Jamie . . . I just needed to get away . . . it's just so horrible . . .'

He stroked her head. 'Why didn't you tell me?'

'I don't know . . . I . . . I just ran. I wanted something new, something different, something not connected with death. So I went shopping. Shopped until I'd nothing left.'

'Tell me about the medicine.'

'It keeps me calm.'

'In what way.'

'As opposed to not calm.'

'Marie . . .'

'I mean . . . I have . . . what the doctors call a chemical imbalance. If I don't take my pills . . . I'm on, like, a permanent high, you know, euphoria. I think I can do anything . . . the pills keep me down . . . but . . .'

'Well, what's the problem, if they keep you . . .'

'Miller . . . I want to have a baby . . .' She began to sob again. Miller brushed a thumb across her face, diverting the tears.

'I don't understand . . .'

'The pills . . . I'm on them for life, but they're so strong, I'm not allowed to conceive . . . do you understand? For me to remain . . . normal, sane, whatever you want, means I have to stay on them. If I got pregnant I'd have to have an abortion because the chances are they'd affect the baby. Do you see? Can you understand?'

Miller nodded a no.

'I don't understand where a baby comes into it at all. Do you mean you came down here specifically to get pregnant?'

'No! Will you listen to me! I came down here to get away from Jamie . . .'

'Jesus, okay, but . . .'

'Part of getting away from Jamie, from the whole Crossmaheart thing . . . Miller, it's all tied up with the baby . . .'

'You're not . . .'

'I'm not! I was . . .'

'Christ, when . . . I mean, Jamie?'

'No, Miller, look . . . look . . .' She quietened her voice, mother-calm. 'It was a very long time ago, way back when.'

'Not from the car? Those bastards in the car?'

Her voice faltered. 'I . . . didn't tell my parents . . . God, I didn't know myself till the doctor told me and I was four months gone by then, I wasn't big or anything, you would hardly have noticed 'less you were looking for it . . . but I had to tell them eventually. My dad went off the handle, really off the handle, after everything that had happened, all of it . . . maybe he had a right to . . . but when I told him he started into me, shouting, storming. I shouted back and he started slapping me, so I slapped back and he really lost it. I ended up on the floor. He kicked me in the stomach. He kicked me everywhere, but you remember the kicks in the stomach. He just went mad, kicked me again and again. It wasn't like him, y'know? He just snapped. Called me all the names of the day, swearing, screaming, kicking. Miller, he killed the baby. Maybe he had a point . . .'

'Christ, Marie, don't say that. There's no excuse . . .'

'It was my fault, if I hadn't . . .'

'Marie!'

'I know, I know, but . . .'

'But nothing, Jesus . . .'

'And that's when it happened. I don't know. The trauma, I suppose. I went a bit gaga . . .'

'Chemical imbalance . . .'

'Yeah, nuts. So I was away with the fairies for a while. It took them months to work out what was wrong with me, and then to get me stabilized. I couldn't hack it at home, for obvious reasons, after that. I haven't spoken to him since. I see him the odd time, about the streets. He looks old, sick. I should forgive him, before it's too late. I'll be saying that until he's gone. I know that. That's the way these things go, isn't it?'

Miller nodded. It was.

'That's when I moved in with Mrs Hardy. She's been an angel.'

'What about your mum?'

'She left him. She died. It was all too much for her. She was never strong, physically, mentally. Maybe I get it all

194

from her. And some violence from my dad. Some legacy, huh?'

'I think I love you,' Miller said.

'Oh,' said Marie.

Miller talked McKeown into letting them stay on. He agreed on the condition that they switched rooms. The only room available was one with twin beds. Miller didn't hesitate. It was no time to think of the temptations of sex. No time to think of babies. No time to think at all. It was time to relax, luxuriate in her company, think of nothing, nothing but love and romance.

Besides the shoes there were dresses and skirts, jeans and earrings, books and CDs. It took him three trips to move it all to the new room. On the last trip he took Marie with him, clutching her under his arm like another expensive acquisition; she clung to him wearily. He put her to bed immediately. He pulled up a chair beside her and sat stroking her hand until she dozed off. Miller slowed his stroking motion right down, then finally lifted his hand and put himself to bed.

He slept dreamlessly. When he woke the room was bathed in sunny winter light. Marie stood by the window, staring out over the city.

'Good view?' he asked, groggily.

She turned to him and smiled. Her face was already a much better colour. Although her eyes were still red there was a jaunty brightness about them which had been missing the night before. 'Lovely,' she said with such feeling that for a moment he thought she must be talking not just of the view, but about him as well.

Marie was too embarrassed to go down for breakfast, so they had it on room service. Then, after they had washed, they went out walking in the city. Miller loved the Dublin pubs, but he thought it better to steer clear of alcohol until

Marie was completely recovered. They browsed in and out of book shops, then spent half an hour watching a succession of street entertainers, most of them, for some reason, English. They lunched in McDonald's, then caught a bus out to the zoo where Marie spent an hour cooing over the prairie dogs.

They returned to the hotel in the early evening. Marie said she fancied a drink. He didn't think it was wise, but he couldn't bring himself to say so. So he turned romantic.

'How does a candlit dinner for two sound?'

She held up a thumb and forefinger, just touching at the tip. 'Fssssss,' she said.

Miller nodded. 'Is that a yes?'

'Ysssssss.'

'I'm sure you'll be able to find something to wear.'

'That's not fair.'

Miller shrugged and laughed. She laughed back. They looked at each other for a long moment. I do love her, Miller thought.

He got a tin of beer from the mini-bar and lay on the bed while she played with her hair in front of the mirror. She produced a foot-long aerosol can from her bag and began spraying her hair. And spraying. And spraying.

'It just won't bloody sit,' she said.

'It looks fine.'

Her eyes turned to him in the mirror. 'Are you anyone to be talking hairstyles?'

'I wondered when you'd mention it.'

'You look like you've had a fight with the demon barber.'

'You might say that.'

Marie tutted at her reflection. 'It's like it doesn't want to go out,' she said through a cloud of Harmony.

'Your contribution to the hole in the ozone layer.'

She turned those eyes on him again. 'As Oscar Wilde often said, fuck off.'

'I wish I'd said that.'

'You will.'

The first three restaurants they went to all had tables available. But no candles.

'I insist on candles,' said Marie.

'Likewise.'

They continued the hunt and eventually found one they both thought suitable on Baggot Street. Italian. Pink candles.

They ate lustily. Drank likewise. A couple of bottles of wine. She looked ravishing. When the meal was finished and the plates cleared, they held hands across the table.

'I'm sorry to put you through this,' she said.

'Holding hands isn't all that big a problem.'

'No, I mean the whole ting. Running away like that.'

'It's okay. Now. I thought you were dead.'

'I didn't think.'

'Mrs Hardy too.'

'I know. I've been awful. I've been stupid. I'm sorry.'

'We thought the people who killed Jamie might have killed you.'

'I just had to get away.'

'I know. It's over now. But you could have run to me.'

'I know. But I didn't want to do that to you. You can do without a crazy woman in your life.'

'You're not crazy. You just don't trust me yet, do you?'

She squeezed his hand. 'I think I do. It's just . . .'

'You don't need to explain.'

'Thank you.'

'You didn't really say anything when I said I loved you.'

'I know.'

'So?'

She looked up from beneath a spray-defying fallen fringe. 'This is a bit public.'

197

'You think?' There were only half a dozen other diners in the whole restaurant, the nearest four tables away. 'You won't even whisper your response?'

She gave him what he thought was the sweetest smile he had ever seen, then leant forward across the table. He turned his head slightly, ready for words of love. Marie screamed, then shot backwards as her lacquered hair wisped across the naked candle flame and erupted.

12

William Craig had been a constable for a very long time. In the normal course of things promotion would have come his way as naturally as puberty to a teenager; he was intelligent, brave, resourceful and experienced, but this police officer's career suffered from an arrested development entirely of his own making. He refused to compromise.

It had become police practice to promote good community relations, to foster in Crossmaheart an image of the happy village bobby going about his daily duty with a smile and a helping hand. Craig could never quite get to grips with that. The one time he had cried while on duty was when a police woman, a good friend, had her helping hand blown off carrying a suspect device out of a crowded restaurant. He had had to carry the hand to the hospital where the surgeons made a failed attempt to reconnect it. When his superiors related their plans for a friendlier face to local policing, he recounted his own story; and so they remained his superiors. When he saw a suspect on the streets, and in Crossmaheart it is more difficult not to see a suspect, he gave them hell.

There were sergeants, there were detectives, there were inspectors, but Craig was the man who knew it all in Crossmaheart. For advice, for opinion, for expertise, they turned to him. He had fingers in every pie, pies in every shop, shops in every street. He had a small office at the rear of the heavily fortified police station. Ostensibly it was a clerk's office; that's what they told visiting officers from divisional headquarters in Ballyblack; but in reality it was

Craig's private domain. Here he kept his own private computer, his own files on Crossmaheart's low life and high life. And right now the file that was absorbing most of his attention was that on Miller.

Once he was satisfied that he had made most of the connections, he went to see him. He knew the way to the flat, of course, having already put him to bed, a claim he could make of few other murderers. Despite what he now knew about the journalist, he quite liked him. He liked the way he hid his sharpness under a mask of vulnerability. He liked the way he had gone about his task with such precision, yet managed to make it look haphazard and accidental. If anything he conformed to the psychological profile of a rootless meanderer rather than that of a serial killer. It was a chameleon performance of epic quality.

Constable Craig arrived at the flat shortly after 10 pm. He rapped sharply on the door. It was answered swiftly. Miller peeked out of a three-inch gap, nodded, then put his finger to his lips and shushed him.

'Come on in,' he said quietly.

Craig followed him into the flat. The main room was dominated by a large double bed. Above the blankets lay a woman, her head swathed in bandages. Miller crossed to the bed and knelt beside it. 'It's okay,' he said softly, 'just a friend . . .'

'Do you want me to go?' the woman said, her voice slurred. Craig craned over Miller's shoulders for a better look. Marie Young. Puffy-faced. Her eyebrows looked singed. Her eyes were closed.

'No, of course not, don't be silly.' Miller stroked her arm. 'You have a wee sleep there, okay? I'm just going into the kitchen for a chat. You give me a shout if you want anything, eh?'

'Okay, love.'

Miller raised himself slowly, stood for a moment looking

down at her disconsolately and then motioned for Craig to follow him into the kitchen.

'Take some tea?' Miller asked, quietly closing the door. Craig nodded. 'I've nothing stronger, I'm afraid.'

'Tea'll do rightly.' He nodded towards the door. 'What happened to her?'

'Bit of an accident. We were in Dublin at the weekend. There was a fire in a restaurant. I'm afraid Marie got the worst of it.'

'Shouldn't she be in hospital or something? It looks serious.'

'It's not as bad as it looks. She's just a bit drugged up. Her hair's all gone and she's got some burns over her head but they're not too bad.'

'Worse for a woman, that, to lose her hair.'

Miller nodded, and started to fill the kettle. 'I suppose you could call us the Three Degrees. Me with my degree from Queens, and Marie with her second and third degree burns.' He forced a smile onto his face. 'Marie said that. Not me.'

Miller folded the kitchen table down from the wall. Craig pulled a stool up and sat down, placing his hat before him.

'So, to what do I owe the honour?'

'Well, I thought we could build on our relationship.'

Miller put the teapot on the cooker, sat down, and concentrated on perfecting a perplexed look. 'Meaning?'

'Well, you were good enough to point us in the right direction about the fox and the late Jamie Milburn.'

Miller nodded.

'So I thought you might be good enough to tell us a little about Michael Rainey, and Curly Bap, and the other one up in town.' Craig gave him the professional police stare. 'The last person I saw whose face drained quite so dramatically of colour had just been shot.'

201

Miller stumbled. 'What ... like, background information, uh ... ?'

'I think you know what I mean.'

'I'm not sure I ...'

'Maybe it might be easier if I tell what I know, or have
been able to surmise, eh?'

'Sure. Sure. Tea first?'

'Fuck the tea.'

Miller reached back and turned off the pot. 'Tea fucked,'
he said tartly.

'Okay. Let's start with Michael Rainey. He was there in
the pub when you got beaten up. That much you told me.
A few days later you call to see him, according to his
appointments book. His wife comes home to find him
extremely agitated, and the next day he commits suicide.
A few days later a bomb attack on one of our most notorious
terrorists is bungled by the UVF, but nevertheless its
intended target, Curly Bap Blair, is found dead, victim of a
bizarre accident which left him impaled on a shard of glass
... in case you're wondering, forensic science has come on
in leaps and bounds in the last few years, the bigwigs from
the city have been able to deduce that people are rarely
thrown forward towards the force of a blast ... and you
are just about the nearest witness, though of course you
can remember nothing ...'

Miller opened his mouth ...

'Shhhh. Let me finish. Third, Tom Callaghan, apparently
a pedestrian in a tragic road accident. Except his sister
reports that he met with a man answering your rather
unique description shortly before his death.'

Miller stood up. 'I was only joking,' he said, and reached
up into a cupboard. Craig was halfway to pulling out his
gun when he saw Miller turn with half a bottle of whiskey
in his hand. 'I do have stronger stuff. I was keeping it for
an intriguing occasion. This intrigues me more than most.'

He got two plastic tumblers and poured out unhealthy measures. For a moment they drank silently.

'So your theory is what,' Miller began again, 'that I killed these three?'

Craig nodded. 'Or were instrumental in their deaths.'

'So we're talking manslaughter rather than murder?'

'Possibly.'

'And what would possibly inspire me to carry out such random acts?'

'Oh, I don't think there's any randomness about it.' Craig caught and held his eyes.

'You think not?'

'I think not. You see, Miller, I am a meticulous man, and the RUC, for all its faults, is a meticulous force. It has information on people you wouldn't dream of. But that information in itself is pretty useless unless you know how to use it. How to make one thing relate to another. Take Michael Rainey, on the face of it a quite straightforward suicide. There's been no inquest as yet, but that will be the finding, and I don't doubt that it was suicide. Now you don't expect a man of the cloth to have a record of any description, but you check it out anyway. And lo and behold, he has a conviction for a sex offence. So you pull his file and you see who his co-defendants were. One of them was the famous Curly Bap. Then he ends up dead a couple of days later and you think, well, that's a bit of a coincidence. You naturally keep your eye out then for any other names that might be in that file as well – and there you go, body number three turns up. That, Miller, is a pattern.'

'It's a crochet pattern, it's got that many holes in it.'

'Oh, I think not. Especially when you consider the family background of that young girl out there. See? You have motive. There is certain circumstantial evidence.'

'What more do you need?'

'Another drink.'

Miller poured. 'So, there's a point to all this? Like an arrest, or something.'

'On the contrary, I just popped round to congratulate you.'

Miller took a big slug. 'I'm not entirely sure I follow you.'

'You helped me, I'm going to help you. Call me old-fashioned, but I kind of hanker after the days when we could go after someone without our hands tied behind our backs.'

'You sound like a cowboy.'

'Yeah, well, maybe. A marshal maybe.' He grinned, took a drink. 'The trouble with this place, Crossmaheart, the whole Province, is that we know exactly who the trouble-makers are, but we can't touch them. We know the killers, the bombers, the rapists, but they're safe as houses unless we have cast-iron proof, and you can't get that in a place where no one talks to the police. Understand?' Miller nodded. 'You know how galling it is to have someone you know has blown up one of your friends laugh in your face? To see someone you know has interfered with a wee girl hanging about outside a school, but knowing you can't touch him because he's in the IRA? I'm a good policeman, Miller, a very good policeman – you don't stay alive in Crossmaheart this many years without being one – and despite the provocation I have never taken the law into my own hands. I took an oath of loyalty to the crown and I shall honour it. But at certain times I have seen fit to look the other way if something wrong, but for the greater good, takes place. There is a lot of scum about in this town, Miller. If you're doing a little bit to get rid of some of that scum, I won't get in your way.'

'You make it sound like *Death Wish*.'

'Isn't it?'

Miller shook his head. 'It's more like *Carry On Constable*.

Is this some cockeyed way of getting a confession out of me? Do you have a tape strapped to your chest?'

'Straight up, no tape. No nothing.'

'Of course, I could be taping you. That was quite a confession, looking the other way while someone bumps off the local hoods. It would make a good story.'

'Yes — on *Jackanory*.'

'So, uh, there's a point to all this? I mean, I'm not admitting for one moment that any of what you say is true, but if you mean to let me go about my business, what's the point in telling me all this? Why not just leave me be, now that the job's done?'

'If you weren't involved, how would you know that the job was done?'

'What I mean is, I'm sufficiently aware of the background to the sexual abuse to know that the three men involved have suffered violent deaths. Mission accomplished, so to speak.'

'But is it?'

'Is it what?'

'Accomplished.'

'Yes, of course.'

'You're sure?'

'I'm sure.'

'Did you ever see *All the President's Men*?'

'The film? Dustin Hoffman and Robert Redford.'

'Yes.'

'I don't know a journalist who hasn't.'

'Well, think of me as your Deep Throat.'

'You want me to turn the light off?'

'This isn't a time for levity.'

'No. You're right. I just don't follow . . .'

'You were good to me, you gave me information on Jamie Milburn. I'd like to reciprocate. Point you in the right direction.'

'The direction of what?'

'Finishing your study of the case.'

'I still don't follow.'

'Put it like this. Where did you get your information from, on the three amigos? From Marie, from her family?'

Miller wanted to take a drink, but they'd finished the whiskey. He looked into Craig's eyes. Drink-dulled or emotionless, either way, they chilled him.

'From the court report?'

'You're presuming I'm involved . . .'

Craig slammed his fist down on the table. The mugs and the bottle vibrated a couple of inches in Miller's direction. 'Quit fuckin' around,' he snarled. 'I'm trying to do you a favour . . .'

'I'm not . . .'

'From the paper?'

'Look . . .'

'From the paper?'

'Yes!'

'Okay. On the strength of that report, your mission is accomplished, right?'

'Right.'

'But what if the report didn't give the complete picture?'

'As in . . . ?'

'An incomplete picture.'

'That's not very helpful.'

'It's a start. It's the way Deep Throat worked. Push at it a bit.'

'But if you know, why not just tell me?'

'Because.'

'Because why?'

'Just because.'

'Just because is the one answer you can never get round in this fuckin' country.'

'You can get round it, Miller. It's not that difficult. Think about it.'

'You could give me a clue.'

'I have given you a clue. An incomplete picture.'

Craig pushed his stool back and stood up. He lifted his cap and fitted it onto his head. 'You'll work it out,' he said. 'I have every confidence in you.'

'I don't see why you just don't fuckin' tell me . . .'

'Miller, this is half the fun . . .'

'It's not meant to be about fun.'

'What's it meant to be about?'

Miller shrugged. 'I could pay you.'

'Hey, I'm Deep Throat, not Deep Fuckin' Pockets. I'm not in this for profit, Miller, I'm in it for justice. I know that sounds pretty pathetic, but that's the way it is.'

'But . . . I mean, Deep Throat was protecting himself, that was why he couldn't give everything away . . . I mean what have you got to protect?'

'Miller, get serious. It was only a movie.'

'Uuuugh?'

Craig pulled the kitchen door open and strode purposefully, although with a certain respectful lightness, across the main room. He glanced briefly at Marie; she'd drifted off. Miller followed him to the front door, then reached round him to open it.

Miller put out his hand. 'I suppose I should thank you.'

Craig grasped it and gave it a light squeeze. 'Have you worked out what for yet?'

Miller shook his head. 'Give me a chance.'

'You will,' said Craig, and left.

Miller crossed to the bed again and stood looking down at the easy-breathing, bandaged form beneath him. He bit at his lip. 'I could just ask you for the details, love, couldn't I? What murky corridors would that open up in you, eh?'

Marie slept on, oblivious.

* * *

207

Marie's return to form was slow, gradual, sometimes painful, but a delight to watch. The first days she spent in bed, mostly sleeping. When she woke Miller was always there, always awake. He slept next to her, but was always magically aware when she emerged from sleep. He fed her banana on toast. He made her ham and coleslaw sandwiches. On a Sunday he microwaved a chicken so badly that it came out like a ball of string. His Brussels sprouts exploded.

He tried to educate her in good music, happy, boppy stuff a million miles from Cohen and sometimes she rewarded him with a tapping foot. Her metamorphosis was not perhaps on a par with that of a caterpillar emerging from its cocoon as a beautiful butterfly, more that of a war-weary soldier emerging from a trench as a born-again skinhead. Between the two of them there was more hair on a pubescent boy's chest, but it didn't matter, they weren't there to impress anyone but themselves.

He could tell when he was being too attentive; her chat would recede into grunt and her eyes glaze in faraway thought, and at times like that he would slink away, hurt, slightly, but aware to some extent of her inner turmoil. Then he would take himself off, walk the streets of Crossmaheart thinking of what the policeman had told him, or not told him. He thought it through again and again, tried to puzzle out his cryptic clue about an incomplete picture, but a shining path to truth eluded him. In fact, the longer he spent in Marie's company, the less the puzzle concerned him. Yes, it would be nice to know, of course it would, but there was never any pre-ordained plan to ruthlessly track down those involved in Marie's abuse; he had simply embarked on a vague investigation which, due to an unlikely combination of bad temper and unhappy coincidence, had led to the deaths of three people. He had never sat down with his *Death Wish* crusade mapped out. He had been merely filling the sad hole left by Marie's disappearance in the only way he knew how. Now she was safe and getting better, there was no need to follow that path any more. Sure, if it had been laid out in front of him, as Craig had the ability to do, he might saunter down it to satisfy his natural curiosity, but the more he thought about it the more like a dead end it became.

Marie, after five days in bed, finally expressed a wish to go home. He was disappointed at first, he had grown so accustomed to her company, to her body beside him in bed at night, there, but never touched. But he knew it would come; he felt so close to her; she didn't say much, he didn't question her; but it was there okay, in her eyes, in her smile, in her gentle touch.

She was a bit shy about going out in public with her head the way it was. The bandages had long been removed but the burns, although healing nicely, were a sight. In a record shop he bought her a baseball cap with the letters BAD on the front so that she could walk the streets of Crossmaheart not only shielded from public scrutiny, but also promoting a bloody good band.

He had work to return to after an extended sick period. She would return to Mrs Hardy's and concentrate on growing her hair. She had great plans for it. He told her he would love her even if it didn't grow back.

'Is that a promise?'

They stood on the steps outside her lodgings. A light rain fell, pleasant, warm. He nodded enthusiastically, like a big kid. She put her arms around him and held him tight, then angled her face up and gave him a long kiss.

'You know,' she said, pulling her face away but holding onto him, 'we must make love one of these days.'

They locked eyes. He felt suddenly dizzy with promise. 'I may have a free half-hour next month.'

'Is that the month about to start, or the one after it?'

'Both.'

She kissed him again.

'Does this mean you're starting to trust me?'

She nodded. 'Plus I've been halibut for far too long.'

'Celibate,' he said softly.

She shook her head slightly. 'I was only joking. I'm not as stupid as you look.'

'Joking about the fish or about the sex?'

'Who mentioned sex? I was talking about love.'

She turned and entered the house without looking back.

A few days later Frank Galvin called. His old editor sounded tired. 'What's the matter, Frank,' he chided him, 'getting too tough for you?'

'Aaaah, things are hard, Miller. We've had the time and motion people in. I don't think they're looking to cut jobs, but we've been working that much harder trying to look efficient. Then we've been buggered by a computer virus as well, which doesn't help matters.'

'Ah, you'd love it down here, Frank. Four-day week, no pressure, time to work on your stories. They think a computer is someone who gets a train to work. I wouldn't say they're backward, Frank, but the last complaint I had from a reader was written with a quill.'

'If I didn't know better, I'd say you were enjoying life down there.'

'I am, Frank. I've kind of gotten used to it. I've found myself.'

'You've found yourself a woman.'

'There's that as well. How'd you know?'

'Something to do with the bright, chirpy voice.'

'And?'

'And Martin O'Hagan told me.'

'You've been checking up on me.'

'Of course.'

'And?'

'You've been getting some good reports. It looks like you've been behaving yourself, when you haven't been in the wars.'

'Bombed and beaten up. How come I never got as much as dust on my jacket in all the years I worked Belfast, Frank, yet I get bombed and beaten up in the space of a few days down here.'

'Luck, I guess. Maybe you'll bring it with you.'

'Meaning?'

'Meaning you've served your time down there. Time to come back up.'

'You mean I'm forgiven?'

'I wouldn't go that far. But we could do with you back. It's getting into bombing season again, Miller, they're back from their winter breaks itching to get into action. We could do with you here to help out. We're not short-staffed exactly, but half the young bucks we're getting in straight from university in England don't know a drogue bomb from an Oxford brogue. We need your experience. We need the Cycle of Violence out on the streets again.'

'Frank – uh, I don't quite know how to put this, but, well, I'm quite happy here.'

'Miller . . .'

'I'm serious. I know it sounds . . .'

'Miller . . . you're talking about Crossmaheart here. You look it up in the dictionary, it's defined as "a hole" . . .'

'I know what it's . . .'

'Even people who love Crossmaheart hate it . . . it's just full of . . . well . . . cunts . . .'

'I know, but . . .'

'Miller, it's the girl, isn't it?'

'No! Yes, of course it's the girl . . .'

'Miller, it's only forty miles away. You can visit. Bring her with you. Marry her. Just get your arse back up here.

You're a fine reporter, you've been through a rough time but you appear to have sorted yourself out, now come back up here before you die of underexposure.'

'You always were a bit of a sweet talker, Frank.'

'Balls.'

'I'll need to talk it over with Marie.'

'Balls. Your contract with the *Chronicle* expires on Friday. We expect you back here on Monday. The holiday's over.'

But he did need to talk it over with Marie, because he could not bear the thought of leaving her, even to travel such a short distance away. Forty miles, but a world apart. Perhaps it was what she needed as well, a new start in a new town, away from the sordid memories of Crossmaheart, away from a dead-end job in a dead-end town. She could move in with him, try writing her book, study, get a proper job. The possibilities were endless in Belfast, non-existent in Crossmaheart.

At lunch time he took the Cycle of Violence round to her lodgings. Mrs Hardy let him in. She looked radiant. She sat him down in the lounge, then popped upstairs. She returned in a few moments, slightly breathless, and crossed to Miller. She took his hand. 'It's great to have her back, you know, I can't thank you too much.'

Miller shrugged.

'She's just in the bath, she likes to take a long soak.'

'Uh, do you want me to wait down here or should I go up to her room?'

'No, sure you go on up. She said for you to go on up.'

Miller nodded and moved for the door.

'Oh – just one thing.' He stopped and turned. 'I was wondering if, now you're here, like, if you could do me a wee favour.'

'Sure.'

'Would you come up to Jamie's room with me for a second?'

'Sure.'

Mrs Hardy led the way up the stairs. On the first floor they both stopped for a moment and grinned at each other as the sound of Marie singing filtered out of the bathroom. She was attempting 'Teenage Kicks' by the Undertones.

'She's much happier, you know,' Mrs Hardy said quietly, then started up the next flight.

Jamie's room was unlocked. It was bright, airy, tidy. Mrs Hardy brought him into the room. She shook her head slightly. 'It seems like only yesterday . . .' she began, then stopped. 'Still, you don't want to hear an old woman rattle on about the dead.' She knelt down suddenly and reached beneath the bed. She pulled out a small cardboard box, which she lifted and placed on top of the quilt. 'I was wondering if you'd mind going through these.'

Miller crossed to the bed and peered into the box. There were about a dozen spiral-bound reporter's notebooks.

'I didn't like to throw them out in case they were important. I thought that seeing as you're in the same business you might be able to have a quick look through them. Marie and I couldn't make head nor tail of them, they're all in shorthand.'

'Yeah. Sure. Although I'm sure if there was anything to them the police would have taken them away.'

'Oh, the police didn't see them. Do you think I should have shown them? They said they wanted to see his room, but I tidied these away before they arrived. I don't like anyone to see any of the rooms all messed up. Word about something like that gets round town very quickly, you know. It's a small town and gossip travels faster than electricity. Jamie, God rest his soul, just wasn't the tidiest of people. I didn't think these would have been of any use. It just looked like gibberish to me.'

Miller lifted one of the notebooks and began flicking through it. 'You're probably right. Sure leave them with me. I'll have a wee bit of a nosey while her ladyship finishes in the bath, eh?'

'That would be awfully kind of you.'

'No trouble.'

Mrs Hardy left him to it. He sat on the bed, with the first notebook in his lap. He knew immediately that it was not Jamie's. The notebooks were old, their pages grey, the shorthand faded. There appeared to be no clue to the identity of their author, but there was little doubt that he was a reporter on the *Chronicle*. Each book was filled with court case after court case, the names and addresses written in long hand, the charges and evidence in shorthand. They all dated from 1977. It was a few moments before Miller made the connection, then he shivered.

He worked his way through the notebooks methodically, page by page, crime by crime, until he came to the seventh volume, and an account of the case against Michael Rainey, Tyrone Blair and Tom Callaghan. He read it falteringly, his finger following the aged shorthand slowly, his mind racing, impatient for more detail but frustrated by his own rustiness in the language. He had developed his own odd hybrid of speed scrawl and shorthand that defied anyone but himself to understand it. This reporter's account of the case was written in impeccable shorthand, but trying to decipher it was like learning to read all over again.

The more he worked at it, the easier it got, until by the end of the case his finger was easing through the closely set lines. As soon as he was finished he went back to the start again. There was a lot more detail than had appeared in the finished article. Much of it would have been cut for reasons of good taste.

A noise at the door caused him to look up sharply, his heart beating hard, his face red with embarrassment at the thought that Marie might have caught him reading of her own sexual abuse. But it wasn't her; an old woman, grey, stooped, vaguely familiar, stood there, peering in, an odd haunted look in her eyes.

'Have we met before?' Mrs Brady asked, hesitantly.

Miller crossed to the door. 'No,' he said crisply and pushed it shut.

He returned to the bed and began running his finger over the notebook again.

This time he found a line which he'd missed before. It was at the top of the page, squeezed into a right-hand corner; he'd presumed it was just a catchline or a hastily added comment, the shorthand was hurried, messy, not perfectly formed like the main body of work. He puzzled over it for a minute, thrown by the first marking. He realized suddenly that it wasn't a shorthand word at all, but a long-hand letter, J. The line read: J dealt with at a previous court.

J for juvenile.

The complete picture began to emerge, like an oil painting that has been cleaned for the first time in centuries revealing a hidden character. Rainey, Callaghan and Blair had not acted alone. There had been a fourth person in the car. A juvenile. A kid in the eyes of the law, but as capable of sexual activity as any man, yet shielded from public notoriety by the anonymity bestowed upon him by the legal system. Miller cursed silently. As far as he knew the *Chronicle* didn't cover, never had covered, juvenile courts because there was no point if they weren't allowed to name defendants. Only people's names sold papers.

And then he remembered, and then he hoped. He began flicking quickly through the remaining notebooks. The juvenile wouldn't have been named in the paper, but the chances were that his first appearance in court would have been in an adult court with the other three, from which he would have been remanded to appear at a juvenile court. There was a very strong possibility that such a meticulous reporter would have taken a note of his name and address anyway, even though denied the opportunity to publicize it. How Jamie had come by them at all didn't concern him. It didn't matter.

In the last notebook, very nearly the last page, Miller found what he was looking for. And a familiar name at that.

Marie, from the doorway, said: 'Fascinating, are they?'

Miller, surprised, dropped the notebook. 'Not really, no,' he said quickly, his voice shaky.

'You look like you've seen a ghost.'

He forced a laugh and shook his head. 'Things do have a habit of coming back to haunt you, don't they?'

'Meaning what?'

'Nothing. A cryptic meaningless reply. Lunch?'

'With a BAD girl?'

'The baddest.'

'Okay.'

He put the notebooks back in the box. 'You can tell Mrs Hardy to throw that lot out. They're of no value to anyone.'

But he knew that they were. He knew that he should ignore them. Get back to Belfast. Take Marie with him. Start all over again. There was no need for confrontation, not after all the deaths. No need for it at all.

13

They sat kissing in Riley's. Miller knew this was the night they had been building up to all week, perhaps even since their first meeting. They had abandoned the negligible intimacy of sleeping together as brother and sister; now she slept alone, but their goodnights, each and every night, on the steps of her lodgings, grew steadily more intimate, more passionate, until they had explored each other's bodies as thoroughly as two people can in public without being arrested.

Even Pearse Riley knew something was up. 'You two look like you've just come out of the closet,' he said cheerfully, wiping at their corner table.

'I wouldn't put it quite in those terms,' Miller said, disengaging momentarily.

This night they both had work to do, Marie her first night back in the bar, Miller putting the paper to bed. They would meet back in the bar later. Nothing had been said about their plans for after that, but Miller knew what he was going to do. There would be no fond farewells on those cold steps, instead he would walk her on to his flat, he would take her upstairs and he would make love to her, with her, for her. Then he would ask her to move to Belfast with him. It would be a momentous night, the night of his life, and, he hoped, he prayed, of hers.

He raced home, bathed, changed, cycled back to work. Along the way he found himself talking to his father. His dad looked understandably gaunt. He laboured inexpertly

at the big old butcher's bike; Miller slowed the easy glide
of the Cycle of Violence, until they were level.

'Nice girl,' his dad said, his voice dry-sandy.

'I know.'

'Nice of you to set fire to her.'

'I didn't set fire to her.'

'As near as damn it.'

'Sure, Dad, you know all about it.'

'I know I do. And about the other guy.'

'What other guy?'

'Son, I'm not a fool. I keep an eye out for you. The other
guy.'

'The penile delinquent.'

'The very same. Leave him alone, son.'

'I have no plans to do anything.'

'I know you. Leave it alone. Leave well alone.'

'It's not well.'

'You know what I mean.'

'Whatever you say.'

'I do care about you, you know.'

'I know.'

'You know what?'

Miller turned to his right. An elderly man was perched on
the kerb, ready to cross the road. He was about the same size
as his father and had a similar angular face, but he clearly
still enjoyed the benefits of breathing and had none of the
giveaway signs of recently having been cremated. Miller, feet
on either side of the Cycle of Violence, said, 'What?'

'You know what?'

'What?'

'You know what?'

'I don't follow.'

The old guy shook his head. 'You're nuts, you are. Or
pissed. Or both.'

'Maybe.'

Miller pushed the bike forward.

'You shouldn't drink and drive, sonny.'

'I'm not driving. I'm not drinking.'

'Sure.'

Miller shook himself out of his trance. Thursdays were always the longest days at work. Everyone was in from nine until five, then from six until the paper was finished, generally around eleven. It wasn't hard, exactly. Miller was used to much worse in Belfast, but it was long when you were restless and in love. Normally Miller motored through his work, keen to be off, but it never did much good; he couldn't go until the paper was finished, and no one else ever showed the same enthusiasm. Enthusiasm interfered with overtime payments. This night Miller idled.

Anne and Helen passed the evening finishing off court and council reports before moving on to some proofreading. Once they were finished they went on home, leaving Martin O'Hagan and Miller to oversee the make-up of pages in the printworks.

Miller listened in to the ten o'clock news to see if there were any last-minute stories of any relevance. There had been a couple of bombs in Belfast, but nothing likely to affect anyone in Crossmaheart. They liked their bombs home-grown. With the front and last page finished, the printers left by the rear entrance. They would return early in the morning to begin printing the completed paper. O'Hagan and Miller returned to the newsroom. O'Hagan produced a half-bottle of whiskey and two mugs from a drawer in his desk.

'Will you join me, Miller, in a drink?' he asked.

'What's the occasion?'

'Well, to celebrate . . . not celebrate, I mean, mark this as your final late night on the *Chronicle* . . . uh, you have been talking to Belfast, haven't you?'

'I've been talking to them, sure. But nothing's decided.'

'Oh.'

'You've heard otherwise?'

O'Hagan handed Miller a mug, then started to pour. 'Well, put it this way, your replacement arrives on Monday.'

Miller raised his hand to stop the flow halfway up. 'Nice to be consulted.'

They chinked cups. 'You know what they're like up there. God, they sent you here in the first place, didn't they?'

'There's that.'

'I thought you'd be glad to get out of here anyway. I mean, it can't compare to all the exposure you get up there, can it?'

'You get used to exposure. I was kind of getting used to things down here.'

'Yeah, like you get used to piles. Still, if it's any compensation, we were . . . well, we were starting to warm to you a bit. We take our time down here, you might have noticed.'

'Perfectly understandable, considering that I came here by way of punishment. And youse having lost a reporter under mysterious circumstances. It must be hard. I mean, the poor bugger was cut into little pieces.'

'Our suffering was negligible.'

'What about Jamie's?'

'Who can say?'

'Who indeed.'

O'Hagan sat back at his desk, reclined in his executive chair. He stretched his arms out behind him, yawning. 'Ah, well, another hard week over, just about,' he said.

Miller perched himself on the edge of his editor's desk. 'Did I tell you,' he began, 'that Jamie's landlady asked me to go through some of his belongings?'

O'Hagan lifted his mug and took a little sip, his eyes carefully watching Miller over the rim. 'Anything interesting?' he said into the mug.

'Ah, this and that, y'know. Some stuff that wasn't his actually. A lot of old notebooks.'

'What, like just notes, or reporter's books?'

'Reporter's. I presume they came from someone here originally. They go back to 1977 most of them.'

'Do you know whose they were?'

'No idea, I'm afraid. Well before your time here, anyway, I'll warrant.'

'Well before.'

'What age would you have been back then anyway?'

'When, '77?' O'Hagan shrugged. 'Fifteen, sixteen, I suppose.'

Miller nodded. 'A juvenile.'

O'Hagan lifted the bottle of whiskey again and inclined it towards Miller. 'More tea, vicar?'

Miller reached forward. O'Hagan clipped the bottle sideways sharply, catching Miller on the side of the head, and he toppled off the desk. But he wasn't out. The blow had been glancing and his skull was thick. He had an arm out before him to stop his head bouncing off the floor and he managed to raise a foot before O'Hagan landed on top of him. Dizzy, stars everywhere, he crashed his hand upwards, his fingers tightly clasped around the handle of the mug, as O'Hagan came down. The mug shattered in the editor's face and with a scream he rolled off. Miller was up, woozy, in a second. He gripped the side of the desk, steadied himself and then launched a kick at O'Hagan's midriff as he struggled to raise himself, one hand clawing at his bloody face. O'Hagan groaned once, then collapsed.

Miller left him there for a minute while he ran to the printworks. He returned with a length of packing tape. O'Hagan lay where he'd left him. His eyes were open and he was dabbing at a lengthy gash on his cheek, but he showed no inclination to move, or to try to escape. Miller got his hands on the lapels of O'Hagan's jacket and yanked

221

him up and into his big executive chair. Then he bound him securely. He didn't resist. When he was finished Miller sat back again on the edge of the desk and felt the side of his head. It was swelling up, but there was no blood. He didn't know if that was a good sign or not. He retrieved the whiskey bottle from the floor and took a mouthful.

Miller splashed a little of the whiskey onto O'Hagan's face. His head winced back. 'There was no need for that,' the editor mewed.

Miller leant forward. 'It was medicinal. It was meant to sting.' Then he punched him flush on the nose. 'That, on the other hand, was meant to hurt.'

A fresh trickle of blood appeared from the left nostril. then dripped onto his tongue. 'You're a bloody sadist.'

'A fine one to talk. One more word I'll take your trousers down and play with your balls.'

O'Hagan's eyes widened in horror.

'Don't like the sound of that, do you?'

Miller reached across and grabbed O'Hagan's crotch.

'Jesus Christ.'

'You're all man, aren't you? You're the sort would rather die than be touched by another man, aren't you? That would be a good revenge wouldn't it, O'Hagan? The penalty you pay for interfering with a wee girl is having a man ride you. How do you feel about that?' Miller squeezed a little harder, then pushed his face into O'Hagan's. 'You're getting tense. I hope you're not going to stiffen up.'

Abruptly Miller let go and sat back. 'I didn't know you existed until the other day, you know?'

O'Hagan shook his head in confusion.

'I mean, obviously you existed as Martin O'Hagan, captain my captain, the ignorant editor. But not Martin O'Hagan, juvenile sex offender. Do you know what concerns me most about it, Martin? Not the fact that you did it, but that you got away with it.'

'I didn't get away with anything, I . . .'

'Ah, now, Martin, you more than most know what the punishment for this type of offence is. It's not the few months you get to spend in a borstal. You might as well be in Butlin's or the army. It's the publicity. It's the people pointing at you in the street, going, "There he is, the filthy pervert." It's never being trusted to babysit. It's parents not allowing you near their daughters. You escaped it all by virtue of the fact that you were born a few years after the others, qualified for juvenile court rather than the magistrates'. You've lived a perfectly normal life, haven't you, Martin? Look at you, a pillar of the community, editor of the local paper. You wouldn't have gotten that far if everyone had known your past, would you?'

'It was a long time ago. I was very young. You have to let bygones be bygones.'

'Do you think she was able to, Martin?'

O'Hagan shook his head. 'No. I know she wasn't. There was nothing I could do about that.'

'Bygones, Martin? Was it a case of bygones? You make it sound like a falling-out amongst old friends.'

'I'm sorry. I don't mean to.'

'Of course, you weren't the only one to thrive, were you? Michael Rainey did well for himself, didn't he? Studied for the ministry.'

'We didn't keep in touch.'

'And Curly Bap did well in his chosen sphere, not so much study involved of course. Only poor Tom Callaghan. Struck down blind, ill. The only one really punished for it, eh?'

'They're all dead.'

'Yes, they are. Dead after fruitful lives, or at least their own interpretation of fruitful lives. Rainey for God, Curly Bap for God and Ireland, Callaghan for God and good deeds.'

223

'And now you're going to kill me, like you killed the others.'

'Mmmm. This is generally a misconception, but at least it shows you've been following this pilgrim's progress. And never let on. However, I'll let it lie for the meantime. Do you think you deserve to die, Martin?'

O'Hagan nodded slowly. 'Probably,' he said.

'For your filthy assault?'

O'Hagan shook his head. 'I've been punished for that.'

Miller tutted. 'What then?'

'You know.'

'What then?'

'Christ.'

'For Christ?'

'No, fuck you. You know fine well what for.'

'Speak to me then.'

'For Jamie.'

A tear appeared and slowly descended his cheek until it splashed into the gash left by the mug.

'Ah, now,' said Miller, 'we're getting somewhere. Tell me about Jamie.'

'What can I say? I'm sorry. I deserve to die for it. Kill me.'

'Come on now, give me the details, Marty. What'd you do to him? Howja chop him up?'

'Oh, for Christ's sake, stop it. Who could do that? Who the fuck could do that?'

'Well, you did.'

'It wasn't like that. Jesus, if only . . . what's the point?'

'You tell me, Marty. Howja do it?'

'You're enjoying this, aren't you?'

'Better than workin', Marty.'

'You are a sadist.'

'I'm not, Marty. And if you say that again I'll set fire to your trousers.'

'How can you laugh?'

'Who's laughing? I'm grinning with pleasure. However, less of my pleasure, more of yours. How'd you cut Jamie up?'

'I didn't! Jesus Christ. Look. He came at me out of the blue. One night we were working late. Just like this. I mean I'd forgotten all about the girl and all that business – no, I mean, I hadn't forgotten, I didn't mean that, but I'd ignored it for so long. And then out of the blue Jamie started accusing me of all these things. That wee mad bitch Marie had put him up to it, started him looking into it all. I mean, he was angry, upset, but he wasn't going around killing people the way you have. He said he couldn't work with me any more. He was going to resign. He was going to tell people. I tried to reason with him, but he wouldn't listen. He was going out the door, I pulled him back, he hit me, I hit him, we started fighting, he was getting the better of me, he lifted a paperweight, started cracking me about the head with it, I grabbed the first thing came to hand, happened to be a scalpel, struck out blindly a couple of times, then he rolled over. I mean, Jesus, what could I do? I was just protecting myself. I . . . Jesus, there was just blood everywhere, pumping out of him. I hit a vein. An artery. I don't know. Whichever one kills you. It was just pishing out of him. I . . . once I realized what had happened I tried to save him . . . I gave him the kiss of life . . . I pressed his heart, y'know pumped it . . . but he just faded away . . .'

'You didn't think maybe of calling a doctor or something, Marty?'

'There wasn't time, it was only a minute, only a minute at the most, what could I do? He just died there in front of me. I was panicked. I was . . . my head was revolving . . . you ever been whacked round the head with a paperweight?'

'So what'd you do then, Marty? You had the scalpel still?

225

You cut him up with that? Must have taken you all bloody night.'

'Jesus, no . . . don't be bloody stupid . . . I don't know. I was there for hours . . . just looking at him . . . talking to him . . . apologizing . . .'

'He must have appreciated that.'

'Apologizing. Apologizing to him, to God, to my family . . . I knew everything was ruined . . . but I had to do something. Who would believe it was self-defence?'

'Man's laughter, Marty. God giggling at you.'

'I knew I had to hide the body but I didn't even have the car with me that night . . .'

'And you couldn't order a taxi.'

'So I got some bin bags, cut them up, wrapped him up in them, got him out into the yard and loaded him into the big trade waste bin. It was just somewhere to put him, y'know? I was going to come back later with the car and bury him somewhere properly. I didn't mean for him to end up like that. I went back into the office and started cleaning up, I mean there was blood everywhere. The carpet wasn't too bad . . . you know what it's like, those carpet tiles come up easy enough and there's a pile of spares in the store, so I got rid of those . . . cleaning, cleaning, blood on everything, by the time I was finished it wasn't that far off seven, and that's when Rosie comes in to do the cleaning . . . it just didn't leave me time to shift him . . . and then the fuckin' binmen changed their schedule. They weren't meant to come that morning. They always come on Wednesdays. I don't know, it was the bank holiday or the Queen's birthday or they just did it for bloody badness, but they weren't meant to come. And that's how he got . . . cut up. Just went into the back of the lorry. It wasn't meant to be like that. None of it was meant to be, but that especially, I wouldn't wish it on anyone.'

'I don't see that it makes much difference if he was dead.'

'It does.'

'You're sure he was dead?'

'Of course I'm sure!'

'Only asking, Marty. As a matter of fact I believe you.'

'And that's it. That's all of it, God help me.'

'You think he will?'

'Help me into heaven, help me into hell, yeah, sure.' O'Hagan shook his head ruefully. His face was white, his eyes a sickly yellow. He'd aged ten years in the course of ten minutes. 'What happens now, Miller, they find me dead here in the morning?'

Miller rose from the desk and reached for the bottle of whiskey. There wasn't much left. He took a mouthful, then held it to O'Hagan's lips. He took a big swallow, half-spluttered with it. 'What is tomorrow, Marty, anyway?' Miller asked. 'Wednesday, is it?' O'Hagan nodded. 'There's a bin collection, isn't there?'

Miller was feeling quite pleased with himself. He had a taped confession of Martin O'Hagan over the killing of Jamie Milburn, and he had only had to resort to the minimum of provoked violence to obtain it. Leaving O'Hagan to stew, he returned to the print room and phoned Constable Craig about the next step. Except he didn't know Craig's name.

'I'd like to speak to . . .'

'Yes, sir?'

'Ahm . . .'

'Sir?'

'I'm sorry. I've forgotten his name. Uh, tall bloke, green uniform with a moustache.'

'The uniform has a moustache?'

'No, the . . .'

'Sir, that description fits us all. It goes with the job.'

'Well, he's kind of . . .' As if it would make any

difference, he lowered his voice. 'Does the name Deep Throat mean anything to you?'

'Deep Throat? Sure, hold on.'

In a moment Craig's voice barked down the phone. 'What?'

'Uh, Deep Throat?'

'Yes.'

'They actually know you as Deep Throat at the station?'

'Who is this?'

'Sorry. Miller. The journalist . . . We . . .'

'Right. Miller. How are you?'

'Fine. They actually know you as Deep Throat?'

'It's just a nickname.'

'Weird.'

'It doesn't worry me. Does it worry you?'

'No. No. Not at all.'

'So what can I do for you?'

'I've completed the picture.'

'Which picture?'

'The one we were talking about last week. The fourth man.'

'Ah. Right. Told you it wasn't hard.'

'It wasn't. Martin O'Hagan, right?'

'Right. Is there any point in me asking after his health?'

'Of course. He's here with me now.'

'Of his own accord?'

'He's tied to a chair.'

'So what are you going to do with him?'

'I was going to bring him in.'

'Where? Here? What on earth for?'

'So you can charge him with the murder of Jamie Milburn.'

'You have evidence?'

'I have a taped confession.'

'Witnessed?'

228

'What?'

'Was anybody else present when you made it?'

'He was.'

'I mean anyone else.'

'No.'

'He volunteered it?'

'After I tied him up and hit him.'

'And you expect that to stand up in court?'

'No, of course not, but if he can confess to me, he can confess to you.'

'What, after his solicitors get hold of him? Are you crazy? He wouldn't open his mouth. There's no point in us getting involved, Miller. You haven't involved us up to the present, what's the point in getting started now? You know what to do. I led you to the man, now you do the business.'

'Listen, all I want . . .'

'Do the business, Miller, it's got nothing to do with me.'

'You're the law . . .'

'No, Miller, not down here. We're the little green men. You're the law as much as anyone. You're certainly the only man handing out punishments that fit the crime.'

'Fuck it,' Miller snapped, 'I'm not killing him. I'm bringing him in, accept him or not, it's all I can do.' He slammed the receiver down.

The blood had congealed in an ugly, jagged mess on O'Hagan's cheek. There was a haunted, death-row look in his eyes. Miller gave him a reassuring smile.

'I wish you'd get this over with,' O'Hagan said.

'I don't know you at all, do I?' Miller said, perching himself again on the side of the desk. 'I've never been to your house, met your wife, played with your children. I only know you as an editor, and a murderer and child sex abuser.'

'I'd rather you just killed me straight out, rather than start philosophizing.'

'How do you tell your wife something like that, mmmm? I mean, does she know about your conviction?'

O'Hagan shook his head.

'What about Jamie?'

'Of course not.'

'Why of course? Husbands are meant to tell their wives everything. Of course I wouldn't know, never having been married, whether it actually turns out like that. I do plan to get married. Hopefully to Marie.'

'And what a lovely couple you'll be!' O'Hagan flashed bitterly. 'You the murderer, she the master, mistress architect. What charming children you'll produce. I can't imagine what sort of small talk you'll have.'

Miller tutted. 'You're not arguing a very good case for your survival, Marty.'

'I've long given up on that. I don't think it's right, I don't think it's fair. I think I'm being over-punished for something I did wrong. But I'm resigned to it. I just don't understand. What you've been doing, killing all these people, is in revenge for something that happened years ago. It should have been a closed chapter, a closed, unsavoury chapter if you want, but it was so long ago. I took my punishment. What got into her, Miller? First Jamie was her boyfriend, and she got him looking into it. Then you became her boyfriend, and she has you investigating.'

'She doesn't have me doing anything, Marty. It's all off my own bat.'

'Doubtless Jamie would have said the same.'

'Well, we can't know that, can we?'

'No. I know.'

'So?'

'So, it still amounts to the same. The both of you on the trail of this age-old case − a case with no point to it, everyone involved took their punishment, paid their debt.'

'Marie is still being punished.'

'Bollocks.'

Miller reached across and slapped O'Hagan across his injured face. He let out a yelp and tried to raise his trapped hands to the wound. Blood began to drip again.

'You know nothing about anything, Marty. How can you get to the exalted position of editor without knowing at least a little about how people are affected by the sort of experience Marie went through?'

'How was she affected? Go on, tell me that. How?'

'I can't believe I'm hearing this.'

'Okay, a little mental anguish, that's bound to happen, I'm sorry about that. But why for fifteen years?'

'Marty, if you'd been interfered with when you were a boy, you not think you'd still be suffering fifteen years on?'

'But I wasn't.'

'But Marie was.'

'No, she wasn't.'

'Marty, what the fuck are you talking about?'

'What the fuck are you talking about?'

'I'm talking about Marie and what you did to her.'

'I never touched her.'

'You just said you took your punishment for doing it, Marty. You're talking shite.'

'Miller, I think we're talking at cross purposes here. I swear to God I never touched Marie. Michael Rainey never touched her. Tyrone Blair never touched her. Tom Callaghan never laid a finger on her. If you're into all this because we're supposed to have touched your girlfriend, forget it.'

Miller shook his head in disbelief. 'To tell you the truth, Marty, I've no intention of killing you. So you can stop this crazy wriggling to get out of it. Relax, don't do it.'

'I'm serious.'

'Yeah, yeah.'

'Check it out, Miller. I'm sure you have your sources. It wasn't Marie we touched. It was her sister. She died years ago. She killed herself. That's what we've had on our conscience all this time. Something we can do nothing about.'

14

'You are looking particularly lovely tonight,' Miller said, taking Marie's hand and leading her from the raucous after-hours singing in Riley's into the cool black of a street-lamp-smashed Crossmaheart night.

'And you're turning into a smarmy bastard.' Marie reached up and kissed him as they walked. Her arm slipped around his back and she squeezed his side. 'And you feel tense. Hard night?'

'And it's going to get harder.'

'Meaning what?'

'Nothing.'

'Meaning what?'

'Nothing. Just a little bit of innocent sexual innuendo.'

'Can you have innocent innuendo?'

'Good point.'

They smooched on and off down the road to Miller's flat. Marie stopped at the steps up to the front door. Miller nudged her up the first one. She barely resisted.

'What're you up to?' she asked.

'I thought you might appreciate some supper.'

'Supper?'

'Banana on toast. Beans on toast. Cornflakes. Whatever takes your fancy.'

'I thought sex might be on the menu.'

'You don't beat about the bush.'

'I hope you will.'

He smiled. 'That is guilty sexual innuendo.'

'Bugger innuendo.'

'On a first date?'

'And don't get literal.'

'Whatever you say, honey.'

'And stay off the smarm pills.'

Miller stopped her and kissed her properly. 'This is going to be a good night,' he said softly.

'I know,' she said.

They were just entering the apartment building when a car, a blue Ford Escort parked about thirty yards further up, flashed its lights. There was a dark figure behind the steering wheel, the glow of a cigarette. The driver's window was rolled down. An arm hung out of the window, the fingers tapping lightly against the door. As Miller peered up, the drumming ceased and the fingers formed into a little fist which was shaken in his direction. It didn't feel particularly threatening. He took out his keys and handed them to Marie.

'Someone to see me, I think. Away on in, I'll be with you in a mo.'

Marie hesitated. 'Who is it?'

'Just a friend. Don't worry. I'll only be a minute.'

She clutched suddenly at his lapels. 'Don't,' she said, 'people have a habit of disappearing on me.'

Miller eased her hands off. 'Look who's talking?' He smiled and kissed her.

She looked sheepish. 'That's not fair.'

'All's fair in love and war.'

'Okay. I'll trust you. Be quick. Ooze back to me as soon as you can.'

She turned and took the steps two at a time. Miller walked up to the car, peered in the driver's window, nodded and went round to the passenger door and climbed in.

'I was getting worried when you didn't turn up at the station with O'Hagan,' Constable Craig said.

'You told me not to bring him in.'

'I didn't expect you to pay any attention to that.'

Miller shrugged.

'So you took my advice?' the policeman asked.

'No, I didn't kill him.'

'What then?'

'He took the gentleman's way out.'

'Jesus. How'd you persuade him to do that? You are one sweet talker, Miller, I'll give you that.'

'I don't think you quite follow. I was bringing him down to the station. I had him tied up and all, but after what he'd been through, confessing everything, he was dying to use the toilet. I let him loose in the gents and gave him a bit of privacy. He broke a window and did a runner. God knows where he is now.'

'You want me to go after him?'

'That's up to you. It's your job.'

'But up till now you've made it yours.'

'By accident.'

'Yeah. Sure.'

'Marie wasn't assaulted at all. It was her sister. You knew that, didn't you?'

'Sure.'

'Why didn't you say?'

'I thought you knew. Besides, what difference does it make? You got rid of a lot of scum.'

'It makes a big difference.'

'Does it?'

'Of course it does. The only reason those people died is because of Marie and what happened to her. If nothing happened to her, why did they need to die?'

'You think nothing happened to her, Miller? You know her. I know her. A lot of people know her. You think she's unaffected by all of this? You think she's a reasonable, well-balanced person?'

'She has her moments.'

'Miller, they may not have fucked her up physically, but they fucked her up mentally. You can't deny that. They deserved their punishment.'

Miller opened the door and stepped out. 'Either way,' he said, leaning back in, 'that's me finished with it.'

'You think it's finished with her, Miller?'

He closed the door and turned back towards the flat. He knew it would never be finished with her. It would never be finished with him. But some things you have to learn to live with.

They'd reached the underwear stage. He laid her down on top of the bed. 'Can we get under the quilt?' she asked.

'Sure.'

They kissed for a long time before he tried moving his hands, first behind her back, she lifting slightly to allow him access. His greedy but civilized fingers slipped under her bra strap and then circled round to the front until he cupped her left breast in his hand. He arched his hand then so that the breast popped out from beneath the cup, repeated the trick with his other hand, so that the bra hung above her chest like a discarded cocoon. She reached back herself and unclipped it, and as she pushed it out and under the edge of the quilt he moved his mouth to her left breast, enveloping the small, soft nipple with his lips as if it was the smallest, finest grape on a perfect vine. A little squeeze, a little hiss of breath, were all that indicated her pleasure. His lips still clamped around her nipple, he moved one hand along her spine until it slipped inside her knickers; he followed the outline of her cheeks, moving his hand in a steady, reassuring circle, squeezing lightly. He moved it cautiously to the front, his fingers combing her pubic hair playfully, then down into the . . .

'Stop.' Breathless. Frightened. Her hand on his, pressure, but not decisive.

'Shhhhhhh . . .'

'Please . . .'

'Trust me . . .'

'Miller . . .'

'Trust me.'

A finger entered her.

'It's okay,' he whispered.

She held him tighter. He penetrated deeper; her nails cut into his back; he slipped his finger out and up to her clitoris . . .

'I love you,' he said.

'I love you back.'

She bit into his neck.

He moved her knickers down. She kicked them off. He moved on top of her. She guided him in. Her first touch sent a shiver of delight through him. He fought to remain in control. She came first, quickly, a shallow, almost imperceptible orgasm which shook her gently against him, soft waves on a warm holiday beach, unthreatening, unpolluted, steady, dependable, but each one slightly different, seeming to go on for ever. Then he came, loud, a convict released.

He remained inside her. 'That was perfect,' she said. 'That was perfect,' he said. And they laughed and hugged. 'You're the best hugger in the world,' she said.

You can satiate lust, you can't satiate love, he thought as they lay stickily in the dark, she under his arm, her head on his chest. You're getting profound in your old age, he thought. She couldn't see it, but there was a big smile on his face. She had said it: perfection. He couldn't imagine anything better, ever. No Nobel Prize for Literature. No singing a duet with Smokey Robinson. Not even having his father back so that he could tell him everything he should have.

And yet. 'Tell me about your sister,' he whispered.

Her breathing had been steady for a while and he thought she might have drifted off, but then he felt her eyelashes fluttering against his chest and knew that she was awake.

'What was she called?'

Marie shifted uneasily, murmured fake-sleepily, 'Erin.'

'What happened to her?'

'She died.'

'How did she die, Marie?'

'I need to sleep.'

'Marie, tell me.'

'She died. Does it matter?'

He knew he was spoiling the moment. He knew he would not have asked if they had not already made love. He would blame it on his hormones, if pressed. He knew that was inexcusable, but he didn't claim to carry the flag for modern man. He didn't love her any the less now that he had loved her, but they were unified now, one nation under the sun, and now that the boundaries were set he could look at the internal conflicts without endangering the whole.

'It matters,' he said.

Marie pulled away from him. She reached across and switched on the bedside lamp and for a few moments they both rubbed at their eyes. He drank in her nakedness; she flashed her eyes shyly at him and pulled the quilt up around her, revealing his flaccid penis; he left it out in the open; perhaps the promise of it would coax her into revelation; perhaps it would scare her off as it lay drained of power, a slug on a bed of wrinkled marshmallows.

'I loved her.'

'I'm sure you did.'

'She killed herself. She hung herself.'

'Why?'

'Because. Because of what happened. Those men. In the car.'

'It wasn't you in the car, was it?'

Marie shook her head sadly. 'It should have been.'

'But it wasn't you.'

'No. It was Erin. They got her but they wanted me.'

'Tell me what happened, Marie. It's important.'

'Why is it important? What difference does it make?'

'Because I need to know about you. I'm in love with you. We can't have any secrets. I thought it was you that was assaulted.'

'I was '85 I . . . fuck it, Miller . . .'

'Tell me . . .'

'You'll hate me. I don't want you to hate me.'

'I won't hate you.'

'You say that now.'

'I won't hate you.'

Marie slumped on the bed beside him, lay with her head buried in his shoulder. She turned her mouth up to him once, kissed him on the cheek and then returned to a mumbling darkness. 'We were at the Girls' Brigade, me and Erin. She was a year younger than me, we weren't twins or anything, but we looked a lot alike. I was . . . more advanced . . . I'd started messing about . . . you know . . . with boys . . . doing things . . . far more than I should have . . . I thought it was just good fun . . . looking back on it now I must have had a bit of a reputation for it . . . these boys, older boys, had been hanging around outside for weeks . . . I'd been flirting with them a bit . . . kissing a bit, y'know . . . Jesus, it seems so whorey now . . . but then you were just glad that someone was interested . . . that night I was kept behind for slabbering at someone, one of the officers, and Erin left without me . . . in the rain, in the dark, they took her for me . . . Jesus . . . there was only a year between us, but it might as well have been five . . . she was so . . . innocent . . . and they took her and they destroyed her . . . she was just . . . white . . . when she got home . . . just

239

stunned and sick and . . . I washed her . . . she was just so different after it . . . all the life had gone out of her . . . and then one day it really did. She hung herself. It seems funny now, I mean, I didn't think she could tie, and there she was, proved me wrong with a big hangman's knot, swinging off the bar of the swing in the back garden . . . and all because I'd been letting people touch me . . .'

He hugged her to him. 'You can't blame yourself, Marie . . .'

'Of course I can. Who else?'

'You can't! You think anyone who engages in a bit of innocent foreplay is saying, sure, okay, rape me?'

'But Erin hadn't even kissed a boy . . .'

'That's not your fault and it's not her fault. It's their fault. Them ones in the car. No one has a right to do that. They deserved to die.'

'They do.'

She patted nervously at his chest. 'It gets worse,' she said.

'How?'

'Not worse, different. Worse for me.'

'Tell me.'

'Well, how do you think something like that would affect me? Your sister assaulted. How should that affect me, my sex life?'

'I know how it affected you. But it's okay now, isn't it? You trust me, don't you? We made love, didn't we?'

'You would think that, wouldn't you, that it would put me off? It didn't though. Not then. I got worse. I went for it, sex, in a big way. What do you think of that?'

'It's okay. People react like that sometimes. In the opposite way.'

'Stop being so bloody understanding!' she snapped suddenly, slapping his chest.

'I'm not . . .'

'Call me a whore, call me . . .'

'Marie!' He grabbed at her, held her close, waiting for her to cry. She didn't. She was rigid against him. Breathing deep. The hiss of her breath might have been the cogs of her mind racing, a thousand jumbled thoughts fighting for the use of her tongue. She started several sentences, then lapsed into silence. After a couple of minutes her body began to relax and she pressed herself against him.

'I don't know why . . . I wasn't enjoying it . . . and then after a few months I stopped . . . I knew it was wrong . . . stopped completely . . . but then I found I was pregnant . . . I mean, I thought I was just getting fat, I thought I'd give birth to a Twix or something . . . I knew Mum and Dad wouldn't be pleased . . . but I thought they'd come round . . . thought they'd maybe have a replacement for Erin . . . you think these stupid bloody thoughts . . . but Dad . . . when I think now, he hadn't reacted at all to her dying . . . and then it all came out, took it out on me . . . I remember a sunny day, a lovely day, all warm and dusty inside the house, and I told them and Dad flew off the handle, called me all the names of the day. I shouted back, he slapped me, I slapped back and that really sent him off. He kicked me. Imagine that. Kicking your own pregnant daughter in the stomach. He was never a violent man. Never hit us as kids. He did it because of Erin. And Erin died because of me. So I deserved to get kicked and lose my child. What goes around comes around, eh?'

'You didn't deserve any of it.'

'So you say.' She laughed, a sad funereal laugh of resignation. 'It would make a good soap opera, wouldn't it?'

'If you were sick.'

'I am sick.'

'I didn't mean it like that.'

'I know. I'm sorry. But you understand . . . don't you? Why I want to have a child?'

'I understand . . . I don't know if I understand how . . .'

241

'We've done . . . how.'

'I mean, with your . . .'

'Problem.'

'Medication.'

'It amounts to the same, doesn't it?'

'Maybe. But you know what I mean.'

'You mean you don't want a nut on your hands. That's what you mean. That's what you're scared of . . .'

'I didn't say . . .'

'I know what you said . . . but what's the craziest thing I've done without the drugs . . . I mean, Miller, you're going to write me off 'cause I went shopping in Dublin . . .'

'I'm not going to write you off . . . I just want you to be well . . .'

'Am I well now?'

'Yes . . . of course . . . but you're taking your . . .'

'Am I?'

'I took it that . . .'

'You took it wrong.'

'Marie . . .'

'Aren't I okay?'

'You seem . . .'

'Aren't I okay?'

'Okay, you're fine . . . but you have them for a reason Marie, they're not just sweeties . . .'

'But I've been taking them like sweeties . . . little rewards to keep me on the ground . . . but I don't need rewards any more, Miller. I need to be myself whatever that is, not whatever I become when I take pills . . .'

'But the pills keep you yourself . . .'

'Do they?'

Miller shook his head. 'I don't know.'

'Do I seem any different?'

'No.'

'So no pills, and the same old me.'

'I suppose.'

'Don't suppose. The truth.'

'Okay, you're you, but . . .'

'Stop fussin' . . . let's make babies, Miller.'

That stopped him. He couldn't help the smile. 'Aren't we getting a bit ahead of ourselves? I haven't asked you to move to Belfast with me yet.'

'Are you going to ask me?'

'I had planned to.'

'When?'

'Tonight. After we'd finished making love.'

'Have we finished making love?'

'No.'

She turned her face up to him and they kissed.

Marie was gone when he woke. Not long gone. Her side of the bed was still warm. Miller rested his hand on the sheet. He couldn't help smiling. He dozed off again.

The second time he woke his hand brushed against her pillow and he felt something . . . paper . . . he blinked in the gloom, then reached for the bedside lamp. A single sheet of paper, a note from Marie in a curiously child-like script. 'That was absolute perfection, all my love, Marie.'

His smile grew wider. He beat the bed with his hand. 'Yes! Yes! Yes!' he shouted aloud.

Things were going to be okay. They had reached an as-near-as-damn-it perfection in bed, considering it was their first time – so much more to try, to experiment, to learn – and they had all the time in the world ahead of them. Marie would work out her notice at the bar, maybe a week, maybe two, then she'd follow him to Belfast. They'd live in his dad's house for a while, but they'd sell it as quickly as possible and buy something of their own, something new. She would get a job, maybe one in a pub, maybe not, and do some serious thinking about her book. Until she got pregnant. Then they'd think about getting married. Of course it was all of a rush; he'd hardly known her more than a few weeks. Everyone else might write it off as a bereaved man's version of a holiday romance, but he knew just as well that his heart and mind were of the same opinion: that this was love, love of mind and body, this was a romance of the soul, that he had to go for it, because it would never come his way again.

As he washed he spoke to his reflection in the bathroom mirror. 'Absolute perfection,' he said, then drummed out an approximation of a one-sticked drum solo with his toothbrush on the rim of the basin.

He danced across the kitchen, yanked open the fridge and surveyed the contents. He removed bacon and eggs. Snipped off three sausages from a string. 'This is a day for the frying pan,' he told the kettle. 'You buggers don't get grilled today. Let's celebrate! Out with healthy living! Let's live on the edge!'

He set to frying it all up. Crackle and frizzle, crackle and frizzle. Twice he had to leap back from the pan as hot bubbles of fat spat at him. He took a slice of bread and dipped it into the fat. 'Yum yum yum,' he said.

Out came a plate. On went the food. 'Look at that, didn't even break the egg,' he told the kettle.

Copious amounts of salt. A good squirt of tomato sauce. And then the first mouthful. A little of everything squelched onto the fork. He chewed six times, swallowed. After a moment of rumination he said, 'Absolute perfection.'

Later, when he was washing up, he said 'Absolute perfection' twenty-three times in a row. He said it in a Scottish accent. He said it as a Texan. He said it in Welsh, but it came out Pakistani. He tried Chinese, then changed so subtly to Japanese that even he couldn't tell the difference. Then he said it as Marie would have, husky, panting in his ear. But her voice came to him not from the night before, but from a night of drunken talk in her room long before. What had she said of sexual perfection then? 'Better to go out on top, eh? Kill myself. Achieve this elusive perfection and then have done with it all.'

The words chilled him. He stood staring into nothing, his bubbled hands scratching absently at the frying pan. Why had those words come back at the height of his happiness? He unplugged the sink and wiped his hands on the dishcloth. He went and sat on the edge of the bed. He felt clammy. She hadn't been speaking in jest, exactly, but the words had not been meant with any great seriousness, a cynic's response to a tangled life, a mock threat. Even if she had been serious, it had to be set in the context of the time, of missing a loved one. Now there was a new loved one, hope, romance, a future. And yet.

Miller went to the phone. He lifted the receiver, then put it down again. 'Don't be stupid,' he said aloud. He switched on the CD player. Kylie Minogue started singing about being lucky. 'That's more like it,' he said and danced across the room.

Halfway through he phoned her. Mrs Hardy answered. 'Hold on, I'll get her,' she said.

Miller smiled into the receiver. I'll tell her I love her, he thought. I'll take her to dinner. Somewhere without candles. She'll wear her BAD cap all through the meal and the waiters'll look daggers at her, and she won't give a damn. We'll talk about her book. We'll talk about my book. I'll turn the Cycle of Violence into a tandem and we'll ride through the South of France. She will be my Paris Bun. It will be the Cycle of Romance. We will get married on the top of the Eiffel Tower. Then we'll bungy jump off.

Footsteps. 'No reply, I'm afraid,' said Mrs Hardy. She hardly changed her tone at all, but Miller could tell it was a reprimand. 'She was out all night. She'll be fast asleep.'

Miller put the phone down. He put on Kylie again. Then switched her off. He had packing to do. He started emptying drawers. She'd worked until late, then they'd made love for a long time, of course she was tired. He was tired himself still, a happy, lazy fatigue born of good love and sex. He looked at his bike. The Cycle of Romance. He would go and see her.

God, don't be stupid, Miller. Give her space. She went home for a reason. We've done our bonding, now leave it for a little while. She'll feel cornered if you pursue her. She's a wild, free spirit. Don't try to pen her in. She's said she loves you. She's said she's moving to Belfast with you. She's had mad passionate sex with you. 'Don't call me mad,' she'd said. She wasn't mad. She . . .

'Fuck it,' Miller said, grabbing hold of the handlebars and wheeling the bike to the front door.

He tried to make it a leisurely ride round to her lodgings. A little light exercise, a little sightseeing of Crossmaheart's boarded-up commercial heart. He nodded at a couple of vague acquaintances. Stopped to buy a paper, rolled it up and slipped it into the back pocket of his jeans. But still that clammy feeling. As her lodgings came into sight he increased his speed; by the time he got there he was pedalling as fast as he ever had before.

He rested the bike against the garden wall, then rang the front door bell. He took a deep breath, tried to compose himself. Mrs Hardy answered.

'I need to see her,' he said quickly, stepping forward.

She put her hand out to stop him. 'Just one second there, my boy,' she said testily.

'But . . .'

'But nothing. I'll see if she wants to see you.'

Miller stepped back. 'Okay. Right. Would you?'

'She was asleep. She was out all of last night.'

'I know. I know. Could you?'

'Just hold on there. Go into the lounge. I'll see if she's awake.'

Mrs Hardy led him into the lounge, pointed at a chair. She switched on the TV. 'There's nothing much on this time of the day,' she said.

'That's okay.'

He ignored the screen, sat staring at the wall. It was a huge armchair. It made him feel like a child, sitting there small and unloved, waiting for a punishment. From upstairs, faintly, he could hear Mrs Hardy drumming on Marie's door. Then the clump of steps.

'I can't raise her. Must be a deep one. Do you want to leave a message?'

Miller stood up. 'I have to see her.'

'I've told you . . .'

'Now!'

He brushed past her. She grabbed at his arm. He pulled free. 'Listen here, young man, this is my . . .'

'I'm worried about her, okay?' he snapped.

'She likes to be alone sometimes . . .'

'I don't care!'

Miller took the stairs three at a time. Mrs Hardy followed, single-stepping, panting.

He reached her door and banged hard on it. 'Marie? Marie? Marie?'

The door to the next room opened and the McCauleys looked out together, as if they were Siamese. 'Anything wrong?' Mrs McCauley asked.

'No,' said Miller. The McCauleys nodded, but remained in the doorway. Mrs Hardy arrived at the top of the stairs.

'I do wish you'd keep it down . . .'

Miller knelt and peered through the keyhole. The room was bright enough, but he could see nothing beyond a chest of drawers and a poster of Leonard Cohen.

247

'Do you have a spare key?'

'Really, I don't . . .'

'Do you have a fuckin' spare key or not?'

Mr McCauley stepped from the doorway. 'Take it easy there, fella . . .'

Mrs McCauley put a restraining hand on his shoulder. 'Are you a friend of . . . ?'

'No, I'm the fuckin' Avon lady . . .'

'Mrs Hardy, do you know this man?' Mrs McCauley asked.

'Yes. Well, of course. It's Marie's friend, but I don't . . .'

'Look,' snapped Miller, 'will you just get the spare key?'

Mrs Hardy looked from Miller to the McCauleys, shrugged and turned back to the stairs. 'This isn't good for my heart, you know.'

As she disappeared round the bend, Mrs Brady appeared. 'What is all this racket?' she demanded, her voice high. Then her eyes fell on Miller and she stopped three steps from the top. 'I know you,' she said.

Miller turned his gaze back to the keyhole.

'What's the silly wee girl done now?' Mrs Brady asked, still loitering beneath them, one hand clutching the banister.

'She's not answering her door,' Mrs McCauley said.

'Obviously,' said Mr McCauley.

'Silly wee girl,' said Mrs Brady and turned back down the stairs. 'The sooner she sees a doctor the better. Disruptive's what she is.'

Mrs Hardy passed her on the stairs. 'That girl . . .' Mrs Brady began.

'Shut up,' said Mrs Hardy.

She handed Miller the key. He fitted it into the lock. He turned to Mrs Hardy and the McCauleys. 'I'll talk to her myself,' he said.

They stepped back reluctantly. He opened the door and slipped into the room, closing it sharply behind him.

Later Mrs Hardy would say Marie looked very peaceful in death.

15

'Happy now?' his father said.

'What do you think?'

'I don't know. That's why I'm asking.'

'Your sarcasm hasn't improved much with death.'

'Yes, it has, it's come on immeasurably.'

'I was being sarcastic.'

'So was I.'

A car honked behind him. He shook himself back to reality, looked round. He was at the lights. A damson Fiesta, pockmarked like it had been continually shot up, engine revving. A shaggy head appeared out the driver's window.

'Are you fuckin' movin' or what?'

Miller, legs astride the Cycle of Violence, nodded slowly. 'I'm going to a funeral.'

'There'll be another fuckin' funeral if you don't get a move on.'

Miller pulled the bike over to the side of the road. Yes, there will, he thought, you talk to me, you end up dead. Four other vehicles were backed up behind the Fiesta; one by one the drivers, sometimes whole families, stared at him as they moved past. He watched them, his eyes set hollowly, hair spikily unwashed, his face heavy with stubble. In the mirror of other people's eyes he saw himself as the convict in a Laurel and Hardy comedy.

The bread was blue-mouldy. He bought it from the Good Neighbour on the way home from the funeral. Goodmorninggoodayhowarya? Nicedaylookslikerainwhatashame. Notbadburiedthegirlfriendnowamgonnagetpished.

He hadn't eaten for three days, the slow rumble killed each time it threatened by another shot of vodka. Now, Marie gone, it was time to break the habit, climb back on the cycle of life. Eat. But the bread was blue. Otherwise it looked fine. But you couldn't eat blue food. You didn't have blue bread, blue potatoes, blue sausages. It meant bad. It was rotting, rotting like Crossmaheart, rotting like Marie in her grave.

'It was a cry for help,' Mrs Hardy said, clutching his arm.

He pulled free, a child shrugging off his mother. 'Bollocks,' he said, loud enough for heads to turn. He lowered his voice, but it still came out like a bitter hiss. 'Slitting your wrists crossways is a cry for help. Doing it from wrist to elbow is a cry for death.'

Voices shushed him.

It was a fine day, sun high, sky blue, birds singing. He thought nature was laughing at them, turning death on its head. It wasn't meant to be like this, the mourners weren't meant to look incongruous on the hillside, clustered darkly about the grave as if they were about to plunge into its dank interior to gain refuge from the noisy brightness of the world. There was meant to be rain and wind and menacing clouds, the minister's eulogy should have been lost in a stormy drumming on the church roof. It had been like that for his dad. But for Marie it shone, the wonders of life promoted in the presence of death.

He sat with his vodka, his bottle of Diet Pepsi, staring out the window which had a view of nothing. Nothing but bricks and mortar. He found solace in Leonard Cohen.

'Leonard,' he said to the speaker, 'you're a miserable bastard, but I'm starting to see your point.'

He slipped out of the service early, walked up the hill to the grave. A couple of yards down, he spotted Erin's gravestone. The bare details, the only hint of her violent death in the close proximity of the dates of her birth and demise.

The mourners snaked up the hill towards him. The minister led, behind him her father, then maybe a hundred others. He picked out the faces he knew: the Rileys, maybe a dozen from their pub, Mrs Hardy, the McCauleys, Helen and Anne from the paper, Deep Throat. Her dad had been tall, but age had stooped him; maybe something else as well. He looked at Miller out of hooded grey eyes. Miller glowered back. He wanted to push him into the grave, pile the soil in on top until he choked.

And the box, wheeled up on a trolley, sticking once, twice, in the mud. She was in there. The husk. All prettied up with the make-up she rarely wore. In the prettiest dress she always despised. He had wandered up and down outside her father's house for two hours, trying to make up his mind whether to go in. Not to speak to him. Jesus, no. To see her, one last time.

In the end the father had made up his mind for him. He'd seen him out in the rain shadows, his long coat, his shaven head, and called the police.

Bloody, bloody blue-mouldy bread.

He stared at it. 'Fuck it,' he said, and stabbed the loaf with the bread knife. He took a slug from the vodka bottle, swished it down with some Pepsi. Bloody, bloody blue mould. 'Imperfect,' he said to the loaf, 'you are imperfect. I want a ham sandwich. I demand a ham sandwich. I do not demand blue bread. Blue bloody bread.'

He stood with the loaf poised above the waste bin, foot on the pedal.

Bloody Good Neighbour.

Bloody Good Neighbour.

See what happens when you put your trust in the traditional corner shop, victim of a ceaseless onslaught from the giant hypermarkets? They give you blue bread.

He let the lid slip closed again. You can't just sell people blue bread like that.

'Are you okay?'

Helen arrived from the other side of the grave. Now there was a thought. Could Marie come from the other side as well, the way his father managed? Miller nodded. Marie was down there now. Some people were throwing in single flowers. He hadn't thought to bring one.

'Are you here by yourself?' she asked.

'I'm with my girlfriend.'

'I mean . . .'

'I know what you mean. Sorry. Yes.'

'Had you met her dad?'

'No.'

'Do you want me to introduce you? I know him vaguely.'

'No.'

'We're thinking of you.' Helen squeezed his arm and moved off.

But what are you thinking of me?

They made a cup of tea downstairs. It was so proper. Mrs Hardy with her tea-cosied pot, the McCauleys hand in hand on the settee, Miller drumming his fingers on the table. If only Marie hadn't been congealing on the bed upstairs it would have made a perfect tea party.

The doctor, flushed, joined them. He shook his head. Tutted. 'Awful, awful,' he said. 'I was her doctor, you know. Since she was a baby.'

'I don't want to know,' Miller said.

'Such a difficult life.'

'I don't want to know.'

'I told her she was playing with fire . . . .'

'Please . . .'

'You can't just stop taking pills like that, you're never aware that you're getting sick . . .'

'Fuck up!'

Miller was across the table and had him pinned against the wall. Man McCauley was up in a second, pulling him back, shouting, and in a moment there was the thud of policemen's feet down the stairs and more hands pulling at him, but he held on, grinding his forehead into the shocked physician's nose.

'Deep Throat.'

'Death Wish.'

'Enjoy the funeral?'

'Marvellous.' Craig clasped Miller's hand. 'I hope you realize you've singlehandedly revived the undertaking business in Crossmaheart.'

'I like to do my bit.'

They held each other's gaze for a moment, then Craig looked away, into the grave. 'If it's any consolation, I'm very sorry. I know you were close.'

'It's no consolation, but thank you. We were very close. Not close enough. Or too close. Who knows?'

Craig nodded. 'I understand it could have happened at any time. Manic depressives are like that. '

'That's a sweeping understanding.'

'That's what the experts tell me.'

'You've consulted experts.'

'I like to know the whys and wherefores. I talked to her doctor.'

'I talked to her doctor.'

'I know. I've seen the scar.'

'Emotional.'

'Understandable.'

'I loved her an awful lot.'

'I'm sure you did.'

'But I killed her.'

'The way you killed the others.'

Miller nodded.

'Makes me worry about my own well being really, being around you. Maybe it's time I retired.'

'People like you don't retire.'

'Which cliché book did you get that out of? We retire early and get a nice fat pension. It's one of the benefits of being a bastard for twenty years.'

Craig took out a packet of cigarettes and offered one to Miller. The journalist shook his head.

The policeman put the packet away without taking one. Together they looked down the hill at the departing mourners. 'Nice day for it,' said Craig.

'Beautiful,' said Miller.

'What will you do now?'

'Cry.'

'Fair enough.'

He decided to take the Cycle of Violence. He gripped the familiar handlebars and spoke to the bell. 'It's only a hundred yards, but I'm too bloody drunk to walk.'

The loaf was hugged inside his coat, haphazardly pushed back into its plastic bag like the innards of a cat squeezed back beneath the fur after being struck by a car.

The bike laboured from side to side, touching here, scratching there, as if he rode into a gale, but the sunny

funeral weather held firm, barely a breath along the quiet
road.

'I hear you've had some bad news.'
    'Word travels slow.'
    'I heard earlier. I would have phoned. Jesus, I would
have come, but things have been bedlam here. You know
what it's like.'
    'I know what it's like.'
    'But you're okay?'
    'Sure.'
    'You'll be wanting to take some time off? Strictly
speaking it's not next of kin, but I think I can swing it
for you.'
    'Thanks, yeah.'
    'A week enough?'
    'Plenty.'
    'There is an alternative, of course.'
    'Two weeks.'
    'No, I mean to coming back. You could stay there.'
    'I could?'
    'You're not masking your sarcasm very well. Still, you
could. We were a bit thrown by O'Hagan's resignation.
Health reasons, my arse, but he's gone. To tell you the truth,
Miller, those girls that are doing it now, I mean, they're
doing a fine job, but they simply don't have the experience
for the long haul. Do you fancy taking over for a while?
Sorting the place out? And if it works out for everyone
we'll make it full time? Run your own show, you've always
wanted that, haven't you? Pull the reins? Make the
decisions? Make the policy, within reason? Pay's good. No
shortage of stories. Do good in Crossmaheart, there's no
telling where you might end up – leap frog over me, for
goodness' sake! What do you think?'
    'I think not.'

'Why not, for heaven's sake?'
'Because.'

He fumbled with the padlock for a couple of minutes. It was a tiny little lock, the type any self-respecting thief could snap off with his teeth, but it had done the job successfully for years. Once connected to the drainpipe, Miller left the Cycle of Violence and entered the Good Neighbour.

The toothpaste smile. 'Good afternoon!' she said with the exaggerated enthusiasm which had only begun to grate on him from his very first encounter with her on his first day in Crossmaheart. Before that it had hardly bothered him at all.

He withdrew the loaf from his coat and set it on top of the copies of the *Chronicle* displayed in front of her. 'Afternoon,' he said, 'I wonder if you could help me?'

'Of course,' she said, eyeing the loaf.

'I bought this here earlier. When I got it home it was all blue-mouldy – do you mind if I change it?'

He was half moving towards the rack of bread on the long display unit which neatly divided the shop, when she said: 'Just hold on a moment – I'll get my husband.'

She lifted the loaf and disappeared into the back of the shop. Miller turned back to her counter and studied the familiar headlines. In a moment a curtain swished and the woman appeared again, accompanied by her husband. Fat, balding, and that was just the wife. He was carrying the loaf. He set it down on the papers, she hovered behind him.

'Can I help you, sir?'

'Yes, I was just telling your wife. I bought this loaf in here this morning, but it's all blue-mouldy. Do you mind if I just change it for another one?'

The Good Neighbour lifted the loaf. 'This one, sir?'

'Yes.'

257

'It looks a bit battered.'

'I know. I had a bit of an accident opening it. But you can see where it's all mouldy.'

'Yes, I see that. But how do I know you bought it here?'

'You sold it to me a couple of hours ago.'

'Do you have a receipt?'

'No, I don't have a receipt. But you only sold it to me a couple of hours ago.'

'Without a receipt I can't change it, I'm afraid.'

'But you sold it to me.'

'I don't recall, sir. We get so many customers.'

'In here?'

'Yes, sir.'

'It was only a couple of hours ago. We exchanged pleasantries. All I want to do is change the loaf. I'm not going to report you to the Public Health or anything.'

'I'm afraid I can't do that, sir.'

'Why the fuck not?'

'Because.'

'Look, I've been in this shop every day for about the past six weeks, sometimes two or three times a day. Every day I have spent at least three pounds, sometimes five, that's hundreds of pounds I've spent in here. You know me. You've spoken to me every day. You're supposed to be the goddamn Good Neighbour. Now all I'm asking you to do is simply replace this rotting fuckin' loaf with a fresh one, is that too much to ask?'

'I'm afraid I can't do that, sir.'

'Why the fuck not?'

'You could just be making all that up.'

'Why on earth would I?'

'To steal a loaf from us.'

'I don't believe this. I don't fuckin' believe this.'

Miller lifted his loaf back. He shook his head, then suddenly threw it at the Good Neighbour. 'You fuckin' keep it!' he shouted as the bread bounced off the man's chest. Miller wheeled, stepped over to the bread stack and quickly grabbed a loaf and turned for the door. Before he could get there the Good Neighbour had barred his way. Miller turned again and walked quickly to the back of the shop. The Good Neighbour set off after him.

Miller rounded the corner of the aisle and made for the door again. Mrs Neighbour emerged from behind the counter to head him off. He slipped past her and began his second circuit of the display unit, this time upping his pace until he was jogging, every step matched by the Good Neighbour, then running. Drunk, he knew how ridiculous it was. Like a scene from the Keystone Kops.

On his fourth lap, when he glanced back to see if the Good Neighbour was gaining on him, Mrs Neighbour stepped forward and felled him with a tin of Heinz Lentil Soup.

He hit the deck, scattering a pyramid of cereal boxes as he fell, but he held onto the loaf.

He shook his head back into consciousness and hauled himself to his feet. Both of the Neighbours guarded the door now. Mr Good Neighbour had a shotgun levelled at him.

'This is ridiculous,' said Miller.

The Neighbours stared at him, unblinking, flush-faced, breathing hard, the both of them.

'I said this is fucking ridiculous.'

'I've never heard such language,' said Mrs Neighbour.

'Put the bread back,' said Mr Neighbour.

'It's my bread,' said Miller.

'No, it's not. You're stealing it. Now put it back.'

'You sold me fuckin' poisoned bread, what do you expect me to do?'

'Leave your name and address and we'll speak to the delivery man when he comes on Friday.'

'All I want is a sandwich.'

259

'Then buy a loaf.'

'I did buy a loaf. It nearly killed me.'

'Well, I will kill you if you don't put it back.'

'Don't be ridiculous.'

'I'm telling you.'

'I'll put it back if you give me a refund on my blue loaf.'

'Leave your name and address, I'll forward it to the wholesaler.'

'It's only fucking 60p.'

'Put the loaf back.'

'I can't do that.'

'I'm going to count to three.'

'Why don't you just call the police? We'll see whose side they're on.'

'One.'

'Go on. See what they say about blue bread.'

'Two.'

'Will you put the gun down?'

'Put our bread back,' said Mrs Neighbour.

'Three.'

'I don't fuckin' believe this.'

He pulled the trigger. Miller shot backwards through the display, then landed on the floor in a cascade of bread and tins and blood.

Somewhere he heard shouting, footsteps, but it was too dark for him to see. Someone nudged his elbow and he looked up into his father's eyes. His dad looked well, not the faded old man of his death-week, but young, vigorous, his voice less raspy. 'Son,' he said, cradling Miller in his arms. 'Son.'

'Have you seen her, Dad?'

'I don't know her dad.'

'No, Dad, I mean, have you seen her? Is she there? Is she comin' to see me?'

'She doesn't finish till eleven, son.'

'But then she's comin'?'

'Aye, son.'

'Dad?'

'What?'

'I'm scared.'

'Don't be.'

'Dut I don't believe in God.'

'Don't worry about it. Sure you can change your mind.'

'Can you do that, Dad, once you're dead?'

'Course you can. All you have to do is convince those three over there.'

Out of the dark he saw them, hovering, wraith-like. They smiled at him leerily. He knew their dead faces. Michael Rainey, Tom Callaghan, Tyrone Blair.

'The Three Wise Men,' said his dad.

'Dad, I don't want to die.'

'It's never been a matter of choice, son.'

He felt the warmth of his father, the shiver of his body, then the dulling of his mind. And then the quiet scream of life departing.

Police sirens. An ambulance. A crowd gathered. The Good Neighbours were escorted away. The body was removed. The shop was shuttered. As darkness descended heavy rain broke and a dour inland wind began to whip along the Main Street. A couple of kids out scavenging came upon the bike. The shop neon was off and the streetlights were smashed, so they took their time with the padlock, working through it patiently with a rusty hacksaw. When they finally released the Cycle of Violence they wheeled it out onto the Main Street and climbed aboard, one standing up to turn the pedals, the other doubling onto the seat and bending round him to steer. They rode into the wind, their anorak hood strings pulled tight, their faces pink and sore with the stinging winter rain.

Divorcing Jack

Colin Bateman

'Richly paranoid and very funny' *Sunday Times*

Dan Starkey is a young journalist in Belfast, who shares with his wife Patricia a prodigious appetite for drinking and partying. Then Dan meets Margaret, a beautiful student, and things begin to get out of hand.

Terrifyingly, Margaret is murdered and Patricia kidnapped. Dan has no idea why, but before long he too is a target, running as fast as he can in a race against time to solve the mystery and to save his marriage.

'A joy from start to finish . . . Witty, fast-paced and throbbing with menace, *Divorcing Jack* reads like *The Thirty-Nine Steps* rewritten for the '90s by Roddy Doyle' *Time Out*

'Grabs you by the throat . . . a magnificent debut. Unlike any thriller you have ever read before . . . like *The Day of the Jackal* out of the Marx Brothers' *Sunday Press*

'Fresh, funny . . . an Ulster Carl Hiaasen' *Mail on Sunday*

ISBN 0 00 647903 0

Of Wee Sweetie Mice and Men

Colin Bateman

'A supremely entertaining piece of work' *GQ*

Smooth operator Geordie McClean has succeeded in setting up a gigantic payday (for all concerned) by arranging a St Patrick's Day fight in New York between his hopeless Irish heavyweight champ Fat Boy McMaster and Mike Tyson. Belfast journalist Dan Starkey is hired to write the book of the whole affair.

Dan is trying to persuade his wife Patricia to give their marriage another go, but he has not succeeded before boarding the plane with McMaster and his deeply suspect entourage. If he thought he was leaving the sectarian conflict of his homeland behind him, Starkey is quite mistaken and McClean's outfit soon falls prey to all the old enmities, while developing an uncanny power to outrage plenty of other interest groups at the same time.

Kidnap, romance and mayhem ensue . . . and all before a punch is thrown in the ring!

'Fast, furious, riotously funny and at the end, never a dry eye in the house'   *Mail on Sunday*

'I have absolutely no interest [in boxing], but such are Bateman's skills with narrative and characterization that one is gripped to the last page, whatever one's sporting predilections'
Literary Review

'If Roddy Doyle was as good as people say, he would probably write novels like this'   *Arena*

ISBN 0 00 649612 1

Empire State

Colin Bateman

'Bateman on epic form in gloriously over-the-top saga'
Daily Telegraph

Possibly because it's been tough living with the same name as a Supremes song, possibly because of the indelible horror of one night in his Northern Irish past, Nathan Jones is a man with a temper.

When his girlfriend Lisa leaves him in New York, Nathan has only his new job for company in the liveliest, loneliest city in the world.

Nathan is a security guard at the Empire State Building, recently acquired by computer billionaire, Michael Tate, and about to be visited by President Michael Keneally, an army of FBI men and one George Burley of Alabama, a white supremacist with the President at the top of his assassination Top Ten.

Soon the stage is set for a vintage Bateman adventure, wild, romantic and darkly, dangerously funny. *Empire State* takes the world of politics – international, racial and sexual – and holds it hostage atop the most famous building on Earth.

'A hugely enjoyable novel . . . blessed with a beautiful sense of irony . . . It's like Carl Hiaasen, Tom Wolfe, and Roddy Doyle at their best'   *The Herald*

'There is more to Bateman than a racy plot. His prose is intelligent as well as aesthetically satisfying, his dialogue toughly funny and tone-perfect, his American observations queasily true'   *Mail on Sunday*

ISBN 0 00 649802 7

fireandwater
The book lover's website

www.**fireandwater**.com

The latest news from the book world

Interviews with leading authors

Win great prizes every week

Join in lively discussions

Read exclusive sample chapters

Catalogue & ordering service

www.**fireandwater**.com
Brought to you by HarperCollins*Publishers*